THE AFFAIR ON
THE PAINTED DESERT

BY CLIFFORD KNIGHT

CLIFFORD KNIGHT'S new "affair" is steeped in the mysterious, garish spell of the Painted Desert. Navajo Canyon, in the Western Navajo Indian Reservation, is one of the few places in America where actual ruins of the ancient cliff dwellers still remain. It was here that Huntoon Rogers went to spend his vacation, supposedly to study and rest. Naturally, he did not expect that a brutal murder would be committed practically on his doorstep, and when they found Bernice Patterson's body deep in the maw of the great canyon, he knew that there was work to be done.

For a time there seemed to be no possible solution until Rogers remembered the significant fact that a white man on the Navajo reservation can do practically nothing unobserved by an Indian. Then he knew where to seek the clue to his riddle; and subsequent developments proved him right, but only in the nick of time.

THE AFFAIR ON THE PAINTED DESERT

by

CLIFFORD KNIGHT

WILDSIDE PRESS

To
MABEL,
HELEN LOUISE
and DICK

1

It was thirty miles from the turnoff on Highway 66 to where the little girl's diary lay in the road. So small a thing in so vast a country could very easily have been overlooked. For the eyes as one approaches that fantastic region known as the Painted Desert are drawn by the pinkish golden splendor of the far view, to the neglect of small things by the roadside.

My own eyes missed it altogether. I was marveling once more after an absence of several years at the intense blue of the sky, which in northern Arizona is something to be felt rather than expressed by mere words, when Huntoon Rogers on the seat beside me suddenly called out for me to stop. He climbed out of the station wagon and walked back, his heavy shoes crunching on the hard surface of the road. There was only this sound and the purring of the warm motor between us and absolute silence, for there was no wind.

He came back within a few moments, climbed in and tossed the little leather-bound book upon the seat between us; and we drove onward. The sun was dropping lower and our destination for the night was now not far ahead, for we had planned to stop at Cameron where the road crosses the Little Colorado River.

To one familiar with the ways of the Southwest, our

presence in this part of Arizona is easily explained by the words Indian fever. Throughout the spring months the inner gnawings of this affliction of the spirit, which prods the physical man into forsaking the comforts of home to go upon the hard trails of the Indian country and suffer the blight of poor food and camp beds and impossible roads, had tormented me. Even so I might not have yielded to the lure of it had it not been for Huntoon Rogers. I ran across him at the Authors Club in Hollywood one day in the early part of June.

"Chuck," he said, taking hold of my elbow, "do you know what I'd like to do, now that school is out at the university?" There was an eager twinkle in his mild blue eyes. He towered above me, being all of six feet tall and broad and powerful in proportion. "The spring winds in the Indian country ought to have blown themselves out by now, and the summer rains haven't started. I'd like to drive over onto the Navajo Reservation, say, to Kaibito or to Rainbow Lodge, get some horses and go exploring down in Navajo Canyon among the ruins of the cliff dwellers."

"Gold hunting?" I inquired soberly. A puzzled frown gathered momentarily on his wide forehead.

"Gold hunting?" he repeated. "Oh"—he smiled broadly, giving me a dig in the ribs—"I thought you were serious for a moment. No, the hidden gold supposedly cached in Navajo Canyon can remain hidden for all I care, Chuck. I'm interested in ruins, rather than legends, this time."

"You're on, then," I answered to my great regret, now that I look back on the tragic events that dogged our trail. But here we were, heading into the Indian country on the first leg of a trip into what even today remains a primitive wilderness. The space behind the extra seat in the station wagon held our camp equipment and supplies, and, with a sense of holiday, of release from the confining groove of humdrum life in town, we rolled steadily along the road. We had come by way of Flagstaff instead of by the Grand Canyon, as we had first talked of doing. Behind us was the cool highland region of pine and fir; ahead lay pink mesas and deep shadowy canyons, terrifying gorges, a broken and tumbled world which might very well be the borrow pits and abandoned quarries from which had come the building materials of a continent.

"What did you find back there, Hunt?" I inquired, indicating the little book on the seat between us.

"Oh," he answered casually, picking it up and turning the pages, "it's just a diary. Queer place to find a diary."

"Any name in it?"

"Barbara W.," he answered, glancing at the fly leaf, "of London, England."

"The owner will never see it again, then, I suppose."

"Not unless there's something more than that to aid us in finding her." He sat turning through the pages, pausing here and there to read what was written in a rather unformed hand.

"Some young lady," I remarked several minutes later, "confessing her secret thoughts to Dear Diary. How can you be so shameless, Hunt?"

"On the contrary, Chuck," he said, glancing at me, "if it were such a person as you imagine, there would be intimate confessions, such as, 'Oh, Diary, I want to dance, dance, dance!' or, 'He was just too divine. I loved the little frown on his forehead, the way he smiled, the thrill of his arm around my waist.' But there's none of that stuff. Our diarist is a younger person, not yet interested in the opposite sex—possibly thirteen years old—and she struggles nobly to record her impressions of a region that has always stumped the best of writers. She sees it, I suspect, through the rather round and popping eyes of a young girl brought up in England."

"What a shame she lost her diary."

"Yes," Rogers replied absent-mindedly. "Probably fell out of her pocket when she climbed back into the car." His gaze returned to its pages. "Listen to this," he said, reading: " 'The child's name was Fat Boy, and he was terribly plump. Indian names, I think, are awfully funny. We saw Mrs. Slim Woman and Mr. Small Legs, and Daddy met one man the trader said was named Mr. Cactus Mustache. Fat Boy's mother couldn't speak English and was very thin. She wore a plum-colored velvet jacket and a red calico skirt, very full, and leather moccasins and lots of turquoise and silver. She and two other squaws were skinning a sheep without even changing their dresses, which I think is insanitary, but they all do it, we were told, in Navajo land. The sight of the blood made Mummy seasick, and we went and climbed in the trader's car.' "

"Rather observing for a young girl," I commented.

"Yes. Here's another passage: 'Cameron is only some tiny little buildings huddled in the great big desert, just like sheep when they are frightened. Mummy and Daddy

went to an Indian hogan to buy a rug and a silver brace-
let to take home to England, but I stayed and played
checkers with a cowboy and almost beat him twice. He
had crinkled eyes and smiled all the time, which I believe
is a good sign in strangers, although when I asked him
his name he said he'd tell me his Indian name which the
Indians gave him. He said he didn't tell everybody. I
couldn't pronounce it, though. He said it means Man-
borrows-horse. I think he was pulling my leg. He had
an old guitar and played some quaint songs which he
sang while he played. It wasn't very good singing, but
we parted friends. Of course we never expect to see each
other again.' "

Rogers closed the book and dropped it on the seat
between us. The roofs of Cameron which, as the little
girl had observed, seemed to huddle like frightened sheep
on the desert, were before us; the sun was almost touching the horizon, making long shadows stretch away from
the few forlorn cottonwoods.

"Chuck, you know every water hole, every trader,
every wanderer in this back country," began Rogers.
"I was just wondering if you know a singing cowboy."

"I've known several in my time. Why?"

"I was just thinking that Barbara betrays a senti-
mental leaning—it's slight, of course—toward this one.
It's just possible she may have given him her address
in England. If so, and if we run across him, I could return the diary."

"Sorry, Hunt. We may run across him, though."

The subject was dropped there and did not come up
again until after we reached Cameron where Rogers

sought information of the trader at the trading post.

"Professor Rogers wants to ask you some questions, Charlie," I said, after I had introduced them. Charlie Richmond leaned back against the shelves and listened to Rogers' inquiry about the English girl.

"Oh, yes," said Charlie, "she and her folks were here only last night."

"Which way were they going?"

"Going out; they'd been up to Navajo Mountain."

"Do you happen to know whether or not they were stopping anywhere around close?" Rogers pressed.

"They didn't say; I didn't ask."

"And now tell me, if you can, about a singing cowboy here recently."

"Do you mean a fellow named Caldwell?"

"I don't know whether I do or not. He had a guitar and smiled all the time."

"His name's Ernie Caldwell. He's drifted in and out of this country for a long time. Everybody knows Ernie."

"Do you know where he is now?"

"No. I didn't see which way he come from or which way he went."

Rogers had taken the diary from his pocket and it lay on the counter. His hand strayed to it to finger the leaves as he turned over in his mind the information the trader had given him. An Indian was waiting to buy a sack of flour, and Charlie, deciding that there were no other questions, turned away. Rogers picked up the diary and in doing so something in its pages caught his attention. He glanced at me.

"Listen to this one, Chuck," and he began to read: " 'We walked half a mile over to a hogan among the trees. The squaw was carding wool. She was very pretty, and her husband had brought water to wash the wool from a spring which is a mile or more away. He said, "Here it is, dear. I'll get some more, if you want it." Which I thought was considerate for an Indian, and then we walked away and the trader said they weren't Indians at all, but a young couple from Baltimore who were trying to live like the Indians, because they didn't have much money. But they looked like Indians to me, and the trader said they were just two screwballs in the desert. Daddy put down the word in his notebook to remember when we got back to England. But I don't know exactly what screwball means. It does seem, though, that there are unnumerable different sorts of people in this strange land.' "

"Nothing truer has ever been said about it than that, Hunt," I laughed.

A hand reached forward and laid hold of the diary. Huntoon Rogers' muscles tensed and he snapped the diary shut, dislodging the hand that had sought to seize it.

"Let me have that," said a man's voice at my side.

"Why?" asked Rogers, his tone crisp and unfriendly.

For a moment the stranger did not reply but stood glaring at Rogers from somewhat watery gray eyes in a veined, reddish face. He was dressed in golf knickers, a sweater and coat, and a soft felt hat was pulled tightly down upon a rather large head. He was close upon six feet tall; his figure once must have been athletic, but he sagged now at the belt line and his legs were thin and spindling, which made his heavy torso seem top-heavy. He didn't belong in the desert but he was of a type not infrequently seen there.

"Sorry," he apologized to Rogers after a moment, the hostile look fading from his eyes. "I didn't mean to be rude. But—I was interested in what you were reading. May I see it?" There was an arrogant air about him which set me instinctively against him.

Rogers gave it to him and the stranger's eyes sought the paragraph which Rogers indicated. He read it through silently, scanned the paragraph preceding and the one that followed, then returned the diary to Rogers.

"Thank you, sir," he said. "I'm interested in the two screwballs."

A young woman who had been standing back against the wall now put her arm through the stranger's. The latter dropped his large soft hand upon her small one without so much as a glance at her, his gaze continuing to be drawn to Rogers. She was young, perhaps not more than twenty. She might have been his daughter, except for the fact that she was so different in type that they could not possibly be kin. Her nose was straight and delicately molded; her eyes and hair were a deep dark brown.

"You have really learned something, Norman, about them?" she inquired interestedly.

"Yes, Emily. They're somewhere about, but I haven't yet discovered just where." He addressed Rogers. "My name is Norman Kimball," he said. "And this is Emily Millspaw, my ward," he added.

Rogers bowed and introduced me and told them his name.

"As I say," the man went on, "I'm interested in the two so-called screwballs; one is my daughter, the other —well, he's my son-in-law. I'm wondering if you can tell me just where I'll find them." He eyed inquiringly the diary which Rogers continued to hold in his hand.

Rogers disclaimed any knowledge of the pair's whereabouts and explained that we had found the diary on the road that afternoon, and that he was interested only in returning it to its owner.

"Why not ask Charlie Richmond?" I suggested. I called to the trader behind the counter, and he came up once more. "Do you know where to find a couple of white folks living as Indians somewhere around here?"

"They're not around here, Chuck," he answered. "You'll find 'em up near Kaibito, about eighty miles from here." His eyes sought the stranger. "They've been there about a year now, I guess. They've managed some way, I hear, to keep from starving, but that's all. They can't own sheep, you know—only an Indian can do that on the reservation."

"Thank you, sir," replied Kimball. "But how do I get to Kaibito?"

"Drive. Fair enough road this time of year. The turn-off is at Red Lake the other side of Tuba City."

"We'd better stay here tonight, I guess."

"The hotel can take care of you."

The girl sighed. Obviously she was tired. She caught my glance and I noted how deep and alive her eyes were.

"We've driven so far and very fast," she explained.

"From Albuquerque——"

The pressure of the man's arm upon hers halted her in midsentence. Rogers turned away toward the door and we went outside. The sun was setting. It was closing time for the trading post. I thought from Rogers' action that he was beginning to think about supper, but when I mentioned it he said that he was not hungry yet.

"What is there, Chuck, about that fellow Kimball that's so—so disturbing?" he asked suddenly.

"Nothing," I answered after a moment's reflection upon the fact that I seldom had heard Rogers hesitate over a word, "except that he's the type I've always wanted to kick. Why?"

Before he could reply, the door to the trading post opened and Kimball and the girl came out. Their feet crunched for a few yards upon the gravel, then the two separated, the girl going toward the gray, expensive coupé at the roadside, Kimball continuing resolutely in our direction. Norman Kimball's voice broke the silence.

"It's awfully dark here on the desert when the sun goes down, isn't it?" he remarked in a conversational tone, gazing at the fiery sunset.

"Yes," Rogers answered.

The pause lengthened. Kimball's feet stirred in the gravel. He cleared his throat lightly as one will who would speak but hesitates to do so.

"I say," he began rather abruptly, "the desert does something to you. It's the awful silence; it's the fact that Nature can be so vast, so terribly vast, and yet be without sound. It crushes the spirit—it's positively devastating to one's customary poise. I don't see how my daughter can stand it. She resembles me; I mean that she likes the city, crowds, parties, a gay life. She must hate me very much to do this to herself—and me. Believe me, Mr. Rogers, it's hatred of me and not that there's a screw loose in her make-up that brought her to do such a crazy thing. Of course, Fletcher Wicks is different— the husband, you know. It's obvious, if you knew them both. His grandfather had to be confined, and Fletcher's parents kicked him about for years between them after they were divorced. Those things leave their mark. He persuaded Marian to do this. Perhaps you can recall the stir in the daily press when they left the comforts of civilization and came out here on the desert to live like the Indians. They did it to humiliate me—and Emily, of course. Her mother and the late Mrs. Kimball were lifelong friends and I took charge of Emily legally, you understand. A sacred trust, as it were—"

"I recall the incident," said Rogers casually. "Rather interesting as an example of behaviorism."

"Yes; isn't it? That a daughter should hate her father so! Two strong-minded people—that's what we are. Of course she had a right to marry Fletcher Wicks, but it was a stupid thing to do. One can forgive everything but stupidity. Came out here where there are only Indians and cowboys who smile all the time, and a hodgepodge of people. What was the man's name, Caldwell—the cowboy?"

"That's what the trader said," I answered.

"No matter. I never heard of him before. I'm reminded of something about a serpent's tooth when I think of my daughter Marian, though."

" 'How sharper than a serpent's tooth it is to have a thankless child!' " Rogers quoted.

"Yes. Yes, that's it, Mr. Rogers. I've been trying to think of the words all the way out here from Baltimore. A thankless child! That's Marian exactly. Well—" He halted as abruptly as he had begun and the intense silence that ensued indicated that Norman Kimball was recovering his poise. He cleared his throat. "I'm sorry, gentlemen. This is all very personal. We're complete strangers to each other, and I've bored you, but, as I observed a moment ago, the desert does something to you. Pardon me—and thank you for being patient with a man who's talked too much."

2

THE desert sunrise was tinting the horizon a delicate rose and blue when we finished breakfast and began preparations to leave Cameron. Early as we were astir, however, Norman Kimball and the small dark-haired Emily Millspaw were before us. A full half hour before we were planning to leave, Kimball emerged from the small hotel, tossed an overnight case and a large traveling bag into the luggage compartment of the coupé and slammed it shut. He espied us at the station wagon and walked over to us, a friendly expression on his reddish face.

"Good morning," he said. "Isn't this unbelievable! Perfectly beyond human comprehension!" His gesturing hands indicated the sunrise. "I haven't been up this early in twenty years. To think it could be like this."

"It's lovely," said Rogers. "It does something to you."

"That's right. It does do something." Kimball's ecstatic feelings promptly gave way to more practical matters. "The trader said I'd find my daughter near Kaibito, didn't he?"

"Yes," I answered.

"Can you give me directions again now, please?"

I pointed into the desert. "That road," I said. "About ten miles out it forks. Take the right fork. You'll cross the Moenkopi at Tuba City. Keep going till you come to Red Lake. Turn left there. You can't miss it."

"All desert?"

"Yes. You may see an Indian or two—"

"Indians?"

"Yes, of course. This is Indian country. Strangers are not any too welcome, but they won't bother you."

"They'd better not," he answered darkly, moving toward the coupé. "Well—I'll be starting. Thank you." He climbed briskly into the driver's seat. The girl looked in our direction and smiled, and a moment later the car shot away across the bridge over the Little Colorado and went humming out into the desert.

I walked from the station wagon over to the trading post to get some matches and say good-by to Charlie Richmond, leaving Rogers to stow our stuff. When I returned a small green car was pulling off the road. It had come up from the south and was desert stained; it looked as if it had been driven far and fast. A young woman whose trim figure was clad in a blue flannel slack suit climbed out when the car rolled to a stop. She wore no hat, no gloves. The blond hair was bound tightly under a blue silk scarf. The nose was rather small, the mouth was youthful, the lips full and red. She was a woman perhaps thirty years of age. As she passed me she not so much as bowed or inclined her head, but the next moment she whirled and called out:

"Mr. Graham!" I turned around. "Chuck Graham, isn't it?" she asked, advancing a step toward me, smiling a little.

"Yes, ma'am," I replied, searching my mind for some

recollection of her.

"I'm Bernice Patterson—perhaps you may not remember."

"Yes, I do, Miss Patterson," I said, the mention of her name having awakened memories. She had a firm, almost hard handclasp for a woman.

"It's been three years since I've seen you."

"All of that, I guess, Miss Patterson," I agreed. "This is the first time I've been up in this country for at least that long. Did you ever finish your book on the cliff dwellers?"

"Not—not entirely," she said hesitantly. "I hope to wind it up after this trip. You see—well, I've been sick during the last year. And my notes are—well, not adequate now; that is, I hope to refresh my memory and make a few more notes—"

"I remember now," I said, interrupting, as recollections of several years ago came back. "Jeff Draper was helping you get your facts together. Heavy Woman's Son—that's his Indian name, isn't it?"

"Yes," she said. After a pause she added: "Jeff—helped, as you say—yes. As a sort of guide."

I was sure that her face flushed slightly, that somehow my recalling Jeff Draper to her was unexpected and a trifle embarrassing. She turned away and started toward the trading post.

"Glad to have seen you, Miss Patterson," I called after her.

"Yes, of course. Good-by," she replied.

We rolled across the suspension bridge which spanned a little brother to the Grand Canyon and headed northward into the fantastic pinkness of the Painted Desert.

"Jeff Draper is his school name?" Rogers inquired as he settled down into the seat beside me, prepared for the next lap into the wilderness.

"Yes. Jeff is one of those Indians you meet now and then; he's Indian with all an Indian's instincts and traditions, but with a white man's education."

"I'm more or less familiar with the type. Gone back to tribal ways, I suppose?"

"Yes. Practically all of them do."

"Navajo?"

"Yes."

We rode on in silence. The sun was up and the differing densities of the rapidly warming layers of air made even more weird the outlines of distant buttes and ledges.

"Why would she blush, do you think, at your recalling Jeff Draper to her?" Rogers persisted.

"How should I know the answer to that one, Hunt? The ways of women are unknown to me; I'm a bachelor, you know."

"That's why I asked." Rogers laughed. "I'm ignorant for the same reason." He hummed a tune for a brief moment, something I'd never heard him do before, then picked up the English girl's diary, which lay on the seat between us. "You know this thing, this diary, is an excellent guidebook for people like us. We've seen all this country before, and, while there's always a peculiar joy in getting back to it, we can't see it with the rapt attention, the first-timeness with which a stranger, and especially a youthful stranger from a foreign land, sees it." He fingered through several pages then selected a brief paragraph:

" 'Everything is so big and strange. I never saw so many red rocks and rusty rocks, and pink ones. I saw maroon and vermilion, and even mustard looking hills where hardly nothing grows. And there are lots of dinosaur tracks in some places. It was bitterly cold last night on Navajo Mountain and the wind blew terribly. Something made me afraid. Daddy and Mummy were with me, but I felt so lonesome I began to cry. This morning it is bright and warm.' "

"You rather take those things for granted," I remarked. "The colored rocks and the overwhelming lonesomeness."

"But even so I still marvel at this country. The Spaniards were the first to name it *el desierto pintado*, but they never described its boundaries. We've come to call this area along the Little Colorado, which we're crossing now, the Painted Desert, but I think the name should be applied to all this Indian country—eastward into Colorado and New Mexico and northward to take in Bryce and Zion canyons in Utah. It's all more or less desert country, and it's painted."

"I agree with you, Hunt."

Rogers did not reply at once. He began turning the leaves of the diary.

"She's more concerned with people, though, than scenery," he observed. "Apparently she overlooked nobody, Indian and white man alike." He began to read. " 'The man in the trailer was awfully funny looking, and I was afraid of his wife, because she just stared and stared at me and sort of bit her lips together like a

turtle. He asked my name and when I told him he said
he was Uncle Lester. But he couldn't be, because my
only uncle lives in England and his name is Horace. I
found out that his name is Lester Andrews and he hates
Indians. I don't see why he came to Navajo land in a
trailer which is painted green, if he hates Indians. He
said he had two for breakfast, but I don't believe that.
He didn't have any hair, except a little fringe behind
his ears. He wasn't very tall, but he was wide and thick
through his stummick. And there aren't any cannibals
any more. Daddy says so.' "

Rogers put the book on the seat. Tuba City was just
ahead. We dropped down into it and rolled on through
the place without stopping.

"Do you know Lester Andrews and his wife, who bites
her lips together like a turtle, Chuck?" Rogers asked, as
Tuba City sank from sight behind us.

"Know them? Why should I? Never heard of 'em before."

"I was just asking. I'm expecting to see them,
though, and the two screwballs. Barbara's guidebook to
the Painted Desert has made me want to see these won-
ders."

"We may at that," I said. "Curious how in so big and
sparsely settled a country as this one is you soon get to
know everybody who is in it. Especially if they're white.
And although you see few Indians, a white man can't do
anything unnoticed by some one of them. If you have
car trouble, or your horse throws a shoe, or if you do
something you shouldn't and are trying to hide out in
here, you can be sure that some Indian knows all

about it."

"Yes, I know," he responded, sinking his large figure deeper in his seat. As was customary our conversation began to lag, and soon it ceased altogether. The miles began to flow beneath our wheels. We did not speak again until we had turned off at Red Lake on the Kaibito road. We had gone only a mile or so when ahead of us at the side of the road appeared a mounted figure, leading a pack horse. He heard us coming and halted, sitting hunched over the pommel of his saddle as he waited for us to come up. From his action it was plain that he expected us to stop, and to make sure we did he held up a hand in a gesture to halt as we rolled up beside him.

"Morning," he said pleasantly. "I don't suppose you've got a match on you. I'm plumb out."

Rogers reached into his pocket and passed a paper of matches to him. Lean, bronzed fingers seized it, opened it and struck a light and touched the tip of a cigarette which he held between his lips. He shook out the match and tossed it away.

"Thanks, friend," he said. "Mind if I keep these? I haven't had a smoke all morning. Must have lost my matches back there at Red Lake. That's why I ain't got any."

"Of course. Here," and Rogers passed two more packets to him.

"Thank you, friend." He was a lean, sunburned man of perhaps forty-five; his face was deeply lined, his eyes were a dark, smoldering blue almost hidden by lids, as if he had spent a lifetime squinting in the bright sunlight. However, his was a pleasant face. He had about him an air of immense loneliness. "A gray car went by a while ago, but the man wouldn't stop. Looked at me, then went on like he was afraid I'd hold him up," he said.

"That was a fellow named Norman Kimball," I offered, "trying to find his daughter. She and her husband are living in a hogan."

"I know those people; they're at Kaibito."

"Isn't your name Caldwell?" asked Rogers of a sudden.

The man may have started inwardly but if he did there was no outward sign of it. He looked searchingly at Rogers, removed the cigarette from his lips and emptied his lungs before he replied.

"Yes—but how did you guess it, friend?"

"Quite simple," Rogers smiled. "I have a description of you."

"Description?" the tone was guarded. "I haven't done anything. I'm just a cow hand passin' through."

"Sorry." Rogers hastened to amplify his statement. "Didn't mean to imply that you'd done anything wrong, Caldwell—"

"Ernie Caldwell," he interrupted, obviously relieved. "You had me bothered for a minute, friend, because I've lived a blameless life, except, of course, I gamble a little and once in a while I go on a bender. Not so frequent nowadays as I used to. That's personal, though; hurts nobody but me. But how'd you happen to have a description of me and where'd you get it?"

"Do you remember a little English girl you met a

few days ago?"

"Oh, yes, Barbara. That was at Tuba City. Played some checkers with her. Smart little girl she was, too. Where'd you see her?"

"We didn't. She lost her diary and we found it."

"She wrote me up, did she? What did she say?"

"She was quite complimentary. Thought the way you smiled all the time was a good sign—"

"Hell!" the cowboy said, and looked away at Wild Cat Peak. "I didn't lay myself out just to get her to say something nice about me," he said apologetically. "That's like a woman, though—didn't tell me she was keepin' a diary."

"What I want to know," said Rogers, "is this: did she happen to give you her address in England? I'd like to send the thing to her."

"Well—yes," he replied hesitantly. "She wanted me to write to her sometime. But—hell, I ain't written nothing to anybody for twenty years, I guess. She wrote her address down on a piece of paper—but—I lost it. She wouldn't be interested in hearin' from me."

"I'm not so sure about that. At her age it would be very romantic to correspond with a man in America, especially a cowboy."

"Don't kid me, friend. What did you say your name was? I didn't catch it."

"Sorry," apologized Rogers. "I didn't tell you. My name's Rogers. This is Chuck Graham."

Caldwell looked at me closely and nodded. "Seems I've heard your name, Graham. Don't think I ever met you, though. I've got a lame mare," he said, changing the subject abruptly, indicating with a jerk of his head the sorry looking animal upon which was a meager pack including a battered guitar case. The animal's ribs were visible under the skin; it stood listlessly and patiently, its thin tail stirred by the light breeze. The other horse was in much better condition, and a younger animal.

"What's the matter with it?" I asked.

"Sprain, I guess, Graham. She's gettin' old. She's held me up two days now. Thought I'd best get goin' this morning. But I find she's still lame, so I guess I better go on to the first water hole and wait till she can travel."

"Well," I said, "so long, Caldwell."

"So long, friends." He waved an indifferent salute. "And thanks for the matches."

We left him hunched and lonely in his saddle at the side of the road, smoking his cigarette and staring with brooding eyes out across the desert.

Wild Cat Peak had gradually slipped behind us on our left when Rogers at length was roused to remark, "Our friend Kimball once more." His eyes caught sight of the gray coupé ahead before I saw it.

The car was parked at the edge of the road. There was no one about it as we slowed. I stopped a few yards beyond.

"They can't be far," I said. "Neither of them is likely to hike off any distance into the desert."

"There they are," Rogers said, as the two of them appeared from behind some rocks.

The moment he espied us, Norman Kimball began shouting and waving his arms. We waited for the two to come up. Kimball looked hot. His face was a reddish purple.

"I can't find any hogans along here." His voice was filled with complaint. "I've wasted a half hour already. Have you any idea where those two screwballs would be? The trader said near Kaibito."

"You're still about twenty miles from Kaibito," I reminded him.

"I thought I'd better start inquiring," returned Kimball. "I've got to find Marian and that crazy husband of hers."

The bleating of sheep came faintly to our ears, and the first of a small flock began to pour out like a dusty bedraggled liquid from behind the rocks. A slender Indian boy was driving them and a mongrel dog tagged at his heels.

"Oh! Oh, look, Norman! How picturesque! I must have a few feet of them." Emily Millspaw ran to the coupé, climbed upon the running board, and after a moment dropped to the ground again carrying a small motion picture camera which she adjusted to her eye. She moved forward in the direction of the approaching sheep and the flock began to veer. The boy shouted at his charges, ignoring the girl completely, determined that the sheep should go forward along the line they were moving. The girl dropped back out of the pathway when she saw that she was frigtening them but continued to hold the camera upon the flock.

The next moment something happened which for a time threatened serious trouble. An Indian mounted on a pony followed the flock of sheep from behind the rocks. He was dressed in overalls and moccasins and a red shirt. His long straight black hair was confined by a faded green headband. He wore a silver ring with a turquoise setting. He was directly in line with the camera and Emily Millspaw let the reel run, adding him to her celluloid record of the reservation.

The Indian had been sitting his horse lazily, but the moment he saw what she was doing he tensed noticeably. A second later he was kicking the pony's flanks. Instead of running away from her, however, he continued in a straight line directly at the small figure. The girl did not realize her danger until the pony and rider were almost upon her; then, with a startled expression on her dark face, she left off with the camera, lowering it slightly and holding it before her as she backed out of the way of the charging Indian. To our amazement he snatched the camera from her unresisting hands and with a sweep of his arm hurled it against a rock where it shattered in hopeless wreck.

Norman Kimball exploded in profanity. He shook his fists and his voice rose to a shriek. He ran to see if the girl had been injured. Finding that she was unharmed, he next trotted on his long spindly legs to where the broken camera lay. All the time he kept up a shouting: "Come back here! Come back here, you lousy Indian! Come back here and I'll take the hide off you! Come back!"

"That happens to be Jeff Draper," I said to Rogers, keeping my voice under Kimball's shouting.

"Is that so? Interesting."

Jeff had galloped onward a short distance as if he

meant to continue on into the desert, but suddenly he wheeled his horse and came loping back. Kimball's shouts quieted down at his approach, but he still was hostile and threatening. Emily Millspaw climbed hastily into the coupé for safety. Jeff jerked up his pony before Kimball and looked scornfully at him.

"I'm back. What you do about it now?" he asked.

"Do? Why—why, blast your impudence! You might have hurt the lady! You're going to pay for her camera, if you don't do anything else."

"What with? No money."

"I'll take it out of your hide, then. I'm still man enough to whip an Indian."

Jeff Draper slipped off his pony and advanced upon the middle-aged man. Norman Kimball turned and ran toward the coupé. He fumbled in the glove compartment for a moment and brought out a bluish ugly-looking automatic pistol.

"Now, I'll make you dance, damn you!"

But Huntoon Rogers of a sudden was out of the station wagon. He crossed the few yards separating Kimball from us, seized him from behind and had disarmed him before the man knew what had happened. I climbed out.

"Jeff," I said, "what's the trouble?"

At the sound of my voice he turned his back upon Norman Kimball and faced me.

"Oh—hello, Chuck," he said, smiling for the first time, exhibiting his strong white teeth. "Glad to see you again." He held out his hand which I shook heartily. "You ask what's the trouble. You see. I get fed up;

that's all. Indian is a man; he's not to be snapped by every amateur who comes to reservation. Let us alone; that's all the Indian wants."

"Oh—an educated Indian," sneered Kimball from behind us.

"Friend of yours?" inquired Jeff Draper, indicating Kimball, who was rapidly cooling off.

"Chance acquaintance. I've a friend here, though, I'd like to have you meet. Oh, Hunt," I called. Rogers came up, carrying Kimball's pistol. I introduced them. Jeff Draper continued to hold Rogers' hand as his dark eyes searched the mild blue ones of the man who towered above him.

"Oh, yes. I'm glad to meet you."

"Jeff," I said, interrupting, lest I should forget it, "I saw Bernice Patterson at Cameron this morning."

There was no change of expression on Jeff's face as his eyes shifted swiftly to me.

"She come back, then," he said.

"Yes. That is, I saw her just as we were pulling out. Driven all night, I think. I recalled to her that you had helped her before as a guide."

"That's so."

"I'm telling you, Jeff, in case she might be looking for you. She didn't say that she was."

"*Ohk*—thanks, Chuck." His gaze shifted down the road in the direction we had come, then back to Kimball who stood leaning against the side of the coupé, talking to Emily Millspaw. From Kimball it returned to Rogers. He held out his hand to him "Glad to meet you, Mr.

Rogers," he said. "I go now. Good-by, Chuck. Be here long?"

"Couple of weeks perhaps."

"I see you."

With an Indian's amazing energy once he was determined upon action, he leaped upon his pony and went loping away among the rocks. Emily Millspaw called out to us and we walked over to the coupé.

"Not a very happy introduction to the reservation, do you think?" she said, smiling now.

"I'll say it wasn't," Norman Kimball snorted. "That's the Indian for you; destroy someone else's property, then run off without paying for it."

"He said he didn't have any money, Norman," the girl reminded him.

"That's just the point. Say——!" He straightened up at the thought that had suddenly struck him. "He could have told us where to find Marian. Why didn't we think to ask him?"

"Too late now," I pointed out. "You can't call him back, and you can't go after him through those rocks in a car."

"There's the boy herding sheep over there," Rogers suggested. "You'd probably have to talk Navajo to him, though."

"That's so. Well, I can't do that."

"If I were you, Mr. Kimball," I said, "I'd go on into Kaibito. Charlie Richmond down at Cameron last night said they were up around there. You'll save time, if you're in a hurry."

"I guess I'd better." He climbed into the coupé and took the wheel. Rogers handed him the pistol, which he accepted casually. "Thanks," he said. "If you fellows hadn't been here I might have needed that."

He switched on the ignition, touched the starter button and, before we could walk ahead to the station wagon, he had pulled around us and was off in a small cloud of dust.

3

WE drove onward, keeping the coupé in sight, but following far enough behind to avoid taking their dust. Rogers was silent for several minutes after we got under way, then he said, "I'm wondering about that pistol, Chuck—whether or not I should have let Kimball have it back."

"What else could you do? It's his property."

"Yes, I know. But he might get himself into trouble before he leaves the reservation."

"You're not having any hunches, are you, Hunt, that things are going to turn out—well, you know?"

"None at all. I have only an abiding confidence that this trip is to be entirely free of fatalities of all sorts. I doubt if there's another area in this country as free of major crime as this region we're in now."

"Perhaps not, Hunt. Just the same it's an ideal hide-out if a fellow knows where to hide and how to live off the country. In the old days many a man wanted by the sheriff has hid out in here until he was forgotten. Lots of folks who come up in here get the idea, too, that you can't get lost in it, either, because they always see one or all three of the big landmarks—Wild Cat Peak, Navajo Mountain, or San Francisco Peak near Flagstaff. But I can take you places where you can't see any one of

29

them. I was lost three days in there myself once."

Miles away across the Utah line the blue domelike peak of Navajo Mountain reared its head into the clear sky. It was serene and beautiful from this distance, but close up I knew it for a scarred and ugly pile resembling pig iron, with canyons rayed out from it like spread fingers from the palm of the hand, canyons some of which even today have not been explored.

We were entering a region of low scrub cedar, juniper and piñon pine on a grayish yellow background. Gray sage and sparse green grass stretched away among the low trees. It was a sign that we were close to Kaibito. The coupé ahead of us stopped suddenly in a cloud of gray dust, which drifted gradually away as we slowed up and prepared to stop behind them.

"What does he see now?" I asked.

"Indian coming on a burro," Rogers answered.

Kimball was getting out of the car, obviously preparing to question the man. The rider was dressed in moccasins, overalls, and a faded orange-colored shirt. His long dark hair was bound with a dingy blue headband. His long legs with feet hanging out of the stirrups seemed almost mixed up with those of the plodding burro. Tied behind his saddle was a somewhat battered tin can which held probably two gallons of water.

A curious transformation swept over Norman Kimball as the Indian approached. He became very still; his reddish face paled slightly, and he began gnawing at his under lip, while the fingers of his soft hands slowly opened and closed as if eager to seize, to grasp and to choke.

"Hey!" he called sharply as the Indian on the burro turned out of the road some fifty yards from us without so much as a glance in our direction. "Hey!" There was no response. Norman Kimball filled his lungs and this time shouted: "Hey, you! Fletcher Wicks! I mean you."

The rider yanked the burro's head in our direction, and the animal reluctantly consented to walk toward us. I saw then that, although the man was dressed as an Indian and his hair was long and his skin burned very dark, he was a white man.

"This must be the son-in-law, Hunt," I said.

Emily Millspaw overheard me. "I can't believe it," she gasped, adding, "although, of course, I've not seen him for more than a year."

If Norman Kimball heard us he gave no sign, so intent was he on the youthful figure so like an Indian in appearance and yet unmistakably a white man. He obviously was endeavoring to control the rage that was sweeping through him like a prairie fire. He rocked slightly on his heels, and his top-heavy body swayed from side to side like a man who is drunk and trying to keep his balance.

"Hello, Fletcher," he said, his voice thickening as he smothered his feelings. "I'm glad to see you." He advanced a step or two as Fletcher Wicks halted the burro and sat staring at his father-in-law. Norman Kimball held out his hand, but the younger man made no effort to reach for it.

"Hello," he replied, but without enthusiasm.

"Aren't you glad to see me, Fletcher?"

"No, I don't think I am," was the frank answer. An

amused smile appeared on the young man's face.

"Well—I didn't expect this!" exclaimed Kimball. "I've come all the way out here from Baltimore to see Marian and you, and now you don't even seem interested."

"I'm really not, you know," Fletcher Wicks replied, making an expressive gesture with his hands. "You kicked us out. Do you expect me to fall on your neck with glad cries now when you arrive after nearly a year to pay us a call? You've got some sort of scheme in your head, of course. Questionable scheme, is it? Unethical? You know what I wrote you to do if you came."

"I say, that's not fair!" shouted Norman Kimball, laying hold of the burro's bridle.

For reply Fletcher Wicks, the amused smile widening into a mischievous grin, twirled the end of his reins and snapped the hard leather at the hand. It left a white mark on the back of the hand which was visible as Kimball jerked it away and rubbed it against his trousers leg.

"I've got Emily with me here," began Kimball placatingly. "We intend to call on Marian. Which way is your house? Emily, my stupid son-in-law—" he said, snapping his head about to look at the girl sitting in the coupé. Fletcher Wicks stared at her. A few seconds later he thought better of it, dismounted before any of us realized what he was doing and walked over to the coupé and offered his lean brown hand.

"Sorry," he said. "I mean I'm sorry for you, because you're not a bad sort at all."

"I'm—I'm sure, Fletcher, it is a pleasure to see

you——"

"It isn't a pleasure. Let's be honest about it, Emily. You never liked me," the amazing young man continued. "There's no use beating about the bush. You're sort of in the family, just like me. Marian thinks she hates you like poison, but she lives pretty much in her imagination at times. Maybe she hates you and again maybe she won't after she sees you. You're really beautiful, you know. But whether you're smart or not depends, I'd say, upon whether by this time you've discovered that your guardian is pretty much of a rotter. I'll wager he's brought you out here to further some crooked purpose connected with Marian and me. Hasn't he?"

The girl made no reply, only stared in amazement at Fletcher Wicks.

"We haven't anything but an Indian hogan," he went on. "It's primitive, but it's home and we pretend that we like it, and it's served our purpose. I suppose that I'll have to take you and the old man over there. We don't have anything to eat usually but mutton, Navajo bread and coffee. Now and then there's a stew with onions and potatoes. So, if you want to go, say so, and we'll start. It's about half a mile in from the road. You'll ride the burro; the old man and I will walk."

Fletcher Wicks spoke with a casually expansive air, his hard blue eyes fastened upon the small, dark-featured Emily. She sat speechless as his words lengthened into a harangue, her lovely mouth slightly open as if she were on the point of speaking but lacked words to do so.

Norman Kimball, standing behind his son-in-law, heard every word of it. Once his fists clenched and were half raised to strike the young man; then he thought better of it and dropped them helplessly at his side, although his watery eyes held a glassy, baleful glare in their moist depths.

"Coming?" demanded Fletcher Wicks. Emily sought Norman Kimball's face with appealing eyes. Taking it for granted that she would go, Fletcher Wicks jerked open the door of the coupé, lifted her out before she had time to protest, and tossed her astride the burro. Her tight skirt slipped up over her knees, exposing her small, slim legs, which she sought hastily and with embarrassment to conceal.

"Norman!" she cried, half frightened, as Fletcher Wicks seized the reins of the burro and started off through the low growth of juniper and piñon pine.

"It's all right, Emily," Kimball grudgingly assured her. He started to follow, hesitated, ran back to the car, fumbled in the glove compartment for some folded papers snapped together with a rubber band, removed the car keys, and started after them. I noted the pocket of his coat sagging from the weight of the pistol, and Rogers and I stood there, the same thought in each of our heads as he made after the slowly moving pair as nimbly as a man of his years and top-heavy bulk could do.

"Not very promising, is it?" Rogers grunted, climbing back into the station wagon.

"It looks like stormy weather in the hogan," I replied, sliding in under the wheel. "Anyway, it's none of our business, Hunt. And, now, we'd better be getting on up to Kaibito."

It was only a mile, and soon the curving road revealed the stone trading post huddled at the base of the two-hundred-foot high grayish-white ledge which was an extension of White Mesa. I had known Kaibito—which means Willow Spring—since the time the trading post was first built, back in the days when the spring yielded only a bucketful of water a day, and the trader, to be sure of this meager supply, visited the spring before dawn.

It lacked an hour or so to noon. We parked the station wagon among the trees and went inside. Harry Easton, the trader, and Peggy, his wife, were both tickled pink to see us. They weren't busy; only a few Indians were around. It was one of those lazy mornings when one could sit and talk endlessly of reservation life, but Rogers was restless, now that we had reached our jumping-off-place.

"You don't want to start over into the canyon this afternoon, do you, Hunt?" I asked as we ate noon dinner with the Eastons.

"Well—no, I guess not. But I should like to get out on a horse for a little exercise, though."

"You boys pick you out your horses from the corral, and start any time you want to," Harry Easton urged, pushing back his plate. An Indian was knocking on the counter out in the bull pen, as the store was known to the traders, but the old custom at Kaibito of not waiting on an Indian while the trader was eating still obtained.

"Supper will be about sundown," Peggy Easton ad-

monished as we got up to go. Peggy was still a beautiful
woman; she was nearing sixty with no gray in her dark
hair and no fat on her rather large frame. Her hands,
of course, showed the marks of toil, but her soft dark
eyes were clear. For years in her early life Peggy had
nursed in a hospital in San Francisco until one day a
convalescing Harry Easton had asked her to marry him.
"That's all behind me now, Chuck," she told me once.
"I loved the work, but I wouldn't go back to it now after
living here on the reservation with Harry." With no
children of her own, Peggy had become a sort of mother
to many a lonesome man in that sparsely settled region.

"It's like getting home again to see you, Peggy,"
Rogers said, pausing at the dining room door.

"I'm glad to hear you say that, Hunt," she answered
with a flash of her sound, white teeth. "You and Chuck
are always welcome at the post. I only hope you two
are not up to any devilment," she joked.

"Devilment?" Rogers echoed. "All we plan to do is
poke around among the ruins in the canyon for a week
or so."

"Well, help yourself. You two know your way about
at Kaibito."

"By the way, Peggy," Rogers said, "there wasn't an
English couple with a little girl here in the last week or
so, was there?"

"Yes. They went from here on horseback to Rainbow
Lodge on Navajo Mountain. Sweet little girl she was
too. Barbara was her name. Why?"

Rogers explained about the diary, but Peggy had no
address to which it could be sent, and so we went down

to the corral, saddled a couple of horses and started for a ride.

We had no particular destination in view when we set out from the trading post; there was merely a desire to be horseback in a country where the horse is still the most effective means of transportation. And it was entirely by accident in the course of that afternoon's ride that we passed close by the hogan where Fletcher Wicks and his wife lived, and to which he had taken his father-in-law and the latter's young ward.

All four of them were sitting outside the hogan as we rode by within fifty yards of the place. It was all too apparent that a heated argument was then in progress. In fact, had it not been for Norman Kimball's voice, we probably would have passed by the hogan without knowing who were the occupants thereof.

"Marian, you've got to sign it, I tell you!" He was shouting at the top of a husky, worn voice. To which Fletcher Wicks replied as heatedly: "Why has she? Just tell me why."

The argument was at that stage where it could go on indefinitely, insistence and denial tossed back and forth between them as when children bicker.

The sound of our horses as we passed close by hushed their shoutings for the moment; heads turned on twisting necks to see who we were, and Fletcher Wicks waved an indifferent hand in our direction, to which we replied and rode onward, hearing the argument resume again before we passed from earshot.

Rogers spoke pessimistically a few moment later. "An argument and inflammable tempers; cross purposes and stubborn natures—plus a gun," he said.

"It's only a family argument," I objected. "Noisier than some, perhaps. Besides," I twitted him, "I thought your hunches all pointed to no fatalities this trip."

He was silent for a moment, then he said, "One can't be sure of hunches until they are proved either right or wrong. Anyway," he added, urging his horse into a gallop, his words coming back to me over his shoulder, "I don't see how it could affect our plans however it terminates."

We were gone from the post probably three hours, being drawn back reluctantly at last by the realization that we ought to check over the stuff in the station wagon and decide just what we were taking on a three-day trip down into Navajo Canyon among the ancient ruins of the cliff dwellers.

We unsaddled the horses and turned them into the corral and walked over to the station wagon which still stood where we had parked it in the small grove of piñon pine. I was busy sorting over the stuff in the wagon while Rogers sat on the seat making a list of it, and noting as we went along things we would have to get from Harry Easton at the trading post. A man walked past, carrying a package. He observed us at our work and paused for a friendly word.

"Hello," he said. Rogers returned his greeting. I looked up to see a man of early middle age, not very tall, wide through the shoulders and heavy through the middle. He was a square block of a man with a bald head and unsteady brownish eyes.

"Mr. Andrews?" I inquired, recalling the description

in the diary.

"Yes," he answered, without curiosity, however, as to how I should know his name. "Nice place up here. I said to my wife when we started out on this trip that I wanted to get as far away from civilization as I could in a trailer. And I guess this is it."

"Have any trouble bringing a trailer up in here?"

"Nope. Oh, there's that sandy stretch down near Red Lake. But it didn't bother me any."

He looked like one of those individuals one encounters on summer roads almost anywhere in the United States. There was no guessing anything about him, however. He could have been a small town merchant, or a plumbing contractor, or he could have been a pensioner of some sort. At any rate he had the carefree air of the footloose, brushed over with a faint suggestion of mystery.

Andrews stood at the side of the station wagon, one foot on the running board, and offered an occasional remark while we worked over our stuff. A hundred yards or so off among the trees I could see a greenish object, which, harking back to the diary again, I concluded must be the trailer from which Mrs. Andrews, who bit her lips together like a turtle, stared and stared at little girls.

The sound of an automobile drew near and soon tires ground over the gravelly surface. An expensive gray coupé pulled in close beside us. Norman Kimball climbed out. He saw us, of course, for we had finished our task and were out upon the ground once more.

"I came to get them something to eat for dinner tonight," he said flourishing an arm in the general direction in which he had come. "Stupid son-in-law! I can't forgive stupidity. Fletcher Wicks hasn't got enough in that hogan for a bird to eat, let alone four human beings. I guess—" His voice sort of trailed off into nothing. I glanced at him to see why he had stopped talking. I was not certain of what I saw. I think that his eyes had encountered the form of Lester Andrews. I think that he started in astonishment and then checked himself before anything of his reaction was visible on the surface, but I'm not sure of it. He turned abruptly away from us and walked rapidly in the direction of the trading post.

Emily Millspaw smiled and nodded to us from her seat in the coupé. She did not appear to recognize Lester Andrews. He stared a moment at her and shifted the package under his arm.

"I'll see you again, gentlemen," he said cheerfully and walked briskly off toward the green trailer.

Ten minutes or so after Andrews had vanished, Norman Kimball came out of the trading post carrying several bundles in his arms. Red-faced and puffing from this exertion he handed the things in to Emily Millspaw.

"By George," he said, calling lightly across to us, "I'm not going to starve. I've got stuff enough for a good dinner and breakfast anyhow." He indicated the bundles which the girl was stowing on the wide seat beside her. "I say—" Kimball came over to the station wagon, lowering his voice somewhat. "I was a bit short with you this morning after that little trouble down

the road with the Indian. I mean when you gave me back
the gun. I don't think I'd have shot him, really. You
might not think so but I control my temper pretty well
in emergencies. I was only going to scare the fellow with
a little gun play, but I didn't need to be short with you
when you meant kindly what you did in disarming me."

"No apologies necessary," smiled Rogers.

"I didn't know how you'd taken it."

"Are things all right down at the hogan?" Rogers
inquired casually. "Sounded like a bit of an argument
when we went by there. Couldn't help overhearing it,
you know——"

"Oh——" Kimball laughed and his watery eyes shifted
to the coupé, "that's nothing. We're a great family that
way. Even when we're agreeing we're apt to sound as
though we're on the point of coming to blows. By the
way, who was the barrel-chested fellow who was here
talking to you when I drove up just now?"

"Name's Andrews," I answered. "Lester Andrews."

"Andrews?" he repeated slowly, reflectively. "Andrews——?"

"Know him?" I inquired. "He's over in that green
trailer."

Kimball's gaze shifted to the trailer, lingered for a
moment then returned to Rogers. "I'll not be here long,"
he said, ignoring my question. "I think the screwballs
will see things my way after we've had a good dinner tonight. I should like to see you two gentlemen again before I start home. I didn't expect to run across your
type in so out of the way a place as this. I'm sure we'd
find several things in common."

"Thank you, Mr. Kimball," Rogers smiled. "Mr. Graham and I will be here a couple of weeks. Come up whenever you can and we'll have a talk."

"I'll do that. Well—" he moved briskly for one of his topheavy bulk toward the coupé and climbed under the wheel, "good day, and I'll see you later."

It was not until after supper that Rogers and I discussed the incident. "Andrews, I thought, looked at Kimball as if he were a stranger," he said in answer to my query. "Kimball obviously was curious, though, about Andrews. Ignored your question too. Well—it's of no consequence, I guess," he ended and we dismissed the subject little dreaming how important the matter was to become. "Wonder if Kimball expects to spend the night down at the hogan."

"I'm sure I don't know," I answered. "I noticed a devilhouse near the daughter's hogan. He could sleep there if he's not superstitious."

Harry Easton came into the living room at the moment and joined our conversation. "That's where Tall Navajo's son died a year ago," he said. "The family, of course, promptly abandoned the hogan, as Navajos always do. Began moving out, in fact, the day before the boy died and there was nobody left at the last, except Tall Navajo himself. I helped him bury the boy. Nice young fellow he was too. The hogan ever since, of course, has been a devilhouse."

"I'll bet Kimball won't stay there, Harry," I remarked, "if he finds that out."

"Maybe not. I know I wouldn't. I've got a great deal

of respect for Navajo notions, if you want to call them that."

Rogers' eyes held a far away look in their mild blue depths as he reflected upon what the trader had said. Presently he broke the silence that had unaccountably fallen upon us.

"The Navajo attitude toward death is so entirely different from that of the white man," he mused. "With us death is a commonplace which leaves us unmoved unless it strikes within our immediate circle of family or friends. We're callous toward it, unfeeling even. But with the Navajo it is the greatest of evils, and personal contact with the dead is to be shunned. With them death is of the very essence of the powers of darkness. Who's right about it, they or we? They live closer to Nature than we do; they've remained fundamentally in touch with the forces of life, whereas we have been civilized into a world of artificialities in which there is no time to reflect upon the great truths.

"I venture," he continued evenly, "that if one of us up here at Kaibito were to die tonight—say, Kimball, for example—it would mean very little to those of us at the post. The daughter and the ward probably would experience an appropriate grief. The son-in-law from all indications would, however, be singularly unmoved; and as for the three of us we very likely would say, when we heard about it: 'Oh, is that so? I'm sorry. What was the cause?' We would experience no profound reaction. We'd do what we could to help, of course, and let it go at that."

"I guess you're right about it, Hunt," said Harry Easton. He yawned and pulled out a thick watch from his pocket and wound it. "I'm sleepy," he announced. "You fellows talk as long as you've a mind to, though. I'm going to bed."

We were sleepy also, although it was early. We said good night to Harry and went to the tiny room assigned to us. I sensed a growing mood which amounted almost to a feeling of depression as we prepared for bed.

"Why Kimball?" I asked suddenly. "Why make him the example?"

"I might have said Andrews. Or Wicks."

"Yes, I know. But there's something mysterious, almost uncanny, about this country. It's not hard to start quiverings in your backbone if you dwell on it. Did I tell you what happened to me the last time I was up here on the reservation?"

"No. What?"

"I had a flat tire down in the desert. I swear there wasn't a hummock or even a rock big enough to conceal a jack rabbit for what seemed miles. I got out the tools and was starting to work when a voice over my shoulder said, 'I fix.' I looked around and there was an Indian. I let him change the tire, gave him a dollar and then stowed the jack. And when I looked around again he was gone. I don't know where he came from or where he went. Now that may not sound so very queer, but let it happen to you while you're alone in the desert. You'll think differently about it. It's things like that in this country, when you let yourself think about them, that stir the hair on the back of your neck."

"Yes, I know," said Rogers quietly. "Talk to any old-timer in this region and he'll tell you stranger things than that. Unbelievable things. Inexplicable."

We went to bed and eventually I dropped off to sleep, although the wind troubled me with its uneasy searching among the branches of the pine trees outside.

The gray light of dawn was in the single window of the room when I wakened. Someone was pounding on the door of the trading post and Harry Easton was shuffling along the hallway to discover what the row was about. I sat straight up in bed, and poked Rogers in the ribs. He merely grunted and rolled out, and without a word began to dress. I heard Harry open the door and begin talking in Navajo to the mysterious knocker. My own understanding of this tricky Indian tongue was rusty. I missed the key words, and the sense of it was lost to me.

"I don't get it, Hunt," I said.

He grunted and looked through the window. "We'll soon find out."

I presumed that he referred to Harry Easton, but the next moment I saw piercing the grayness the lights of an automobile coming swiftly toward the post. It swung in sharply, skidding in the gravel, struck hard against the trunk of a tree and with the hollow metallic sound of a buckling fender came to a sudden stop. A door was either wrenched open by the impact, or was opened hurriedly by the driver, and the next moment a slight figure half leaped, half fell out of the seat, rolled to the ground and lay still.

Rogers reached the girl before I did. He picked her

up and held her in his arms as he stooped over her in the graying light of dawn.

"Are you hurt, Miss Millspaw?" he asked gently.

The girl at the sound of his voice struggled violently; she brushed a hand across her eyes as if to clear away a film before them, and regained her feet.

"No!" she said sharply. "No, no! I'm not hurt. I didn't see the tree in time." She was trembling; her dark eyes were suddenly filled with dread as if some vast fear had laid its hand upon her.

"Tell me," said Rogers quietly.

Suddenly and without warning the girl collapsed and would have fallen had not Rogers caught her and held her. "Oh, it's awful!" she moaned. "It's terrible!"

"What's happened, Miss Millspaw?" Rogers persisted. "Tell me."

There was a footfall upon the gravel behind us and I looked about to see Harry Easton approaching. He had overheard Rogers' question and had taken in the situation.

"It's Kimball," he said strangely. "They've killed him."

"I was afraid so," said Rogers.

4

MANY things happened that morning which stamped
themselves upon my mind, but nothing, I think, remains as vivid as the white, strained face of Emily
Millspaw as she told in short disjointed sentences of
the finding of Norman Kimball's body.

"I ran," she said. "I ran to the car. Through the
trees. And I fell." She held out her left hand and showed
the small, bruised palm. Her skirt was torn at the knees.
"All the time I knew he was dead—"

"How did he die?" Rogers interrupted. The question
startled her, and she turned her dark eyes up to him.
The light of the new day was growing stronger and I
saw fear still lurking in the white face.

"I don't know," she breathed. "He was sort of under
a tree. But it was his hand that frightened me so," she
went on breathlessly. "It reached out—"

"Reached out! How do you mean—?"

"Yes. It must have been reaching out for a long time,
as if to stop me. It was still dark, you know, and reaching out like that it—well, I realized that it was stiff—"
Her lips quivered, and she bit them severely to check
their quivering. "Of course he was dead. And—then I
ran. You—you're going to do something about it, aren't
you?"

"Yes, of course."

We had begun slowly to move toward the trading post. Harry Easton asked a question.

"Where was Fletcher Wicks?"

"Oh—I never thought of him!" she replied, halting in her tracks, her dark, frightened eyes turning curiously upon the trader. "Of course, he could have come with me. I don't know—I just didn't think of him."

Harry refrained from questioning her about the body, for he had had something of it from Big Lefty, the Navajo, who had pounded on the trading post door even before Emily arrived. And Rogers, who might have made further inquiries was strangely silent.

"Well," the trader began, a serious note in his voice as we approached the steps of the porch, "well, it's bad. It's bad business—"

His observation was interrupted by soft, thudding sounds as Emily Millspaw suddenly sank upon the stone steps and began to sob. The three of us gazed ruefully down upon the tiny figure, uncertain just what to do for her. As if in answer to our silent plea for help, Peggy Easton of a sudden slammed out of the trading post door, ran across the porch and dropped down beside the girl on the steps.

"There, there, child," she said comfortingly. "You come with me. I'll take care of you." She lifted the slight figure in her strong arms and carried her inside.

We breathed a sigh of relief and the trader picked up where he left off a moment ago. "It's bad business. I'm deputized, of course, to help preserve the peace up here at the spring, but this is a job for the sheriff at Flagstaff. I'll call him, and after some breakfast, Hunt, you and Chuck and I will go down there," he said looking from me to Rogers. He turned away in the direction of the telephone.

Rogers' face had a wry expression, and he glanced away through the trees at the peaceful morning scene. The sunlight was just beginning to touch the pines. He made a gesture of resignation with his large hands, admitting that at least for that day there would be no excursion into the canyon.

Harry Easton had finished his conversation with the sheriff's office in far away Flagstaff when we entered. "Come on, boys, let's have breakfast."

Only the three of us sat down to bacon and eggs, coffee and toast, and when that was finished very largely in silence, we walked down to the corral, saddled horses and started off. There was no opportunity for conversation, for the distance was only about a mile and the pace that the trader set was fast. He pushed down the road for half a mile or so, then entered the scrub as if it all were still a life and death matter. Rogers rode easily behind him on a big bay horse, and I brought up the rear.

Fletcher Wicks was standing in the doorway of his hogan when we pulled up in front of it. A woman was visible through the doorway, a woman dressed in Navajo costume. Her face was deeply tanned, her feet were shod in moccasins. Obviously, however, she was white. I realized that it was Marian Wicks. In the few minutes we were there she did not emerge from the hogan but left the talking to her husband.

"Where's the body?" asked Harry Easton of Wicks. "There was a man killed near here, wasn't there? Named Kimball?"

"Yes," was the casual answer. "My wife's stepfather, to be exact. It's lying over there the other side of that chindi-hogan."

"What can you tell us about the killing?"

Fletcher Wicks shrugged his shoulders. "I don't know anything to tell you. The Indians found it. The first I heard about it was when some Indians made a racket out there. That was a little before sunup. I went over. He was dead all right. But go see for yourselves. I've seen enough of it and I'm staying here."

We dismounted and dropped our reins. Rogers led the way to the place Fletcher Wicks had indicated. At first I didn't see the body, which lay where it had fallen partly under the sprawling branches of a scrub cedar. Rogers stiffened a trifle as his eyes fell upon the gruesome sight. Harry Easton halted suddenly, threw out an arm to stay our progress and muttered something under his breath.

"Well, there he is, boys," he said quietly. "Not pretty to look at, is he, with his head bashed in like that?"

"They seldom are," Rogers remarked grimly. I knew what he was thinking; he was thinking of the trip into the canyon which Norman Kimball had ruined at least for this day. He sighed lightly. "Well, if it will help any, Harry, I'll look the scene over and see what I can discover of importance. There's no sign of a struggle here."

Thus did Huntoon Rogers set to work on what was

to prove to be one of the strangest of his many investigations. He spent a few minutes examining the body where it lay face up, the eyes staring glassily into the dark, writhing branches of the cedar, the spindly legs clad in golf knickers and the arms thrown out.

"Undoubtedly death was due to a skull fracture, Chuck," he remarked in the course of his examination. "There's an abrasion on the knuckles of the right hand, which indicates that he may have fought his assailant." He felt in the baggy pockets of the coat and sat back on his heels. "The pistol he carried is missing." His gaze strayed to Harry Easton. "That's important, of course, even though he died of a bludgeoning rather than gun shot." He got to his feet, apparently lost in thought.

"Anything, Harry?" Rogers inquired of the trader whose eyes were fixed on something beyond the body.

"Looks like a gun lying over there by that piñon."

"Gun? Let's go take a look at it."

I was glad to quit the immediate presence of the dead man. We walked about fifty feet, Harry Easton leading the way. Suddenly he halted and Rogers and I stopped at his side. On the ground lay an automatic pistol wrapped in an old cloth which once might have been blue but was now somewhat faded. Except for about an inch of the barrel and about half of the grip, the pistol was concealed by the cloth. I stooped to pick it up when Rogers struck my arm away sharply.

"Let it alone," he said. "An Indian always wraps his gun, doesn't he, Harry?"

"It's an old custom—to keep it from rusting."

Rogers dropped down beside the weapon and poked

at it gingerly with the tip of a long yellow lead pencil he took from his pocket. He lifted it gently by inserting the pencil into the end of the barrel, looked under it, gazed into the barrel itself, smelled of it, then placed it gently back. He got slowly to his feet, leaving the weapon on the ground.

"In the first place the gun is Kimball's," he said. "I recognize it, even if it is partly wrapped. It might have been dropped there accidentally, and again it might not. The ground is too hard for it to have left any mark if it had been dropped from the height, say, of a man's pocket as he ran away. The pistol hasn't been fired. And it may or it may not have been the weapon which was used to beat Kimball to death. Assuming that Kimball was killed where the body now lies, the position of the pistol is on the pathway out to the road." He took a piece of string from his pocket and, with the aid of the lead pencil, which I wielded for him, we managed to get the string about the cloth-wrapped pistol and tied securely.

"Was the slayer mounted or on foot?" I asked.

"The only way we can find that out, Chuck, is to do a little tracking," Harry Easton answered.

"Before we do that, though," Rogers countered, getting to his feet, the pistol swinging from the string, "I'd like to know a little more about what happened last night at Fletcher Wicks' hogan. It all may be very simple of solution. Let's go talk to them now."

"All right, Hunt," Harry said, and strode off through the trees, leading the way.

Fletcher Wicks watched in silence as we approached,

a curious look mingled of scorn and apprehension on his face. He pointed to seats on several old, well-worn packing cases, and invited us to sit. He sat down, then, leaning back to call in at the doorway of the hogan, shouted:

"Marian! Come out here!"

The young woman came out. She was an unusually attractive person, despite the fact that she was dressed in Navajo fashion. She had a marvelous complexion, the natural red of her cheeks showing through the deep tan, and she was as graceful as a mountain lion, which fact was evident in the few steps she took in our presence and despite the enveloping fullness of the green skirt. Her manner was quiet, as if the tragedy of the night just past weighed heavily upon her spirits.

"This is my wife," said Fletcher Wicks, making the introductions. "I know what you've come for, of course." He addressed Harry Easton. "The old man is dead, and you and I know how he died. You want to know if I did it. You're hoping maybe that I did, and you mean to get what I know out of me by hook or crook."

As he talked my gaze chanced to rest upon the right side of his face. There was a puffiness about the cheekbone, and the skin was bruised. Rogers saw it, and so did Harry Easton, and I knew that Rogers, at least, was thinking of the skinned knuckle of the dead man lying out under the trees.

"Yes, I know," said Fletcher Wicks, almost as if he were reading our thoughts. An expression of amusement flickered briefly in his hard blue eyes. "The old man landed one on me, but that was early in the evening when the row was just beginning to warm up."

"What was all the trouble about?" interrupted Rogers.

Fletcher Wicks looked at his questioner hesitantly, then he said:

"I might as well tell you that too. He came out here to get Marian to sign away her interest in a piece of business property in Baltimore which she inherited from her mother. His interest in it and Marian's were undivided. The old man was getting hard up and he wanted to sell it, and Marian and I were determined that she shouldn't agree to do so. He could have saved his breath and ours too by not coming out here in the first place."

"You were angry; you lost your tempers?" pursued Rogers.

"He was raving part of the time. I don't think we got even upset about it."

"What happened when he realized that Mrs. Wicks wasn't going to agree to the sale?"

"He never realized it. Never admitted it, so far as I could discover. He was the most stubborn man I ever knew. Thick-headed, I guess, is a better word. He rushed off to the trading post to get some things for dinner. And Marian cooked it for him and Emily. Then the argument started all over again, and finally I pushed him out of the hogan and he belted me one."

"What happened then?"

"He calmed down and went over to the empty hogan and decided he would sleep there. I told him it was a devilhouse to the Indians, and that I was inclined to

believe as the Indians did about it. He laughed and said
what was the difference. He wouldn't go up to the trading post, and he wouldn't let Emily Millspaw go, although I told him that you could sleep them both. Emily,
of course, slept here in the hogan with Marian. We gave
the old man a blanket and an old sheep pelt for a pillow,
and that's the last I saw of him alive."

"Where did you sleep?"

"On the ground over there," he replied, pointing to
a near-by tree.

"Did you hear anything after you separated for the
night? Any sound of quarreling, or anything of an intruder moving about?" Rogers asked.

"No."

"Did you waken in the night?"

"No."

"Have you any information to offer which you think
might have some bearing on what has happened?"

"None."

"Do you know of any enemies Mr. Kimball had?"

"A man like him probably made many enemies in his
lifetime, but I don't know of any particular enemy who
would do him in here on the reservation."

Fletcher Wicks, I believed, had spoken truthfully. As
he talked the apprehension he had manifested earlier
vanished; he remained somewhat casual and amused
throughout at Rogers' questioning. Of a sudden Rogers
turned to Marian Wicks.

"Mrs. Wicks, can you corroborate what your husband has said about your father?"

"Yes. All of it," she said quickly. Her voice was soft

and pleasant. As she talked there were evident faint signs of the shock she must have felt at the violent passing of Norman Kimball. Her face became animated from the moment she opened her lips to speak, and I was drawn to Marian Wicks.

"What can you tell me about the death of your father that your husband hasn't already told me?"

"Very little. But—let me explain. He wasn't my father. He was only my stepfather. He married my mother when I was just a child. I was known, however, as Marian Kimball until I married, and few, excepting Fletcher, knew it wasn't my name."

"Yes?" said Rogers, smiling faintly.

"Mother, of course," the young woman went on, "was a very naïve person. When they married she gave him an interest in her property, and he managed it rather badly. He lost so much because of his poor business sense. He kept me always short of money after mother died. Finally I couldn't endure it longer to even be near him, and I married Fletcher—and we came out here."

Rogers cleared his throat lightly and gazed steadily at the young woman. He said, "It may not seem to have any bearing on the subject, but why did you come here to the Navajo Reservation?"

"Well—you see"—she hesitated, a light half apologetic, half defensive in the depths of her brown eyes— "Fletcher had this idea of his that a white person could adopt the ways of primitive man, such as the Navajo, and thrive on it. That the white man is cousin to the savage. That civilization is much too complicated for his own good, even for his happiness. That man's well-being is much more closely related to the bare soil and hard ways of a primitive wilderness than it is to the city. As soon as we prove it, Fletcher is going to write a book about it."

"And, then," Rogers pressed, "it wasn't because you hated your stepfather and wished to humiliate him that you came out here to the reservation?"

"Did he say that?" she demanded, her eyes firing up.

"Night before last at Cameron. To Mr. Graham and me, who were strangers to him."

"You see what sort he was," said Fletcher Wicks, interrupting.

"Let's get back to what happened last night," suggested Rogers, ignoring the young man's interruption. "Mrs. Wicks, did you hear or see anything after your stepfather went to sleep in the devilhouse that might throw light on our inquiry?"

"Well"—again she was hesitant—"I don't know."

"How do you mean that?"

"I was restless. Naturally such an afternoon and evening as we had, in spite of Fletcher's saying just now that it didn't upset us, was disturbing. I didn't sleep well. I came out here about midnight and stood looking at the stars, thinking over the unusual sort of life I'm leading. Then something happened. You know how it is when all of a sudden you become conscious of a changed situation without knowing exactly how or when it began to change—that is, one moment you didn't know and then suddenly you did without realizing how. You see, I wasn't alone. Somebody else was there near that tree." She pointed with a slim arm.

"Maybe it was the old man, Marian," suggested Fletcher Wicks.

"Perhaps, but I don't think so. Of course, the light was dim, and things are so different at night. It was more like a darker shadow than the other shadows, but it moved. It didn't seem to make any noise. It didn't move rapidly. It was more like a man, moving slowly. Then there was a whistle."

"Could it have been an Indian, Mrs. Wicks?" asked Harry Easton.

"I don't think so. The shadow moved in the direction of the devilhouse where father was sleeping. I was on the point of thinking that I'd seen and heard nothing when all of a sudden there was the sound of voices. I went to the opposite side of the hogan to investigate, but everything was still again, and I could see nothing."

"What happened next?" inquired Rogers.

"Nothing. I concluded that my imagination had played me a trick, and I went back inside and got to sleep again."

Rogers puzzled for a moment over this odd story, then he asked, "Did you hear anything that was said between the shadow and your stepfather, if it were he who spoke with the shadow?"

"No. Only voices; no words."

"Were you aroused later by any noise of a struggle, say, when the crime was committed?"

"No."

"Tell me about the girl, Emily Millspaw, who stayed with you in your hogan last night."

"She's the daughter of an old friend of my mother's.

She's younger than I am—she's twenty; I'm twenty-five."

"How does she happen to have been with Norman Kimball?"

"When her mother died—her father having been dead many years—Norman Kimball became the trustee of the estate. And I'm sure he all but ruined it for her."

"Why did she come along with him to the reservation?"

"I didn't ask her. Perhaps only for the trip; but my guess is that father said to her that if she would help him persuade me to sell that property in Baltimore there would be some money for her."

"Did she take part in the argument yesterday?"

"She joined in once or twice to plead with me to see it their way. Understand, I'm not blaming Emily. She's a sweet girl, and father has influenced her to his way of thinking. He'd made me appear in her eyes as standing unjustifiedly between her and what was rightfully hers. I don't blame her at all."

"Did she sleep in the hogan last night?"

"Yes."

"Could she possibly have had anything to do with the death of Norman Kimball?"

"I don't know; she—"

"She couldn't have killed him, Hunt," Harry Easton interrupted. "As small a woman as she is. Kimball was a big man—"

"Yes, I know," Rogers replied. "What else were you going to say, Mrs. Wicks?"

"Emily was gone this morning when I wakened—just

before daylight."

"What time do you think Kimball died, Hunt?" I asked.

"I'd have to guess, Chuck," Rogers answered. "I'm not a doctor. Probably, though, some time between midnight and four o'clock this morning."

"I venture that you're correct, Mr. Rogers," offered Fletcher Wicks. His head lifted suddenly as he caught sight of someone approaching the hogan. "Here comes John Navajo," he said.

"That's good. I sent for him," said Harry Easton, turning about on his box to catch sight of an Indian on a cream-colored pony. He waved an arm in greeting, then turned back to Rogers. "John Navajo is the Indian police around Kaibito. He'll run down the Indian angles to this thing for us. The sheriff won't get here for several hours maybe."

5

THE Indian police officer swung off his pony and walked solemnly into our circle. Harry Easton addressed him in Navajo. He introduced Rogers and me to him, and the Indian bowed stiffly to us. For a moment he stood beside the packing case Fletcher Wicks had pointed out to him. He was more than six feet tall, straight and slim, yet with muscles, I'm sure, more like steel than mere flesh. Instead of the neat uniform resembling that of a forest ranger which the Indian police were supposed to wear but often as not discarded as the whim dictated, he was dressed in a badly wrinkled blue serge suit which was tight through the trouser legs. His shirt was a delicate orange color, open at the throat, and his long black hair was caught up underneath a small tan, round-crown, stiff-brimmed little hat one would see nowhere but on an Indian reservation. His black eyes were mere slits between the high cheekbones of his copper-colored face.

"John," said Harry Easton, as the Indian sat down, "the body is over there by that big cedar. The name is Norman Kimball." He pointed in the direction of the dead man. "It's murder. Skull broken. This is the weapon, I guess," he ended, indicating the wrapped pistol.

61

Huntoon Rogers lifted it by the string and the weapon dangled, swinging slightly before the Indian's interested gaze. He did not offer to touch it, but nothing of interest about it escaped his little black eyes. Harry went on talking.

"The gun hasn't been fired. Belonged to the dead man. Found about fifty feet from the body. Wrapped like that. Big Lefty discovered body before sunrise. Ran to the post to tell me. I telephoned sheriff's office at Flagstaff. I tell you this, John, to save you work. But you look around too. White man may have done it; Indian may have done it. Don't know yet."

"Yes," the Indian policeman replied. He reached suddenly for the string on which the pistol dangled. Rogers gave it to him, and the Indian held the weapon for a closer inspection. He smelled the muzzle, then gave the weapon back to Rogers.

"Where's Jeff Draper now, Harry?" I asked of the trader.

"Jeff? Went down to Red Lake three days ago to stay a week."

"Jeff home now," announced John Navajo. "I come by his hogan. Why?"

For a moment no one spoke, then Rogers explained. "The dead man threatened Jeff yesterday morning with this," and he held out the dangling pistol. "The argument was over a camera which Jeff smashed on the rocks. It belonged to a girl in Kimball's car. She had tried to take Jeff's picture. He didn't like it."

"I understand," said the Indian. "Was Kimball mad with Jeff?"

"Yes; very. How far does Jeff live from here?" Rogers asked.

"Half mile. I talk to him. Anything else?" He addressed us all, although his gaze was upon Harry Easton.

"I can't think of anything else, John."

"You spoke a while ago, Harry, of doing a little tracking," Rogers reminded him.

"Oh, yes."

"Tracking?" echoed John Navajo.

"Yes. Whether or not the killer was mounted. Which way he went. Anything we might pick up about him."

"*Ohk*," said the policeman. He rose to his full six feet or more.

We left our horses stamping and switching their tails at the flies, and walked in the direction of the body. John Navajo went over to stand beside it for a brief moment while the rest of us walked beyond it in the direction of the Red Lake road. The character of the ground in the vicinity didn't promise much. A horseman would leave a trail, but our feet made no impression on it as we walked. In the open spaces between the piñon pine and scrub cedar there was thin grass growing on the gravelly surface.

We spread out in our attempt to pick up some sign, but without success. It was obvious that the killer had arrived and departed from the immediate scene of his crime on foot. We struck one fairly fresh trail, which for a few minutes seemed to promise something; but, when followed, it led us back to Fletcher Wicks' corral. When Wicks was questioned it was settled that it could have been made only when he brought Emily Millspaw and Norman Kimball in from the road the day before.

John Navajo had joined us by this time and we went back to the dead man and started over again. A half hour later, after careful search, we struck a trail about a quarter of a mile in from the road. It was not more than a few hours old.

"I've got something, boys," shouted Harry Easton.

We converged upon him where he stood looking down at the prints of an unshod horse's hoofs. We looked at John Navajo for confirmation. He grunted then struck off alongside it. It was not difficult for an experienced tracker to follow. At times it vanished on hard ground, but we managed to pick it up again with no trouble. For a quarter of a mile the trail indicated that the rider had plodded along at an easy walk. Then of a sudden he had halted, but not for long. From this point he had ridden fifty yards to a juniper tree and tied his horse to a limb, and been absent some time. It was plain that the horse had been restless and had trampled over a considerable portion of the grassy area. Some time later, as we read the signs, the rider had returned, mounted his horse and ridden away at a slight angle from the course he had followed in from the road, and at a faster pace.

Twenty minutes later we walked up to an Indian hogan. In a corral near by were three ponies with heads together drowsing in the sun and stamping at occasional flies. At first there seemed no one about. John Navajo lifted his voice in the Navajo tongue, and a moment later Jeff Draper appeared in the door of the hogan. He looked sleepy, but when he saw the four of us he straightened up alertly. Whatever he may have thought at sight of us was obscured behind his dark eyes.

"Want to talk," said John Navajo, indicating the seats outside the hogan door. We sat down. Jeff continued for a moment to stand, then squatted on his heels before us. I had time to take out a packet of cigarettes and offer them and light one before anything else was said. John Navajo, looking through his slits of eyes at the young Indian, said, "You kill man named Kimball last night?" He jerked his head in the direction of Fletcher Wicks' hogan perhaps half a mile from the spot where we sat. Jeff Draper did not reply at once. He seemed to consider the question from its many angles, then he said:

"No."

"You know who kill man?"

Again there was the wait, then the answer, "No."

John Navajo leaned forward, and with a small stick drew on the ground a long line which we soon realized was to represent the Red Lake road. "You ride here." The stick scratched along the ground at right angles to it. "You stop here. Then ride to tree and tie pony. You gone long time. You come back and ride to hogan." John Navajo discarded the stick. The sketch remained a graphic picture on the ground before us. "What happen?"

Jeff Draper's face was inscrutable; his manner one of indifference. At length he said:

"Two cars are beside the road. Gray one and another. I turn off. I know the man and girl have gone to Fletcher Wicks' hogan."

"How did you know that?" Rogers interrupted.

"I have heard from a friend down the road." He hesitated as if to give Rogers an opportunity to reply, then he went on: "I ride along, then I see someone walking. He hide behind a tree. By and by I stop. I tie pony, and go back and follow this man. He go to hogan of Fletcher Wicks. I hear whistle. Three times. Pretty soon he is talking to someone. I go away. I cannot see who man is. I go back to pony and ride home. That's all."

"Was there any quarreling between the two men, Jeff?" I asked.

"Just talk. I think it is friendly visit, so I do not stay. I am there maybe ten minutes."

"Was the man an Indian or a white man?" I asked.

"White man. Navajo man no whistle at night."

"Why?" asked Rogers.

Jeff was silent for a moment, then he said, reverting to precise English. "The dead should not be disturbed by whistling, for at night they are up and about their own affairs."

"Why did you come back from Red Lake so soon?" demanded Rogers, shifting the subject. "You went to stay a week, I am told."

There was no resentment in Jeff Draper's face; there was the slightest narrowing of his eyes, so slight as to be almost unnoticeable. Because of that I reasoned it was a question he was not prepared to answer; at least it was one he had not expected. There was no change of expression, however, when he said, "I decide to come home."

Rogers thanked Jeff, and we turned away toward Fletcher Wicks' hogan. There John Navajo separated from us to prosecute his inquiry among the scattered hogans in the vicinity of Kaibito, and we mounted our horses and rode back to the trading post.

"Somebody will be getting up from Flagstaff soon," Harry Easton said as we rode along. "We can turn the whole business over to him. I'm not a detective; I'm an Indian trader. How about you, Hunt?" he twisted in his saddle to address Rogers. For a moment Rogers rode in silence, then he spoke rather decisively.

"I came up here, Harry," he said, "on a little vacation. I want to poke around among the ruins of the cliff dwellers in the canyon. I still mean to do it. But—" he hesitated, "I don't know. There's something strikes me as peculiar about the murder of Norman Kimball. Both Marian Wicks and Jeff Draper saw a shadowy man; both heard a whistle. A Navajo, as Jeff pointed out, doesn't whistle after dark. Yet the gun is wrapped." He indicated the weapon tied to the pommel of his saddle. "An Indian," he went on, "if he had wrested the gun from Kimball and killed him with it, might perhaps wrap it and carry it away from the scene. On the other hand, if an Indian isn't guilty, and it's a white man, the attempt to throw suspicion upon an Indian is rather clumsy. Although the fact would point to somebody familiar with Indian ways."

"And so what, Hunt?" I asked, thinking of Harry Easton's question.

"I may not poke about as much in the cliff dwellers' ruins in the canyon as I had hoped to do. But I'll not give it up entirely."

Little else was said on the remainder of the ride to the

post. We continued to the corral, unsaddled and turned the horses inside and walked back to the stone building in which were both a store and living quarters. There was no sign of the sheriff yet, but near the station wagon was a small desert-stained green coupé. It was the coupé I had seen early the morning before at Cameron.

"Well," I said to Rogers as we walked past it, "it looks as if Bernice Patterson has arrived."

Harry Easton picked up my remark. "Bernice?" he echoed with interest. "She hasn't been up here for a long time. Nice girl. Peggy'll be glad to see her."

We found Bernice Patterson and Peggy in the bull pen. The blond young woman greeted Harry with enthusiasm, which bubbled over to include me and Rogers, whom I introduced. The rather abrupt way she had told me good-by down at Cameron remained in my memory, but whatever had prompted it was forgotten now by her, and she was interested in recalling incidents and individuals, both Indian and white, of several years ago when she was making a study of the ruins in the canyon.

The murder of Norman Kimball was briefly touched upon, for Peggy had passed the news on to her. It meant nothing, however, to Bernice, for Kimball and his ward were strangers, as were also Fletcher Wicks and his wife Marian.

"I don't know any of them," she said. "They're all new since the last time I was up here."

A heavy voice behind us rumbled the request, "Some cigarettes, please, Harry," and a coin clinked on the counter. I turned about to see a somewhat rugged looking individual with soft brown eyes and dark hair which lay thin and flat to his rather round skull. His hat was crushed under his arm. He was solid and heavy-limbed and slow moving. I guessed him at somewhere near fifty years of age, although there was no gray in his hair and only a slight sagging of the muscles of his face and throat. He was tanned, almost weather-beaten, but his hands were soft.

Harry went behind the counter and got out the cigarettes. Bernice Patterson, her arm about Peggy's waist, went into the living quarters of the post, leaving the bull pen to the men.

"Where's your pardner this morning, Mr. Bent?" Harry asked. The reply was not immediate.

"He deserted me for a skirt," the man said finally with a detached casual manner. "Little dark-haired girl hanging around here this morning. It seems that he knows somebody in Philadelphia who knows somebody in Baltimore who knows her by sight. Provides a bond of sympathy and understanding when you're young, you know. All I know, of course, is what I overheard of their conversation. Girl is mixed up in this killing you had last night, I understand."

"That so? Do you know these fellows, Mr. Bent?" said Harry, introducing us. "Mr. Huntoon Rogers and Chuck Graham. Surrey Bent—he paints pictures."

"Glad to meet you, gentlemen," Surrey Bent said, extending a powerful hand in turn to each of us. He broke open the package of cigarettes and offered them. "That your station wagon out there under the trees?"

"Yes," I answered.

"Looks like you came up for business. But tell me,

Harry"—he turned back to the trader—"about this killing last night down at Fletcher Wicks' hogan."

"Well—" Harry Easton hesitated, "we can tell you 'most everything about it but who done it, Mr. Bent. That's what the sheriff's going to want to know, but he'll have to figure it out himself. John Navajo is already working on the Indian angle of it, but nobody's sure an Indian done it—at least I'm not—although there's some signs it might have been." He went on from there to relate the salient facts we had discovered at the scene of the crime, and Surrey Bent listened carefully, smoking his cigarette and staring through the open doorway.

"Rather unfortunate for Fletcher Wicks and his wife," he commented. "It'll be hard for them to keep the sheriff from jumping to conclusions."

"Yes, I imagine so," I said.

Harry Easton continued, telling of the tracking of the unshod pony to Jeff Draper's hogan, and Jeff's denial that he had been the killer.

"Jeff was down at Red Lake as late as seven o'clock last night," Surrey Bent remarked. "Saw him and a couple of other Indians who belong up around here. We stopped, Carter Lamb and I, to eat with Stacy James and his wife at the post, then came on to Kaibito."

"Jeff would have to ride pretty fast to get here when he said he did. It's about thirty-five or six miles," I observed.

"An Indian would, especially a fellow like Jeff," said Harry. "He'd catch up a fresh pony out of some Indian herd down there and ride it to death if he was in a hurry to get some place. A horse doesn't mean much to an Indian. There's lots of 'em on the reservation. He'd make it in five hours—maybe four. That would put him up around here about eleven o'clock, or twelve, if he left Red Lake soon after you saw him, Mr. Bent."

"His story could be true, then," mused Rogers. "About seeing another car parked beside the gray coupé when he turned off to his hogan. Did you see another car on the road there, Mr. Bent?"

"No—I didn't. The gray car was there. Showed up in our headlights, of course. But that was all— I guess." He left us with a feeling that there was something more.

"You guess what, Mr. Bent?" Harry Easton prompted him.

"That's what I'm wondering," the artist replied. "Whether that's all there is to it. I guess not, though. That would be jumping to conclusions, instead of reaching them logically."

"You saw something else, Mr. Bent?" pressed Rogers.

Surrey Bent flipped the unfinished end of his cigarette through the open doorway. He removed the crushed light felt hat from under his arm and smoothed it out and set it on his head, as if he were on the point of leaving us, but instead he put his hands in his pockets and leaned back against the counter.

"I saw something else, yes. But what it means, if it means anything at all, is something I'm not prepared to say."

"What was that?"

"Carter Lamb, this young friend of mine—he's a painter too—was driving, and I was sitting beside him

talking to him about old Thlizzy Thlanny—remember
old Many Goats, to translate his name, over around
Canyon de Chelly? Fine old Indian, he was too. Well,
as we swung around the last curve down here below the
post, I saw the headlights of a car up this way. Looked
to me as if somebody was just starting out somewhere.
And the only way you can go, of course, is down the
way we had come. Then all of a sudden the lights were
switched off, and everything was dark up around here.
Didn't think anything about it, of course. Didn't even
comment on it to Carter. We pulled in beside the station
wagon out there, and I was thinking that maybe the
fellows who owned it might have been about to start
out with it and changed their minds, or had just been
moving it around to park it, or even had just come in
ahead of us. But my hand touched the hood and then
the radiator as I climbed out and they were cold. So it
couldn't have been the station wagon lights." He stopped
abruptly and stood away from the counter.

"Then what?" asked Harry Easton.

"That's all there is to it. Your car was in the shed,
Harry."

"I didn't have it out at that time; the truck neither,"
Harry said.

Surrey Bent pulled out the packet of cigarettes once
more and slowly took one, lighted it and inhaled deeply
before he went on.

"Yes, I guessed you hadn't. Only other car up here
last night besides ours," he said, indicating all of us,
"belongs to that fellow with the trailer over there. But
I didn't go over to see. Wasn't that curious, in other

words. Don't jump to any conclusions, gentlemen. I know I'm not going to. Well," he pulled his hat down on his forehead and started through the doorway, "I've got to do a little piece of work this morning. See you later."

6

I⊤ was not until later on that day that we got around
to questioning Lester Andrews, the man in the green
trailer. For the sheriff, who brought the coroner with
him, arrived soon after Surrey Bent walked out of the
bull pen. He wanted to be taken at once to the scene of
the murder and go over the ground we already had
covered.

I had known Ed Wilson, the sheriff, for fifteen years.
He was one of those Western characters, physically
hard and forthright, who not only knew his duty but
never hesitated in its performance. There was no sub-
tlety about him, no hidden crannies in his mental proc-
esses; he was as obvious as the Grand Canyon, which, as
the crow flies, was less than a hundred miles from where
we were that morning at Kaibito.

He shook my hand with a crushing grip and was introduced to Rogers. Ed Wilson looked Rogers up and
down, a little frown wrinkling his leatherlike forehead.
He dropped Rogers' hand after a moment.

"Are you by any chance the fellow who doesn't claim
to be anything but an English professor, but who's
managed to solve some pretty tough murder cases?"

"Well—yes," grinned Rogers. "I've happened to be
lucky. All it takes, of course, is a curious mind and a

little luck."

"What I'm hoping," said Sheriff Wilson, "is that this isn't a tough one."

"Yes, of course. Personally, I don't want to have a perfectly good vacation spoiled for me. I'd lots rather poke around down among the ruins in the canyon than try to untangle clues."

"Well—maybe you'll get your wish, Professor. I'll look the thing over, then I'll compare notes with you." He turned to Harry Easton. "I suppose you can supply us with horses, Harry," he said. "The coroner will want to pack the body out to the road. He's got a truck down that way."

"Sure; help yourself, Ed. You know where the corral is. Don't think I'll go down again. The Indians are going to hold a 'sing' in a couple of days near here, and already some of them are beginning to drift in to Kaibito. Keeps me busy waiting on trade."

"Okeh, Harry. Maybe the Professor will go down with me."

"Of course."

Rogers and I went back to the scene of the crime with the sheriff and the coroner. The latter was a thin, tall man whose small head seemed on the point of being completely enveloped by the huge hat he wore if it should chance to slip.

There was nothing new to be discovered at the spot where the body still lay. However, we found Emily Millspaw and Carter Lamb at the hogan of Fletcher Wicks. Emily and Marian Wicks, as the two persons most closely connected with the dead man, had been discussing the disposition of the body, and whether or not they should return with it to Baltimore when it was released for burial.

"I've decided I'm not going back," said Emily soberly to Rogers' inquiry. "And neither is Marian." There still were traces of fear in her deep, dark eyes.

Fletcher Wicks hunted out a couple of empty packing boxes to add to those already around the doorway to the hogan, and we all sat down.

"I've offered to make the trip," said Carter Lamb, speaking up and addressing his remarks to the sheriff. Lamb was a well-built young man of medium height. He wore a small black mustache, hardly more than a shadow on his upper lip, and he had a pair of sincere dark-brown eyes set in a wide, deeply tanned face. He hugged his knees, his fingers toying with the laces of his high boots.

"But he's not going," said Marian Wicks. "It's silly to think of letting him. There's a lawyer friend of the family who can look after everything at that end."

"Just as you say, Mrs. Wicks," Carter Lamb replied. "I'm perfectly willing to act for you, since I was planning anyway to start east within the next few days."

The matter was dropped there, giving way before a question directed at Emily Millspaw by Rogers.

"How did you happen to discover the body of Mr. Kimball?" he inquired.

The girl was instantly in a state of confusion. I thought that it was because she had been dreading the questioning which she knew was coming.

"I—I don't know," she began hesitantly, her face

losing somewhat of its bright color.

"Tell us about it," suggested Rogers casually. "Just the facts as you recall them." He smiled at her encouragingly.

"Well—of course, I— You see, everything was so strange last night, so different from things at home in Baltimore. And—there'd been this argument, and Norman was—was so excitable. It was difficult for him to keep his temper under the circumstances. Naturally all that sort of thing did something to my nerves. And the bed I tried to sleep on was hard—" She shot a glance at Fletcher Wicks. "I'm not used to a hard bed on the ground. So I didn't sleep at all. Or at least not very much. Just naps."

Marion Wicks reached out a brown hand and patted the girl on the arm and smiled at her. What feeling there had been between them evidently had been dissolved by the tragic event of the past night.

"Did you hear any sounds of the fight, Miss?" asked Sheriff Wilson.

"None at all," she turned her wide eyes upon the sheriff. "That's why I think I must have dozed a little, although I imagined I didn't sleep a wink."

"What happened? I mean how did you come to discover the body before anybody else did?" Wilson persisted.

"That—" the girl said seriously, "that was so strange. I was very wide awake and suddenly the strangest feeling of dread, of uneasiness, of fear, came over me. Something kept telling me that a terrible thing had happened. At first I believed it must be a nightmare and that I'd wake up in a moment. Then it was so vivid in my mind all at once that something was wrong that I became panicky. I had to get out of the hogan; I just had to get out into the open air, although I was timid about the dark when I went to bed. For it was still dark when this happened." She paused a moment, then went on.

"I got up quietly. I put on my clothes and got outside as quickly as I could. I was even more terrified outside than I had been inside. I started to run and I— stumbled over the body. It was gray in the east. I don't know how I knew it was Norman's body. Maybe it was the feel of his coat; it was a rough tweed. Something told me that he was dead—the stiffness, I guess, in his arm, which brushed my leg. I was too terrified to scream. I ran, though. Toward the east, because it was growing light there. I came out on the road not far from the coupé. I had keys in the pocket of my coat; Norman and I both had keys to the car. By this time I was over my panic, although I was still scared, and so I climbed in and started up to the trading post to tell somebody what had happened."

She was breathless at the end of her recital. A moment's silence intervened and then Rogers said, "Didn't it occur to you to appeal to Mrs. Wicks or her husband for help?"

The girl shook her head slowly. "I just didn't think of it. I was so frightened, so intent on getting away from the spot."

Carter Lamb reached out and laid a hand on the girl's arm and patted it reassuringly. "I'm sure you did just what anybody else would have done, Emily, under the circumstances," he said.

"So help me," Emily Millspaw said, "I didn't think of you, Marian, or of Fletcher. I was never so frightened, so completely out of my mind with fear, ever before."

"It must have been a shock." Rogers smiled toward her. "But that's over now. Tell us, though, did you hear a whistle about midnight? Or voices? Or the sounds of the struggle which ended in Norman Kimball's death?"

Emily Millspaw shook her head blankly. "No," she breathed.

There seemed little else to be gleaned at the scene of the crime. The pockets of the dead man had been searched, but nothing of interest beyond the usual small change, billfold, pocketknife, checkbook and handkerchief was found. The coroner then had wrapped the body in canvas and, with it sprawled upon the back of a pack horse, was seen going out toward the road through the sparse growth of piñon pine and scrub cedar.

"Well," Sheriff Wilson got to his feet, "thanks, folks, for helping us out."

"Do you need me any longer, Sheriff?" inquired Fletcher Wicks, rising also. "If you don't, I think I'll go into Flagstaff. Not that I cared a damn about the old man, but just to make sure that the body is started east all right, and that the lawyer at home is notified."

For a moment Sheriff Wilson stared at the young man, at the Indian costume, the long black hair bound by an orange-colored headband, stared as if probing deeply into and assaying the motives behind this assertion.

"No. Go ahead," he said shortly.

"Thank you, sir. Emily," he turned to the girl, "it's all right if I take the coupé?"

"Of course, Fletcher. It's really mine; my money paid for it."

Fletcher Wicks turned away and we mounted our horses and headed back toward the trading post.

Lester Andrews was riding up the trail from Navajo Canyon when we turned our horses into the corral. Rogers called to him while Sheriff Wilson and I waited at the bars to the corral for him to put up his horse. Andrews swung down from the saddle, his heavy boots crunching upon the gravelly ground.

"Hello," he said cheerfully. The presence of Sheriff Wilson with us excited his curiosity. He didn't know the sheriff even by sight, I was sure, but his sharp eyes must have caught the shine of Ed Wilson's badge.

"Mr. Andrews," I said, "this is Ed Wilson, the sheriff from Flagstaff."

The man stuck out his hand. "Glad to meet you, Sheriff," he said.

The sheriff's flinty eyes scanned the wide shoulders and thick body of the other, then he dropped the hand. "Howdy," he said.

It was Rogers who brought us to the subject in hand. "I suppose you've heard there was a killing last night not far from the trading post," he said.

"Yes," answered Andrews. He was smoking a black, battered pipe and had been holding it in his left hand.

He stuck the stem between his lips and waited for Rogers to continue.

"Man was named Norman Kimball. From the East. Baltimore, I think."

"So I heard earlier down at the post," replied Andrews, removing the pipe from his mouth. He turned to Ed Wilson. "I guess you're inquiring into the thing, Sheriff?"

"Yes, I am."

"Who do you think did it? Some Indian?"

"Maybe. Maybe not."

"I guess it's safe enough around here for us white people, Sheriff. Not been any Indian trouble, has there?" Andrews inquired with a trace of anxiety in his manner.

Sheriff Wilson snorted a denial and looked away toward the post.

"By the way, Mr. Andrews," asked Rogers, "did you happen to know the dead man?"

There was no sign of the effect of this question upon the man, but I wondered afterward about it. "Know him?" he echoed blankly. "No, of course not. Why do you ask?"

"I had a feeling yesterday," Rogers explained, regarding him narrowly, "when Kimball drove up and stopped near where you were talking with Chuck Graham and me, that you might have known each other."

"That so?" Andrews replied blandly. "Of course, I can't say what this man Kimball knew or thought he knew about me, but I'm sure I never saw the fellow before."

"Sorry," apologized Rogers, smiling.

"Are you a detective, or something?" asked Andrews seriously of Rogers.

"No-o," Rogers answered slowly. "I haven't any official connection with this investigation. I am interested, though, in finding out who killed Kimball last night—"

"I'll connect you up officially now, Professor," announced Sheriff Wilson, reaching into his pocket and bringing out a deputy sheriff's badge. "Put this on," he ordered, handing it to Rogers, "and go ahead with your questions."

"Questions?" echoed Lester Andrews, looking first to Sheriff Wilson and then to Rogers, who was pinning the badge on his coat. "You don't think I had any part in what happened last night, do you?" There was a slight resentment in his tone. "I didn't kill the man; didn't know he was dead until I went down to the post this morning after breakfast to hire a horse to take a little ride down into the canyon."

As he voiced his protest my eyes were drawn to the trees beyond the corral where I saw riding slowly along a lone horseman leading a weary-looking pack horse. The meager pack, the battered guitar case, the hunched shoulders of the rider struck a responsive chord in my recollections, and I recalled our meeting with Ernie Caldwell on the road early the day before. It was the cowboy who, according to our youthful diarist, had crinkled eyes and smiled all the time, which was a good sign in strangers. He disappeared from view, and my attention came back to Rogers. He had noted Ernie

Caldwell's arrival too; however, he was still intent upon Lester Andrews.

"By the way," Rogers continued, "did you happen to have your car out last night? Around midnight, say?"

"My car! You mean you're asking me that question?" Andrews retorted with undue emphasis, I thought.

"Yes."

"I was asleep last night by nine-thirty. And my car sat all night right where it is now." He waved a thick arm in the direction of the green trailer and the black sedan beside it. He was very positive; his unsteady brown eyes seemed to fire up in the depths of his round face. "You can't accuse me of killing anybody; I'm not that kind. Do I look like a killer, Sheriff?" he demanded of Wilson.

"Killers always look like themselves, Andrews," replied the sheriff, "which is one way of saying that they don't always look like you expect them to look."

"What do you mean by that?" the man snapped, knocking the ashes from his pipe against the corral gate, his voice rising angrily.

"Keep your shirt on. It was your question and you asked it. All I did was answer it," the sheriff retorted testily.

"You're not going to accuse me and get away with it," Andrews retreated defiantly from his position. "Is that all you want to know?" he inquired coldly of Rogers.

"One more question." Rogers' tone was casual. "Did you some time around midnight last night park your

car near Kimball's coupé on the road, then walk into
the scrub to a hogan next door to Fletcher Wicks'
hogan where Kimball was staying, attract Kimball's
attention by whistling a signal, and hold a conversation
with him?"

"Me?" shrilled Andrew, his voice rising excitedly,
the color fading from his round cheeks. "No, I didn't."
He thought for a moment, then burst out: "You can't
trap me with any trick questions. I just told you I was
asleep at nine-thirty and that my car wasn't moved last
night at all—"

"Did you kill Kimball?" asked the sheriff sharply.

"No, I didn't."

Rogers exchanged glances with the sheriff.

"That's all," the latter said.

Lester Andrews opened his lips to retort something,
thought better of it and his mouth closed like a steel
trap. He turned on his heel and strode away toward the
green trailer.

We watched him walk all the way before we made a
move. When the trailer door slammed upon him we
returned to the trading post, making no comment
among ourselves as to what had been said at the corral.
When we arrived at the post we found Jeff Draper
sitting on the porch as if waiting for someone.

"Hello, Jeff," I greeted him.

"Hello, Chuck," he answered. I was on the point of
going inside the store, when Sheriff Wilson stopped
short and stared at the Indian. Jeff looked at the sheriff
stonily.

"What are you mad about, Jeff?" Sheriff Wilson asked him.

"Not mad."

"Don't let me find out that you killed that man Kimball last night."

"I no kill him."

Rogers interrupted this exchange. He was smiling slightly, and there was a twinkle in his mild blue eyes.

"Jeff," he said, "I think maybe you looked at the other car last night too. Not the gray one, but the other one parked near it. I think you would know it if you saw it again. How about it?"

Jeff Draper's black eyes were on Rogers' face. He seemed to study not only the remark but Rogers as well.

"Maybe," he replied. "I think maybe I could. Why?"

"It would help a lot if we knew whose car that was."

"I guess maybe so," replied the Indian.

"Would you mind going over to that car beside the green trailer and looking at it, and coming back and telling me whether or not it's the car that stood near the gray coupé last night?"

Jeff Draper did not move from his comfortable position with his back against the store front. He glanced in the direction of the trailer and the black sedan beside it, then back at Rogers.

"No," he said indifferently.

"Go on, Jeff," urged the sheriff.

Jeff did not reply. He looked away as if he had dismissed all thought of us and the request that had been made. Rogers continued to wait smilingly. Finally Jeff brushed a fly from the back of his hand, shifted his position slightly, and said: "No need. Same car I saw last night. I looked at it while ago."

7

WE entered the bull pen at the trading post. Harry Easton, the trader, was sitting beside a window at the rear reading a day old newspaper which Sheriff Ed Wilson had brought up with him that morning from Flagstaff. Business had slackened after a morning rush. John Navajo was leaning against a showcase smoking a cigarette, his eyes mere slits in his copper-colored face. I was still turning over in my mind the fact that if Jeff Draper was telling the truth, then Lester Andrews had lied to us and his black sedan had been parked beside the gray coupé on the road at the nearest point to Fletcher Wicks' hogan.

"Any luck, boys?" inquired Harry Easton, putting down his paper. He took off his horn-rimmed spectacles and stowed them carefully in a case he carried in his shirt pocket.

"Not a great deal, Harry," was the sheriff's reply.

"John's been talking to Big Lefty," the trader remarked, jerking his thumb in the direction of the Indian policeman.

"How about it, John?" Sheriff Wilson asked.

John Navajo drew deeply upon the small remainder of his cigarette, dropped it on the floor and stepped on it with a moccasined foot. He blew a great cloud of smoke from his lungs, then said:

"Big Lefty say still dark when he start to post to get sack of flour. No flour in hogan; squaw want biscuits for breakfast. He see man on ground like shadow. Poke him with foot. Man stiff. Dead. Somebody running on path. He think it is a girl. She make crazy noise like crying. Big Lefty keep still on other side of tree till girl go away. Big Lefty run to post with news."

John Navajo ceased his account as abruptly as he began it. The sheriff looked at the policeman thoughtfully.

"Thanks, John," he said, then added as an afterthought, "any moonlight these nights?"

Rogers answered. "Not much," he said. "There's an old moon; it rose last night a little after midnight."

The sheriff turned to the trader. "Harry, where's the gun you brought with you this morning from the killing?"

Harry Easton got up from his chair and went behind the counter. He brought out a pasteboard carton and removed the lid, exposing the weapon still wrapped in the dingy blue cloth and tied as Rogers had tied it with a string.

Sheriff Wilson lifted it out, carefully untied the string and removed the cloth wrapping. It lay on the hard counter, an ugly, heavy automatic pistol; without question it was the weapon Rogers had taken from Norman Kimball the morning before when the latter was about to threaten Jeff Draper with it for smashing Emily Millspaw's camera.

"How about my fingerprint outfit, Harry?"

Harry Easton brought out a small black case from under the counter. Sheriff Wilson took his dusting powder from it and carefully dusted the weapon first one side then the other and blew off the surplus powder, lifting the pistol about as Rogers had done with a lead pencil thrust into the end of the barrel. He pored over the surfaces carefully, finally taking a magnifying glass from the box and re-examining the weapon minutely. At last he stood up straight and shoved back his broad-brimmed hat. Rogers spoke.

"You never find fingerprints, Mr. Sheriff," he said grimly, "when they might be helpful. Not even a blood-stain on the butt, is there?"

Sheriff Wilson swore under his breath and rubbed a hard hand through the graying stubble of his beard. "Wiped clean," he said. "What do you make of it now, Professor?" He picked up the weapon and replaced it in the carton, and tossed the dingy blue cloth upon it. "Save it for me, Harry, till I get ready to go back to Flagstaff." He turned to Huntoon Rogers for a reply to his question.

"The only thing that occurs to me now," Rogers answered slowly, "is that a white man would be more likely to wipe the gun clean than an Indian—the Indian temperament being what it is, and his knowledge of the methods of criminal detection being less extensive than is usually the case with a white man."

"I guess you're right about that," said the sheriff.

"Unless, of course"—Rogers hesitated slightly—"the killer is what you might call an educated Indian."

He did not amplify the statement, but I knew he was

thinking of Jeff Draper still sitting with his back to the stone wall on the porch outside. The frown that crossed the sheriff's leatherlike brow indicated that he followed Rogers' thought perfectly.

"All of which doesn't help us much, does it?" I remarked.

The sheriff ignored my statement and turned to Harry Easton.

"How long has this fellow Andrews in the green trailer been at Kaibito, Harry?" he asked.

"About a week, I guess. This is Wednesday—yes, just a week."

"Know anything about him?"

"Not much. He was up here a couple of years ago in the same outfit. Stayed a week or ten days. Went down into the canyon every day. That wife of his acts like she's stuck tight in that trailer. Peggy tried to talk to her a couple of years ago. But she didn't have much luck. When Peggy can't thaw 'em out, they just don't thaw. She's said howdy-do to her a couple of times now this trip, but that's all. He does the talking. Talks on anything. Seems to know a lot about various things ; seems sort of interested in the history of this country, as though he might be collecting it. Never heard him say, though, that he was going to write it up."

"Well," the sheriff lowered his voice, making sure that there were no outsiders listening in from the porch, "he's a candidate. Either he's lying or Jeff Draper's lying. He says his car wasn't parked on the road near the gray coupé ; Jeff says it was. Who's right?" He paused, then turned to the Indian policeman, who seemed to brood over what we were saying. "John, how about it—does Jeff lie?"

After a long moment John Navajo shifted his moccasined feet and leaned more heavily against the counter. "Um-m-m," he grunted musingly, "sometimes."

"To come back to one point," Rogers interrupted, "there's no reason to doubt Mrs. Wicks' statement that she was aware of the presence or actually saw somebody lurking in the vicinity of the hogan. Jeff Draper's statement corroborated hers. Moreover, why should Jeff manufacture out of whole cloth, so to speak, the black car parked on the road near the gray coupé? If Mrs. Wicks had seen or heard nothing we would have more reason to doubt Jeff's word than we have now."

"I guess you're right about that, Professor," grunted the sheriff. "Well," he went on after a moment, "it begins to look like we'd have to put this guy Andrews on the griddle. I'd like to have somebody else besides Jeff, though, to accuse him of lying to us. You know how a white man is, especially a fellow like Andrews who doesn't seem to know Indians. He thinks an Indian's word ain't any good. And an Indian—especially you Navajos, John"—he turned to grin at the Indian policeman, "is dead certain he's superior to a white man, so it leaves a fellow like me up against it in this kind of an argument. It would sure help out if just one of you fellows here knew something."

I was on the point of reminding Rogers of what Surrey Bent had said that morning about seeing the lights of a car as he and Carter Lamb were pulling into the trading post, when the sound of footsteps on the thresh-

old of the doorway to the living quarters of the post
halted me. We all turned to see who was approaching
and discovered that it was Carter Lamb. Behind him
came Emily Millspaw. The pair paid no attention to us
as they walked up to the counter.

"Two bottles of your very best pop, Harry," Lamb
said with an air of slightly exaggerated humor. "It's
my treat, and the lady is from Baltimore."

Harry Easton took a couple of bottles from the cooler,
removed the caps and set them out. Carter Lamb cere-
moniously presented the girl a bottle of reddish liquid,
then as his hand moved toward the other he paused.

"Oh, pardon me, gentlemen," he said engagingly,
"won't you join us? It's my treat, as I just said." We
were slow to respond, and then Rogers accepted with a
twinkle in his mild blue eyes.

"Thank you, Mr. Lamb," he said, "I don't care if I
do."

"Mr. Sheriff? Mr. Graham?" persisted the youthful
painter. "Oh, by the way, Mr. Sheriff," he said, as we
moved up to the counter alongside them, "I overheard
what you were saying just now about our friend Andrews, the man in the green trailer."

Sheriff Wilson shot a sharp glance at the suave young
man. "Guess we were speaking up. Forgot Harry's room-
ers have the run of the house. But it don't matter, now
that you heard us, if you keep still about it."

"Then you'd really like to find somebody else who
could offer a bit of evidence about the owner of the black
sedan?"

"Yes, we would."

"Well—" Carter Lamb sipped from his bottle then set it down. "Look at me. I'll talk."

"What do you know?" Sheriff Wilson's manner seemed lightly touched with suspicion, as if the young man's airy approach to the serious matter under discussion was to be suspected.

"Well, it depends upon your arithmetic, Mr. Sheriff," Carter Lamb replied lightly, a smile playing about his lips.

"What's arithmetic got to do with it?"

"I mean when you add two and two do you get four for the answer, or five?"

"I thought you said you knew something," retorted the sheriff.

"It's all in the point of view." The young man shrugged his shoulders. Emily Millspaw, her lips red from their contact with the bottle of pop, looked disapprovingly at the young man.

"This is serious business, Carter," she said soberly.

"And I'm serious, Emily," he answered, turning to her. "The sheriff just doesn't want to draw me out. I like to be drawn out, you know."

"Tell us what's on your mind," said Rogers casually.

"Ah—" and the youthful painter addressed Rogers, "a man willing to listen. I'll tell you, sir. Yesterday morning Surrey Bent and I planned a trip down to Tuba City. Surrey Bent, by the way, is the best painter to my knowledge of the Western scene. A bit somber, of course, in his composition, somewhat abstract, but with a most marvelous sense of color. The mystery, the somberness of this country saturates you if you've been in it as long as Surrey has. It's not a happy land; it's no Maryland apple orchard in springtime. Well, as I was saying," Carter Lamb went on, with an impish eye to the stern, rugged face of Sheriff Wilson, "we were bound for Tuba City. A one-day trip. The old car, though, had a bum spark plug. Shorting badly. Harry was entirely out; new supply not in yet. What to do in this crisis? 'Hell,' says Surrey, 'go over to that fellow in the green trailer and borrow one.' "

"You did that?" asked the sheriff.

"Exactly, Mr. Sheriff."

"What does it prove?"

"You're ahead of me now," Carter Lamb retorted. "Mr. Andrews was very helpful; his spares were at our disposal. The bum plug was replaced by a new one and we went gaily down to Tuba City, returning last night. Of course, I brought back a new plug to give to Mr. Andrews, but ten-thirty at night is no time to return a borrowed article. I did go down to the trailer with it about seven-thirty this morning, however. The gentleman wasn't up yet, according to the old sour-puss who eyed me as if she thought I were a redskin come to massacre them. I gave the plug to her, of course, with our thanks for their help, but I couldn't forbear the remark anent her husband's late sleeping. This is what I said: 'This night life at Kaibito gets the best of us down.'

"I thought her head was going to fly off her neck the way she jerked it around at me. She'd started back inside the trailer. 'What business is it of yours?' she shot at me. 'None at all, lady; none at all,' I said, and bowed myself out."

Carter Lamb picked up his bottle of pop from the counter and drank from it. Nobody said anything for a long moment, then Sheriff Wilson asked, "And what does that add up to, Lamb?"

"That's what I observed at the outset, Mr. Sheriff; it depends on your arithmetic entirely. I understand, Professor Rogers, that this sort of problem is up your alley," he turned to Rogers. "What do you say the answer is?"

"Well," Rogers began, a thoughtful light in his mild blue eyes, "granted that the facts are exactly as you have stated them—and I'm not doubting you at all—it would seem that Mrs. Andrews' reaction to your sally conveys the idea that Andrews was out late last night."

"That's the way I get it too, Ed," said Harry Easton.

"Exactly the same thing was in my mind," Carter Lamb went on. "You see, I didn't know then what had happened down at the Wicks' hogan, or what seems now to be in your thoughts—namely, that Andrews is involved some way in the murder. The old gal, in that one brief sentence, when taken with the manner in which she delivered it, expressed surprise, resentment, and a desire to hush me up; also the assumption that we both knew something which we interpreted in the same way. Do you get me now, Mr. Sheriff?"

"I get you, Mr. Lamb. I thought at first that you were trying to kid me about this thing."

"Not at all." Carter Lamb grinned, returning to his unfinished bottle of pop. "I wouldn't kid the law. Emily here knows I wouldn't. Especially when it concerns the manner in which her dear guardian departed this life."

"Please, Carter," begged the girl, turning her wide eyes upon him. "Don't try to be funny when things are so serious. I'm not quite up to it after—last night. And —before that too." She put down her bottle half finished, indicating that she was through with it.

Rogers' eyes were on the girl. He seemed to probe beneath the surface as if seeking the reason for that last remark of hers. "You looked tired night before last at Cameron," he said, "as if you'd been under considerable strain."

"I was tired, Mr. Rogers," she responded, turning her gaze up to him. "We came so fast. And all I could do was sit still in the car. It was so monotonous for so much of the way. If he'd only have let me drive even a little it would have been a help. He worried me with the things he said, the reckless way he drove." There was a strange sort of earnestness on the girl's face, as if something within her was forcing itself out, as if she was finding relief in talking. "And I knew that our reception would not be the pleasantest, and our stay might end— I didn't know how. Certainly, though, I didn't dream that it would be like this."

Rogers set his empty bottle on the counter. He took out a large white handkerchief and wiped his lips. A couple of Indians appeared in the doorway with some wool to sell. Rogers made no response to the girl's remarks. An exchange of glances, however, flashed between him and Harry Easton and the sheriff.

"You folks go on back into the living room," Harry suggested, "while I wait on trade."

"Let's do. Shall we?" said Rogers, taking the girl lightly by the arm. Not until we were seated did Rogers resume the conversation. "There are some questions I want to ask," he said. "You want to help, I'm sure, unravel some of the knots in this problem of ours."

"Yes, of course, I do. But I don't know anything at all helpful."

"One never knows about that," Rogers reminded her. "You indicated just now that Norman Kimball on the trip out was in a state of mind. Can you tell me what was the trouble? Did he, do you think, foresee this sort of ending?"

"I'm sure I don't know about that," replied Emily. "But after we left Oklahoma City he got to talking about my father. He never did that before. You see"— she hesitated, sitting forward in an old-fashioned rocking chair, her feet scarcely touching the floor, "my father disappeared mysteriously years ago. He had a gold mine in Utah, and when I was being born he came back home to New York to see me. He stayed only a day, mother told me, then hurried back out west. But he never arrived. We never did hear from him again. We were unable to trace him. Of course, the court declared him legally dead some years later, but I don't know whether he's dead or still alive."

"How did Norman Kimball come to talk about him, do you think?" Rogers asked.

"Well—he and father were good friends. That's why Norman was named trustee for my money when mother died. And Norman was associated with father in the mine, and was waiting at the mine for father to return from his trip east to see his new daughter."

"What became of the mine?"

"It just sort of played out, Norman told me once. He came back east a few months later. I remember mother saying that he was broke. He married Marian Wicks' mother, you know. She was an old friend of my mother. She had quite a bit of money then, and Norman remained in the East. He gave up mining and just managed her business affairs for her."

"And his talking about your father got on your nerves?"

"Yes. He'd say: 'Emily, what if he's still out here? What if he was a victim of amnesia? What if we'd find him in the West after all these years?' Then he'd jam the accelerator down and we'd go shooting around cars and tear along the highway at eighty miles an hour, or even faster. It was just as if he were trying to run away from himself. I accused him of it, and he looked at me so strangely. That's when we hit a soft shoulder and almost turned over. Only a miracle saved us. I'm still weak when I think of it."

"Did he say anything in answer to that?"

"Nothing. I tried to reason it all out that night at Cameron, when we were so close to our destination, and I was certain then, just as I'm certain as I sit talking to you, that something was worrying him greatly. Something more than whether or not we could talk Marian Wicks into selling the property in Baltimore. And now, after what happened last night, I've changed my mind. I don't think it was worry at all. I think it was fear."

"Fear? Of what?" urged Rogers.

"I don't know, Mr. Rogers. I don't think it was fear of the Indians, although he looked at every one of them suspiciously. He got out his pistol the morning we left Cameron and put it in the glove compartment. I didn't know until then that he had brought one along."

"Did he name any individual? Or make any indication whatever?"

"Oh, no. Maybe it's all imagination on my part. I didn't accuse him of being afraid of anything, and he didn't say that he was afraid. I'm just putting my feelings about it all in words. Maybe it will help you. I don't know."

8

THE placing of Lester Andrews on the griddle, which Sheriff Wilson proposed to do, was postponed until after supper. Peggy Easton came into the living room, at the conclusion of Emily Millspaw's story, and announced that supper would be ready in about half an hour, and that she didn't want any of us who expected to eat straying off anywhere. She wasn't the kind to wait supper on anybody. And so we delayed the visit to the trailer.

In the meantime Rogers and I wandered out into the bull pen. We found Ernie Caldwell there, come to buy coffee. It was the first time I had seen him off his horse. He was tall and wiry, and noticeably stooped at the shoulders, as if from a lifetime hunched over the pommel of his saddle. He wore a pair of faded overalls, heavy shoes, and an old windbreaker stained with years of wear. There was something diffident, almost naïve about him; his voice was soft and carried an apologetic overtone in it when he spoke.

"I just wanted to buy a pound of coffee," he said to Harry after he had shaken hands warmly with the trader. "I'm about out. Was gettin' supper down at my camp and found I wouldn't have none for breakfast tomorrow."

100

"Want it ground, Ernie?" asked Harry Easton.

"Oh, sure, Harry. I finally throwed away that old coffee mill I had. It was just extra weight, and you can get coffee ground anywheres now."

The whirring coffee mill as Harry Easton spun it by hand filled the silence that followed. Rogers, who had been eying the cowboy, moved closer to him.

"I guess your pack horse got all right to travel, didn't it, Caldwell?" he remarked.

"She limps a little yet. I kinda hated to start with her this morning. I come a little ways farther yesterday after I met you fellows, and camped. Decided to come on today. She'll be all right after a few days' rest here, though."

He took the package of coffee and reached deep into his pocket for a dingy leather money pouch which closed and opened by a drawstring, its ends clipped with small brass buttons. I'd not seen another like it for years. He hunted out a greenish coin and dropped it on the counter, picked up his change, put it into the purse, drew the strings tight and dropped it into his pocket.

"I suppose you heard about the murder last night, Ernie," said Harry Easton.

"Yes, I did," he answered, his soft voice drawling slightly. "Stopped to talk with an Indian down below here a piece this afternoon—Red Goat it was—and he was tellin' me about it. Who was the fellow?"

"Name was Norman Kimball. Guess you'd call him a stranger from outside, except that his daughter and her husband have been living down below here a piece in an Indian hogan for the last year."

"What kind of a car did he drive?"

"A big gray coupé."

"Oh, that fellow! I saw him on the road. Tried to stop him to borrow a match. I was all out. He slowed down like he was goin' to stop, took a look at me and then high-tailed it. Never figgered before that I looked so much like a scarecrow I'd scare folks that way."

"Do you think he was afraid of you?" Rogers asked.

"I don't know, Mr. Rogers, about that. All I can go by was his actions. Don't suppose the law knows who done the killin' yet."

"No, but it will."

"I hope so." he started to turn away, hesitated and looked at Harry Easton. "Do you still keep open after sundown, Harry?"

"Only for setting around purposes. Don't sell anything."

"All I was thinkin'," Ernie Caldwell mused, almost as if talking to himself, "is that I get lonesome. I thought if you liked I'd bring up my gittar after supper and play for you."

"Sure. Come ahead, Ernie. We'll listen to you."

The cowboy shuffled out of the front door and disappeared, and I went to wash up for supper. It was a hurried meal when we sat down to it. Surrey Bent had returned with the fading light from his painting. Bernice Patterson came in and sat down. I learned that she had slept most of the day. She preferred now to listen to what conversation there was rather than enter into it. It was mostly a monologue by Surrey Bent about the earlier days on the Hopi Reservation around Keams

Canyon. The rest of us ate hurriedly, my thoughts, as I was sure were the thoughts of Sheriff Wilson and Rogers, on the projected visit to the green trailer.

A light shone cheerfully from the interior of the trailer as the three of us approached it. Dusk had given way to a starry darkness filled with mystery. I recalled Carter Lamb's assertion earlier that this part of Arizona was no Maryland apple orchard in springtime, that its somberness saturated you in time. A horse whinnied piercingly from down in the corral, the sound echoing shrilly in the darkness from the sounding board of the high ledge behind the post. The conversation within the trailer ceased abruptly as our feet crunched on the gravelly surface outside the door.

"Hello!" called the sheriff. "Mr. Andrews!"

A moment of dead silence ensued within, then came the sound of a heavy body hoisting itself out of a cramped space, and the trailer rocked slightly. The door opened, bathing us all in the yellow light of the trailer lamps.

"Oh—hello," said Andrews dubiously, holding the door partly open. "What's up?"

"Thought we'd like to talk to you a little," the sheriff answered, mounting the trailer step. "Can we come in? Or will it hold us all? There's three of us."

"Oh, sure; come in," Andrews replied with a noticeable lack of enthusiasm. "You can all squeeze in, I guess. Sit down." He pointed to the seats about the table which was not yet cleared of the supper dishes. "My wife," he said, indicating the rather thin, dark-haired, dark-eyed woman. She wore gold-rimmed glasses which sat astride the sharpest nose I think I ever saw. Her whole appearance was one of penetrating sharpness. Her eyes seemed to bore like twin dentist drills. To this introduction she nodded stiffly; the faintest of faint smiles parted her thin lips, but she uttered no word. She was a woman about forty years old. But a woman who had crowded twice that much of suspicion into her life, if outward appearance was to be relied upon.

"Go ahead with the dishes, Thelma," Andrews said to her, as we crowded into the seats. I noted that he was nervous. The only reaction upon the part of Thelma Andrews was one of indifference and contempt of us and of our mission, which both of them no doubt suspected.

"We want to talk a little more with you, Mr. Andrews, about the killing of this fellow Kimball," began the sheriff. The approach was unfortunate in its bluntness, but bluntness was to be expected from Ed Wilson. It served, however, to antagonize Andrews.

"I told you all there was to tell this afternoon," Andrews snapped. Rogers came to the sheriff's assistance.

"Yes, we know that, Mr. Andrews," he began quietly. "But in this sorry business of trying to solve such a murder as has occurred here, it's necessary to keep playing the facts over and over, like a phonograph record, to get them firmly fixed in mind."

"What facts have I to give you?" countered Andrews. "I go to bed about nine-thirty, sleep like a baby all night, wake up next morning and hear that there's been a murder. Then you fellows come hinting around that I know something about it, insinuating, in fact, that I killed the fellow."

"I wouldn't put it quite so strong as that, Mr. Andrews," Rogers returned quietly. "By the way, did you lend a spark plug to Carter Lamb yesterday morning?"

"Yes."

"Did he return it this morning about seven-thirty to Mrs. Andrews? Before you got up?"

"Yes," he said suspiciously, glaring across the tiny table at Rogers and the sheriff. I was sitting beside him and could feel the tenseness of his body as he parried this new thrust. "But what's that got to do with the murder?"

Rogers did not reply at once, and when he did he took an entirely different tack. "Kimball drove out here with his ward," he began, his tone still conversational. "She tells us that Kimball had been in this Western country many years ago. And that he seemed—well, disinclined to return to it. He worried over the fact much of the way. Do you know why he should hesitate to come back to it?"

"Know why? No!" Andrews returned explosively, then with a distinct effort his voice softened to a placating, almost pleading tone and he began to expostulate. "Why, Mr. Rogers, why, Mr. Sheriff, do you come to me with questions I can't answer? I never knew the dead man, never even heard of him. To my knowledge never in all our lives did our paths cross. If I could give you any information that would help you in the least, I would be only too glad to do it. I'm a simple, honest citizen who occasionally travels around in summer in a trailer. When I'm at home I live in Tucson. My life has been an open book. So how—why?—I can't understand your attitude in the matter." He laid his hands palm upward on the tiny table in an appealing gesture.

The sheriff's face was a study. He opened his lips and then closed them again without speaking. I sat back in my seat, aware that the tension was going out of Lester Andrews' body. Andrews believed that he had convinced us of our error in suspecting him of any connection with Kimball. My eyes strayed to the thin form of Thelma Andrews. Her face was turned away from me; I saw only her back, but it was eloquent of the tenseness that possessed her.

"Mr. Andrews," said Rogers, then paused for a lengthening period of time which became almost unbearable before he spoke again, "let me ask you a question—a sort of hypothetical question."

"Yes?"

"If an Indian returning home about midnight, last night, saw a car parked near a gray coupé on the road, overtook a man on foot, dismounted and followed him to the vicinity of Fletcher Wicks' hogan, heard him whistle a signal, heard voices of two men in conversation, then today identified your car as the one seen parked on the road, and if Carter Lamb returning a borrowed spark plug at seven-thirty this morning found you still asleep and said to Mrs. Andrews, 'This night life at Kaibito gets the best of us down,' and Mrs. Andrews returned sharply, 'What business is it of yours?' what, Mr. Andrews, would you think?"

"Thelma," Lester Andrews burst out, "why can't you keep your mouth shut?"

The thin, tense woman turned slowly from the tiny

sink, her hands dripping dishwater. Her face became even harder and her eyes smoldered. Her voice was on a dead level tone when she spoke.

"Go on, Lester, and tell them the truth," she commanded.

For a long moment there was a struggle of wills in the deep silence that surrounded us. The woman turned slowly back to her work with an air of secret satisfaction. Our gaze centered upon Andrews. The color had gone from his face, and his lower lip sagged; his breathing was shallow and his heavy body weaved slightly in its seat.

"Well," he said at length, "I guess I have made a mistake. It would have been better if I'd told you the truth in the first place. But before I say another word, I didn't kill Norman Kimball!"

"But you went down there to talk to him," Rogers asserted.

"Yes."

"You started the first time about ten-thirty, then, because Surrey Bent and Carter Lamb drove into Kaibito about that time, you turned off your lights and waited until later?"

"Yes," he said, a glassy film seeming to cover his eyes. "I was afraid all the time you had me. You knew I was covering up. Well—as I say, I didn't kill him. I merely went down to talk to him. I started about ten-thirty, just as you say, then decided to wait till later. I didn't want anybody spying on me. It was my business; it concerned only Kimball and me. And if it hadn't been for this damned Indian, nobody would have found it out."

"Tell us all about it," Sheriff Wilson interrupted. "Why did you go to see Kimball at that time of night? How did you know where to find him?"

"Well—" Andrews took up hesitantly once more, "I had business with Kimball, that's why I went to see him."

"Why go at that odd time of night?" asked Rogers. "Start from the beginning, please, and tell us all about it."

"That's what I'm trying to do," Andrews flared; then his manner became apologetic. He passed his heavy hand over his bald head and down across his face, rubbing hard on his nose and mouth. "I guess Kimball and I both recognized each other yesterday afternoon when he came up to get groceries at the post. He mentioned his son-in-law, Fletcher Wicks. Anybody would know where to look for Kimball after his saying what he did—"

"You knew where the Wicks hogan was?"

"Yes."

"Go on."

"Well—the reason I went down there when I did was that I was afraid Kimball might leave this morning before I could see him. He wouldn't stay long in an Indian hogan—not him. I got to thinking about it last night after supper and decided I'd better go at once, or he'd pull out before I had a chance to talk to him."

"Why? Was he afraid of you?"

"Afraid? I wouldn't know about that. Maybe he was. You see, he owed me money. He and I were in business together once, and he crooked me out of several thousand dollars when we busted up. I hadn't seen him since. Never caught up with him. Didn't know whether he was alive or dead until yesterday afternoon when he drove up to the post. I saw that he recognized me, but I tried to keep from showing that I knew him. Naturally, he'd be expecting me to hunt him up, and naturally, therefore, he would leave again just as soon as he could, and if I was going to have a talk with him I had to move promptly. That's the way I reasoned it out. He'd have been gone early this morning, I'm sure, if he'd lived."

"And you didn't kill him?" Sheriff Wilson asked insistently.

"No! How would I get my money out of him if he was dead?" Andrews spoke sharply, and his eyes fired up. "Besides, I didn't see him last night."

"Didn't see him?" echoed Rogers, taken by surprise. He leaned forward on the tiny table. "How do you mean you didn't see him?"

"I didn't see him," Andrews reiterated. "I whistled, as your Indian says I did. I knew I was followed. Several times I whistled. There were two hogans close together. I didn't know which one he was in. I thought he might recognize it; it was a signal we used to use when we were in business together. But after I whistled a time or two, I realized that that was just the thing that would make him lie low. I'd got down there and discovered I didn't know exactly how I was going to get him outside where I could talk to him—"

"But—"

"Yes, I know, Mr. Sheriff, you're going to ask who it

was I talked to. It was his son-in-law. Wicks was sleeping outside, and he heard me. He came over to where I was and wanted to know what I was after. I told him it was Kimball I wanted to see. I guess I said something about being afraid Kimball would run out on me, and he said to forget it, that he wouldn't run out on me; he didn't intend to let him go. He had several things himself that he hadn't had time to talk over with him. He said Kimball was sleeping in the devilhouse next to his hogan. He told me I'd better go on back to my trailer. I didn't want to. I was going to insist on seeing Kimball. Then Wicks said I'd waked up his wife and that she was watching us from the door of their hogan, and that if I didn't clear out and let them alone, he wouldn't help me to see Kimball next day. He said this, 'I've got the old man where I want him, and he's not going back until I say so.' "

"What did he mean by that?" asked Rogers.

"I wouldn't know, Mr. Rogers. It was pretty much like a threat, I thought. I asked him myself what he meant, and he shut up and told me to go on or he'd kick me out of his front yard, so to speak. I saw there wasn't any use raising a row there at that time of night. Wicks is as strong as I am, and he's younger besides. Anyway, there was no use in advertising what I'd come to see Kimball about, so I decided the best thing was to play in with what Wicks said and trust to luck to see Kimball later." Andrews ceased abruptly and sat back in his seat with a sigh.

"And that's all?" inquired Rogers, a faintly rising inflection in his voice.

"I came on back to the trailer and went to bed. It made me feel pretty queer this morning when I heard that Kimball had been murdered. I didn't think, though, that there would be anybody who could trace my movements last night. I could see that Fletcher Wicks would want to keep still about my visit. It'd be a lot safer for him to stick to it that he slept all night and didn't hear a thing. So I decided to act the way I did with you, gentlemen. I'm sorry. I hope you believe me now."

Sheriff Wilson made no immediate reply. He sat with pursed lips staring down at the table.

"Look here, Andrews," he said suddenly, "what are you up here for?"

"Me? I'm taking a little vacation. Why? I've a right to be here."

"Yes, I know. You don't happen to be hunting the lost gold in the canyon, do you?"

"Lost gold?" A blank look appeared in the unsteady brown eyes. "What lost gold?"

"Well—forget it," Wilson replied, and made as if to get up from his seat.

Andrews' spirits had lifted noticeably by this time. He suddenly thrust out his large soft hand to the sheriff and to Rogers, and shook solemnly with them in token of complete understanding. With that we seemed to have reached an end, and, therefore, said good night.

Sheriff Wilson walked along with us toward the trading post in silence. I had no notion of what he might be thinking until suddenly he said, "That was a fool thing for me to do, letting Wicks get out from under like I did."

"How do you mean, Ed?" I asked.

"Well," he flared slightly as if at my stupidity, "I let him go down to Flagstaff to see about Kimball's body, didn't I?"

"Yes."

"Well, then, where do you suppose he is by this time? Plenty of trains to get out on, and a highway where he can thumb a ride to some place where we can't get him now that I want him. Or he could just keep going in that gray coupé."

Rogers was silent, making no comment whatever upon the possibilities the sheriff had suggested. We walked up the steps to the store porch and went inside. Ernie Caldwell was sitting on a chair at the rear surrounded by Carter Lamb, Emily Millspaw and Bernice Patterson; he was strumming his guitar and singing in a rather good voice a doleful cowboy ballad.

I joined the circle, as did Rogers. Sheriff Wilson hesitated a moment, then jerked his head toward the living quarters.

"I guess I'll go back and do a little telephoning, boys," he said and disappeared through the doorway.

9

SHERIFF WILSON came back from the telephone and stood for a moment looking at Ernie Caldwell whose fingers were lightly plucking the strings of his guitar; then with a lift of his chin he summoned Rogers and me to the front of the bull pen beyond earshot of the others.

"I was just talking with the office in Flagstaff," he said confidentially. "They tell me Kimball's body is all set to go east on Number twenty-four tonight. Wicks attended to it."

"What did they say about Wicks' whereabouts?" I asked.

"They don't know anything about him."

"Haven't seen him?" Rogers inquired.

"No. I told 'em to pick him up; that I want him. But"—his arms swept wide in a gesture of self-accusation—"I guess I slipped up on that angle."

"You think he's your most likely suspect now, Ed?" I asked.

"Who else have we got, Chuck? Jeff Draper's out of it. So's Andrews. Who else would have any motive but Wicks? Family row. Bad blood between them, maybe. I've never been satisfied with the story Wicks has put out as to why he's here on the reservation."

The door opened and Surrey Bent, his soft felt hat

113

pulled tight upon his forehead, entered. The sheriff ceased abruptly and his eyes were for the moment turned calculatingly upon the middle-aged artist.

"Do you know this fellow Wicks, Mr. Bent—who lives down below in a hogan?" Sheriff Wilson asked.

Surrey Bent halted, reached for his pipe and tobacco pouch, opened the latter and filled the bowl of the scarred, blackened pipe.

"Well," he began deliberately, "I know all I want to about him, I guess."

"Just how do you mean that, Mr. Bent?"

"I think he ought to be locked up and charged with cruelty to animals. That wife of his, anatomically speaking, as a painter would, is one of the finest physical specimens I've ever seen. Of course, I don't paint figures any more, but what I was referring to is his keeping her here on the reservation when she ought to be out where a woman of her type belongs—in the social world. Wicks"—he struck a match and touched it to his pipe, talking between puffs—"is just a screwball." He threw the match away. "He's asked me two or three times since I've been up here if I know where the Crossing of the Fathers is. And I don't, of course. I don't suppose there's a dozen men living who know where that place is on the Colorado River where Escalante and Dominguez crossed in seventeen seventy-six. Do you?"

His soft brown eyes in his tanned face were on me searchingly. "No," I answered, "and I don't know any-body who does. I tried to find it several years ago and I nearly lost myself for good and all in the canyons north of here."

I was aware that somebody had come up beside me, drawn by our rising voices, now that Bent was with us and because of the turn our conversation had taken. Ernie Caldwell was folding up, so to speak, for the night. I looked about and discovered Bernice Patterson at my side.

"You were saying something about the Crossing of the Fathers," she said. "Do you know anybody who knows where it is?" The blue eyes of the blond young woman were upon first Surrey Bent then me.

"We were just saying, Miss Patterson," Surrey Bent repeated, "none of us knows where it is."

"I'd like to find somebody who does know. And Hole-in-the-Rock, too, where the Mormons crossed."

"Maybe the cowboy knows," suggested Bent, as Ernie Caldwell, his guitar swinging at the end of his long arm, shuffled along toward our group. "Do you, Caldwell? Know where the Crossing of the Fathers is?"

"Who wants to know?" Ernie Caldwell inquired.

"The young lady here," said the artist, putting his fingers on Bernice's arm.

"I've always wanted to know where it is. Things like that interest me tremendously. I'd like to go there and see what it's like. It's still there, of course——"

"Well," grinned Caldwell, "seeing that this country don't change much, I reckon the crossing is still there. But I'm afraid, ma'am, you'll have to ask somebody else to take you. By the way, ma'am, if I'm not being curious," the cowboy continued, an apologetic note in his voice, "just what is your business? Are you a writer?"

"I'm an archaeologist," Bernice Patterson answered.

"The ruins down in the canyon interest me. One in particular up on the bench where the pecked hand prints are. I can't find a kiva. A kiva must be there and I mean to find it. I may write something, of course." A slight hardness had crept into her voice, although she continued to smile.

"I sure wish you luck, ma'am." Caldwell smiled at her, the corners of his eyes wrinkling.

"Thank you. Oh—by the way," she shifted the subject abruptly, "have any of you seen anything of Jeff Draper?" Her voice was still bright and filled with interest.

"Jeff—" I started to say when Surrey Bent interrupted.

"Jeff's been hanging around here off and on all day, Miss Patterson. He was outside just now when I came in."

"Thank you."

She went outside and we heard her calling Jeff's name. Sheriff Wilson's flinty eyes had been engaged with Ernie Caldwell's lean figure during all this time. He spoke suddenly.

"Caldwell, where were you last night when this fellow Kimball was killed?"

"You don't say just what time he was killed, Sheriff," answered the cowboy, "but I guess that don't make any difference so far as I'm concerned, because I was camped last night down at White Mesa not far from the natural bridge. I pulled out for here this morning after I'd had my breakfast. The Indians all up and down the road as I was comin' along knowed all about the killin' up here."

"How far," said Rogers, "is it from your camp last night to Kaibito?"

"Oh, maybe twenty miles, I guess. I had to stop and rest that mare of mine some on the way. That's why it took so long for me to get here."

"Which leg was she lame in?" pursued Rogers.

"Why," returned Caldwell, cocking his head on one side and regarding Rogers closely, "the right hind one. Just a light sprain, I reckon." Caldwell seemed not so much to await further questioning as to assume a defensive air against whatever effort might be made to obtain further information of him. But as the moment lengthened and there was no other question, he put his hand on the doorknob and made ready to go. "Well, it's my bedtime, so I guess I'll be goin' along," he said, a thousand little creases about his eyes as he gazed at us.

He opened the door suddenly and a thickset figure stumbled from outside across the threshold, caught himself and regained his balance. "Sorry, pardner," said Caldwell with no more than a casual glance at Lester Andrews, and passed through the doorway, closing the door behind him.

Lester Andrews steadied himself with a hand on my arm. He was breathing hard as he stared belligerently at the vanishing figure, weaving slightly on his feet. He blinked rapidly, sighed deeply and let go my arm, aware that our gaze was directed at him inquiringly after his awkward, stumbling entrance.

"Like stepping up for one more stair in the dark and finding there isn't any," he said, looking at me. "I started to lean on the door just now to open it and it wasn't there. Certainly is upsetting," he said, then looked from me to Sheriff Wilson and laughed nervously.

"It's the unexpected, you know," replied Rogers, smiling faintly. "The muscles are all set but the expected resistance is absent."

"Yes, I know; that's it, of course." He seemed to want to dismiss the incident as quickly as possible, for he turned to Harry Easton. "I came up to see if I could get some pipe tobacco," he said. "I'm all out, and I like to smoke a pipe before bedtime."

Harry Easton started behind the counter. "Store's closed at sundown, I suppose you know, Andrews. But I'll sell you this time."

"I'm sorry. I didn't know that."

"Oh, I'll sell to you. I wouldn't to an Indian, though."

Andrews pocketed his change, opened the tobacco and filled his pipe. Now that he had attended to his errand, he was in no hurry to leave. His attitude toward us had changed; he exuded friendliness. It was as if he were one of us, now that he had successfully run the gantlet of our questioning earlier and had cleared himself of suspicion.

"What did they do with the body?" he inquired.

"Sent it east," answered the sheriff, who eyed Andrews calculatingly. "To Baltimore."

"So that's where he lived—was it?"

"So I'm told."

Emily Millspaw and Carter Lamb, who had lingered talking in the rear of the room after Caldwell left off playing, moved toward us as we stood near the front door. With a vague smile for us, the girl followed Lamb outside, and the door closed behind them.

"Who's she?" demanded Andrews of Harry Easton, drawing deeply upon his pipe which was now well lighted.

"Name's Emily Millspaw."

"Millspaw?" he repeated oddly, as if the name struck long sleeping memories. "Where'd she come from?"

"She came out with Kimball," I explained.

"Oh, yes—I remember. She was in the car with him yesterday when Kimball drove up to get something to eat. Millspaw—"

"Name mean anything to you, Andrews?" asked the sheriff pointedly, his flinty eyes still upon the man.

"No—I guess not," he said slowly. "It struck me as an odd name. I was just wondering whether I'd ever heard it before."

"Have you?"

"No. I guess not, Mr. Sheriff."

Conversation seemed to lag. Surrey Bent knocked the ashes from his pipe and slowly put it away in his coat pocket. He yawned sleepily, disclosing a mouthful of discolored, irregularly aligned teeth, glanced at the watch on his wrist and announced that he was going to bed. He said good night and walked slowly and heavily toward the living quarters at the rear.

"Nice fellow," remarked Andrews, as Surrey Bent's form disappeared from view. Andrews apparently was in no hurry to go. He puffed on his pipe, not contentedly as the average man might at the close of day, but with a nervous manner, as if he still felt the effects from his stumbling entrance of a few minutes before.

No one replied to his comment. Rogers, however, a moment or so later turned to the man. "By the way," he said, "there was a little English girl with her parents up around here several days ago. Did you see her, Andrews?"

"Yes," he answered between puffs, "yes, I did. Sweet little girl. Very keen. What about her?"

"I was just wondering if she happened to give you her address in London."

"No, she didn't. I saw her only for a few minutes. Joked with her. She didn't seem to get what I was driving at; English lack of humor, I guess. What made you think she gave me her address in London?"

"I didn't think so; I asked on the chance that she did. Chuck Graham and I found her diary which she lost along the highway below Cameron," Rogers explained.

"I see. You want to return it to her."

"Yes, of course."

"Sorry, Mr. Rogers. I can't help you out." He struck a match and applied it to his pipe and sucked the flame down upon the tobacco. There was about the man by now an air that indicated he expected to stay talking indefinitely. The hour was growing late, for Kaibito. Sheriff Wilson turned to Harry Easton.

"Have you got a bed for me, Harry?"

"I guess so, Ed," the trader replied, "if you can sleep on a cot here in the bull pen."

"Sure, Harry. I've slept worse than that before now."

"So many folks up here now I'm about full up,"

Easton replied, setting about to fix up a bed for the sheriff. At this point the sound of voices from outside broke in upon us. They were muffled, although one was unmistakably that of a woman, an angry woman. For a moment we paid no particular attention to it, then Rogers cocked his head in a listening attitude and the next moment had laid his hand upon the doorknob and jerked the door open.

The light from the store fell upon an interesting scene. Bernice Patterson, arms upraised and fists clenched, was beating herself free from Jeff Draper's embrace. The Indian's arms dropped from her shoulders and he gave ground before her vigorous onslaught. The immense weight of her fury, however, rather than her slender strength drove the Indian backward.

Rogers stepped outside, followed by the rest of us. So intent was Bernice upon the object of her wrath that she was unaware of our approach until Sheriff Wilson seized one of her flailing arms and spoke to her. She ceased her attack instantly, staring in surprise at the sheriff.

"What's the trouble, Miss?" he asked. "Has Jeff done something he shouldn't?"

The question startled her. For a moment she was speechless, then with a vague gesture toward Jeff Draper, which ended before it was completed, she said shortly:

"No, no! It was just an argument."

The sheriff turned his attention to the young Indian. "What were you doing to her, Jeff?" he demanded.

All the scorn and contempt of which an Indian is capable was in Jeff Draper's manner as he glared at the sheriff. He said nothing in reply for a moment, continuing to stare at his questioner. Finally he opened his lips.

"That's my business," he said, shortly, turned on his moccasined heel and strode away into the darkness. We watched him go, and then Sheriff Wilson's voice brought us back to Bernice.

"If he mistreated you, Miss, I wish you'd say so, because—"

"No, no! It's not that," she protested. "It's personal between Jeff and me. Believe me." She turned her blue eyes beseechingly upon the sheriff, staring at him in the dim light from the open door.

"If you want any help now or any other time, Miss Patterson, please say so, and it won't occur again."

"Thank you. I can take care of myself. I always have."

The incident was over; her breathing was calmer. Harry Easton turned back into the bull pen. I was on the point of following him.

"Well," Sheriff Wilson added, with a fatherly touch in his voice, "don't take any chances, will you?"

"Oh, I won't."

We were turning away when the lights of an automobile flashed into view and drew rapidly up to the trading post. We soon discovered that it was the gray coupé. We waited until it pulled up and stopped. The motor was shut off, the door opened and slammed behind

Fletcher Wicks and he stood there before the sheriff.

"Hello, Sheriff," he said, his voice, I thought, subtly mocking in its tone. "I'm back at Kaibito. You thought I wasn't coming back, didn't you?"

10

EARLY as I was awake next morning Huntoon Rogers had been before me. I had not heard him get up. All I know was that when I was wakened in the gray dawn by the sound of a small flock of sheep being driven past the trading post, Rogers' place beside me in the bed was vacant. His clothing had disappeared, and so I reasoned resentfully that he already was astir outside on some matter pertaining no doubt to the murder of Norman Kimball.

Nothing worth recording had occurred the preceding night after Fletcher Wicks returned from Flagstaff in the gray coupé. Sheriff Ed Wilson had looked him up and down rather critically, ignoring the mocking tone in the young man's voice, then said sarcastically, "Why didn't you keep going when you had a good start?"

Fletcher Wicks resented the implication in the sheriff's remark, and he moved closer to the heavy figure of the older man as if to intimidate him by the sheer weight of his disapproval.

"I don't like the inference you intend me to draw from that, Sheriff," he said.

"I don't care whether you like it or not, Wicks. You've got some more explaining to do, now that you're back here, but I'm not going to ask you to do it tonight.

Save it for me until morning."

That had been the end of the incident, and soon there-after Wicks had swung off on foot in the direction of his hogan, and the rest of us went inside and to bed.

Now that a new day had dawned with the promise that our inquiry would be directed to Fletcher Wicks, I got out my razor and, standing before the cracked mir-ror over the washstand, proceeded to shave, wondering where Rogers had gone. I spent the next half hour out of doors in the vicinity of the trading post, hoping to discover what had become of Rogers, but with no result beyond the fact that the station wagon was missing too. There was no sign of life around the green trailer. Harry Easton, with the help of an Indian boy, was feeding the horses down at the corral.

Rogers drove back just as Harry Easton and I were going in to breakfast. He seemed thoughtful and was not inclined to be communicative. He went hungrily to work on a large plate of ham and eggs. He drank two cups of coffee and finished with some fresh peaches grown in one of the near-by canyons.

"Excellent, Peggy," he said, reaching for another peach. "The early day Spaniards were a boon to the Indian. Brought him peaches as well as the horse."

He pushed back his chair and went out into the bull pen. Two or three Indians had arrived to make pur-chases. Harry Easton was occupied behind the counter. Sheriff Wilson bought some cigars and lighted one, and Rogers, Wilson and I drew together as by common agreement to plan the day's activities.

"I suppose you want to pitch into Wicks the first

thing this morning, Mr. Sheriff," suggested Rogers. There was an eagerness in his mild blue eyes.

"Yes, I do. That young fellow knows something he hasn't told us yet. And he's got to come clean."

"I'm ready any time you are," Rogers returned, starting outside.

"You're awfully mysterious this morning, Hunt," I complained as we walked toward the corral.

"I? Mysterious?" he answered.

"You slip out on me before daylight, take the station wagon and don't get back until just in time for breakfast."

"Oh, that!" he laughed. "Nothing mysterious about that, Chuck. I was awake and felt like getting started, and so I drove down the road to the place where the coupé and Andrews' car were parked the other night."

"What for?" asked the sheriff, looking closely at Rogers.

"To make sure nothing had been overlooked. Clues that might help."

"Find anything?"

"No-o," he said hesitantly, "nothing. Just some tracks of a horse that interested me. I'll show them to you later."

As we approached the corral we saw that Jeff Draper was inside saddling a horse. His own Indian pony was tied outside to a rail. We spoke to him and he returned our greeting in a friendly manner for a Navajo, as if, I thought, he regarded the incident of the previous evening as a bygone. We chose our horses and saddled them. As we were riding away, Bernice Patterson, her blond hair bound with a dark silk scarf, dressed in her blue slack suit and wearing heavy shoes, came running down the trail to the corral. She carried a lunch basket on her arm and a small camera, and in her pockets were stuffed a notebook and pencils.

"Going down into the canyon," she shouted at us, her spirits high. "Cliff-dweller ruins."

Sheriff Wilson reined in his horse and studied the trim, blue-clad figure. He removed his cigar. Bernice halted in her tracks expectantly.

"Miss Patterson," he said soberly, "I'm not saying you can't go into the canyon with Jeff Draper. All I'm asking of you is, please, to be careful."

A little smile appeared upon the warm red lips; the blue eyes danced. She shifted the lunch basket to her other arm and took a firmer grip upon her camera.

"Thank you, Mr. Sheriff," she replied lightly. "I'm thirty years old. I've been about quite a bit. I've always managed to take care of myself. Thank you, though, and please don't worry about me, ever."

She didn't wait for a reply but turned away and walked rapidly toward the corral where Jeff Draper waited with her horse. We rode off through the parklike grounds about the trading post, in the direction of Fletcher Wicks' hogan.

"No hunches, have you, Ed, about Miss Patterson?" I asked as we rode along.

"No, Chuck," he answered slowly, lipping his cigar to one corner of his mouth. "No hunches. I try to warn a girl like her, though. I'd feel bad if something happened to her and I hadn't been able to warn her. She's probably safe enough with Jeff, but that little set-to she had with him last night left me wondering whether Jeff hadn't gone sweet on her. If he has, that's something I don't like."

"That reminds me, Ed," I remarked. "Down at Cameron, the other morning, I'd swear she actually blushed when I mentioned Jeff Draper to her. Jeff, you may not know, helped her before with her work when she was up here."

"Perhaps we have the explanation," Rogers said, to the accompaniament of our horses' hoofs, "of why Jeff was in such a hurry to get back to Kaibito, when he'd gone down to Red Lake to stay a week, and why he hung about the post all day yesterday."

"Waiting to see her," I commented. "We told Jeff, you know, Hunt, when we met him that first time, that Bernice was on the reservation."

"Well," Rogers summed up cheerfully, "the whole incident has been a big help to us. If Jeff hadn't come along when he did around midnight the other night, we'd never have known what we know now about Andrews. He'd not have volunteered anything."

"Of course not," I agreed.

"Well," the sheriff countered gloomily, "just the same, boys, I don't like it."

We rode out a few minutes later into the tiny clearing about the hogan of Fletcher Wicks. Marian Wicks was outside washing some wool preparatory to carding it. There was a crude hand loom set up close by the hogan on which was the beginning of a small rug. She spoke to us, smiling engagingly, but went on with her work. We dismounted and anchored our horses with dropped lines. Rogers went over to the loom and examined the work. About six inches of it was done, and the design was beginning to be apparent.

"You do it very well, Mrs. Wicks," he said, turning to her.

"Thank you, Mr. Rogers. I'll never get rich at it, though. This is my first rug. I've been eight months learning the little I know. And when I get it finished it will only be worth at the trading post about three dollars."

Rogers turned from the loom. Sheriff Wilson tossed the stub of his cigar away. "Where's your husband, Mrs. Wicks?" he asked.

"He's gone for water on the burro. He won't be back for another hour at least. Won't you sit down?" She pointed to the packing cases with a gesture of magnificent grace.

"No—thank you," said Rogers. "We'll come back later." He walked over to his horse and mounted. Sheriff Wilson and I followed his example and we rode away. "There'll be time enough to look over something," Rogers called over his shoulder, leading the way at a trot through the scrub cedar and piñon toward the road.

Overhead was an intensely blue sky, with only here and there tiny puffs of white cloud that seemed to have burst out like scattered grains of popcorn. Rogers led us to the road, bringing us out within a few yards of the spot where the two cars had been parked the night of Kimball's murder. He paused briefly to call our attention to this fact, then more slowly led the way beyond the road some hundred yards and dismounted.

"We weren't thorough trackers yesterday, Mr. Sheriff," he said as we walked along. He broke off a twig from a juniper tree as we came to a small cleared space and held the fragrant stem to his nose, then pointed with it to a trampled spot where a horse recently had been tied.

Sheriff Wilson regarded the hoofprints in silence. He walked around them, he noted the marks leading up to the spot and still others which led from it. Abstractedly he pulled a fresh cigar from his shirt pocket, bit off the end and stuck it unlighted in his mouth.

"What do you make of it, Professor?" he asked at last.

"The same thing you do, I imagine," Rogers answered. "My guess is that an unidentified rider tied his horse here at about the same time Jeff Draper's pony was standing only a couple of hundred yards or so from here on the other side of the road."

"This horse was unshod too," observed the sheriff.

"It was an Indian pony," I remarked.

"You're both right," agreed Rogers. "It's plain that somebody rode in from the road at a point a few feet from where the cars were parked, tied his horse to this juniper, that the animal stood here some little time, then the rider rode off to the south, for the tracks angle in that direction. I traced the hoofprints coming and going. The rider walked his horse coming this way, but he went back at a gallop. Take a good look at the signs here and then let's go over to where Jeff Draper tied his horse and see if they were not made at about the same time."

"This sign here," said the sheriff carefully, "is, I'd say, at least twenty-four hours old. Let's look at the other, though, and make sure."

We did that and then came back to this new discovery of Rogers'. We traced the trail in from the road and then away in a southerly direction until it was lost in the road, and found that it was as Rogers had pointed out.

"Well," said Sheriff Wilson, as we returned to our horses, "this much is certain, boys; somebody came in here either just ahead or just behind Jeff Draper, tied his horse for maybe an hour, then rode off again. Maybe it don't mean a thing; maybe the fellow didn't actually ride up till after daylight yesterday morning, somebody who had heard about the killing and came up to see. It wouldn't be a Navajo, because you can't hire an Indian to come near a dead body. It could, of course, have been an Indian spying on somebody before he knew Kimball was killed. Wonder if it could have been Ernie Caldwell, now."

"No," Rogers replied quickly. "Both of his horses are shod—"

"You know that, do you, Professor?" the sheriff interrupted.

"I looked this morning before breakfast and made sure. Besides this new sign was made by an Indian pony. Caldwell's horses are both good-sized animals. There's the track of only one horse here, instead of two. And Caldwell, when he came past this place, continued on to

Kaibito, which is north and not south. Our unidentified rider returned southward. Caldwell was getting breakfast when I was down there. Wanted to know why I was looking his horses over so closely."

"What did you tell him?"

"Told him I was hunting for the slayer of Kimball."

"What did he say to that?"

"He said that he didn't make a practice, and he didn't think anybody else did, either, of going about the country murdering people he'd never seen or heard of before. He was good-natured about it."

"I don't think it could have been Caldwell, Professor," observed the sheriff thoughtfully. "Nothing squares with him in it."

"I don't see how it could be Caldwell, either," Rogers agreed.

"Ernie's an old-timer in these parts. Comes and goes. You run across him every now and then. He moves about. Everybody knows him and likes him. I've known him for sixteen-eighteen years now."

"How does he get along? I mean, does he have work?"

"It don't take much to keep a fellow like Ernie. He works now and then, whenever he can find something to do."

"He asked me one question I couldn't answer," Rogers laughed.

"What was that?" I inquired.

"Was Kimball killed in the hogan or outside?"

"Outside—wasn't he?" the sheriff replied in some surprise.

"We never looked to see. I didn't. Took it for granted

that he was killed where we found the body. I think we'd better make sure," Rogers suggested.

We swung into the saddle once more and rode toward Fletcher Wicks' hogan. Nobody had anything to say as we rode along; all of us were busy with our thoughts, puzzling over the new angle that had developed in the last hour or so.

Although we had been absent for longer than an hour, Fletcher Wicks had not yet returned when we pulled up in front of his hogan. Mrs. Wicks had finished washing the wool and it was hanging on the branches of a juniper tree. She was expecting her husband at any moment, she said.

"We'll wait for him," Sheriff Wilson announced, as he swung out of his saddle.

Rogers started toward the hogan which Norman Kimball had occupied the night he was slain, then halted and turned about to face the young woman.

"Has anything been touched in this hogan, Mrs. Wicks, since your stepfather slept in it?"

"Everything is just as it was. Emily took father's traveling bag up to the post with her. There's nothing else of his in it."

"Thank you."

We paused at the door to the devilhouse. The customary barrier had been removed, but the gaping hole in the north wall remained as mute evidence that death had entered—death prior, that is, to that of Norman Kimball, and it had been abandoned by its Navajo owners as a chindi-hogan, or devilhouse. We paused at the doorway and scanned the rude interior, the bare, hard earth floor, the smoke hole in the roof. There seemed to cling to the blackened walls even yet the faint odor of the juniper fire which for years must have burned in the hogan.

Near the south wall of the hogan lay a blanket and some old sheep pelts, softened by long usage, a thin and dingy wool clinging to the hide.

"They didn't make it very comfortable for the un-welcome guest," observed Rogers, as he surveyed this primitive couch.

"You couldn't expect anything else in a hogan, Hunt," I said.

We still stood close to the entrance of the hogan. There was plenty of light within. As in all hogans, the door was on the east, and sunlight was streaming in; the gaping hole in the north wall let in much light, and the smoke hole in the roof added its bit of daylight, so that scarcely an inch of the interior was obscured. Even so, we advanced cautiously, lest we trample something underfoot, and came at length to the rude bed, where we squatted the better to examine it.

"I've wondered a bit about the body," mused Rogers. "It was fully clothed, even to the necktie and shoes."

"You can understand why, can't you, Hunt?" I asked.

"I suppose he didn't want to undress. Slept with his clothes on if he slept at all. Under like circumstances I'd do the same."

"So would I," Sheriff Wilson agreed.

We fell silent, our eyes intent upon the simple articles on the bare hard floor of earth. Rogers' large hand strayed to the blanket, lifted a corner of it a few inches from the packed dirt and dropped it. He did likewise with one of the pelts. Something in the wool drew his close attention. He made no comment after a long scrutiny, but with an ominously tapping forefinger on the spot drew our attention to something he had discovered.

The sheriff and I bent our heads together over it. I touched it. It was a spot of dried blood. Sheriff Wilson's hard eyes closed to mere slits, and he pursed his lips thoughtfully over this discovery. Before either of us had put our thoughts in words, Rogers said:

"I can see them, now that the light is on them. Three, four more spots on the floor between here and the door."

On hands and knees we traced the trail of blood spots, now more than a day old, from the rude bed to the doorway and out into the bright sunlight. We found three more, all leading in the direction of the place where the body had been found. There were no more until we reached the large stain on the ground where the body had lain.

"That all adds up to something, Professor," remarked the sheriff.

"Norman Kimball was killed in the hogan. Or, rather, he was beaten there and either stumbled out here to die or was carried out by his slayer. Although the latter is very doubtful."

"Don't you think," I suggested, "that he still had strength enough to chase after the man with his gun?"

"How could that be, Chuck? He was clubbed with his own gun. And the gun was found fifty feet or so from the body, and wrapped. That fact, curiously enough, established the gun as the weapon."

"Let's put these questions up to Wicks," said Sheriff Wilson brusquely. "He's coming through the scrub now on his burro."

11

FLETCHER WICKS dismounted, set the water can on the ground, unsaddled the burro and turned the animal into its crude corral. He shouldered the saddle, picked up the water can and walked to his hogan. He looked at us speculatively as he approached. His lower jaw worked slightly from side to side, and he bit gently at his lips. He didn't say anything until after he had thrown down the saddle and given the water can to his wife.

"The men are here to see you again, Fletcher," she said to him.

"So I see," he answered, a note of impatience in his voice. "Well—sit down, gentlemen." He waved a lean brown hand at the worn packing cases, and selected one for himself. "What's on your mind this time?" The steady gaze of his dark eyes was directed at the sheriff.

"Same old murder of your wife's stepfather."

"Well—I've told you all I know about it."

"Maybe. Maybe not," the sheriff's flinty eyes were unrelentingly on the dark face. The faded, orange-colored headband offered a striking contrast to his long black hair. An angry protest welled up inside the young man, but it was not put into words. Instead he crushed it down and with a shrug of his shoulders continued to sit eloquently silent before us. The slight swelling along his cheekbone occasioned by the blow of the murdered man had subsided, but there remained faint marks of the healing abrasion.

"There are several things, Mr. Wicks," Rogers began casually, "which need clearing up—"

"What?" Wicks turned his eyes sharply upon the large figure of Huntoon Rogers, who sat, elbows on knees, leaning forward on his packing case, his brow corrugated as he gazed with steady eyes at the young man.

"In your story yesterday of what happened after Norman Kimball went to bed, you omitted some important details."

"Is that so?" Wicks challenged.

"After everybody went to bed a mysterious person came whistling a signal to Kimball. You got up from wherever it was you were sleeping outside the hogan and talked to the man. Lester Andrews had come to see Kimball—"

"Did Andrews say that?"

"Andrews has been quite frank as to just what happened here night before last. He said he could understand why you would want to keep still about his visit here that night. What does he mean by that?"

"Go on; tell me what else he said," Wicks requested.

"I'd rather you tell us what happened."

"Why should I, if you have the story already?"

"I want to see which one of you is lying to us."

"I'm not lying to you," Wicks retorted, his voice rising angrily. He calmed down a moment later. "Well— you didn't ask me that question yesterday; that's why

I didn't tell you about Andrews."

"Andrews is the man who was hunting Kimball?" the sheriff put in.

"He came stumbling along about as quietly as a horse in a tin stable. Nearly stepped on me. When he began to whistle I got up and asked him what the devil he was up to. He said he wanted to see the old man. 'What for?' I asked him; but he wouldn't tell me his business. Marian had waked up about that time and so I told Andrews to go on and get out, that I'd see that he got to see the old man in the morning. There wasn't any sense in waking everybody up. He insisted, though, that I tell him where the old man was sleeping. And so, to get things quieted down, I went over with him to the devilhouse and woke the old man up and left them talking. I came back to my bed and—"

"Andrews and Kimball were talking together?" interrupted Rogers.

"Yes. Did he tell you something different?"

"Never mind what he said. What else happened?"

"Nothing, except, as I started to say, I came back to my blanket under the piñon over there and tried to sleep."

"Did you?"

"Not right away. I was wondering what Andrews wanted with the old man."

"How long did Andrews talk with him?"

"I don't know. He had a flashlight. So did the old man. I could see the shine of them through the cracks. Then I got sleepy."

"What happened next?"

"I guess I dropped off to sleep."

"Go on."

"Well—that's about all there is to it. I woke up again, but don't know when. There wasn't any shine of the flashlights; everything was quiet over that way, and I believed that Andrews had gone. I remember thinking that I was going to make the old man tell me in the morning what it was Andrews wanted of him."

"Could it have been money?" interposed the sheriff.

"It could have been. Most of the old man's troubles were about money. Why should I know the answer to that one, though?"

The question was ignored; then Rogers asked,

"When did you first know that Kimball was dead?"

"When the row started—when Emily went flying off through the scrub making noise enough to wake up the whole reservation."

"That was when?"

"About daylight."

"Did you carry the body out of the devilhouse?"

"Me?"

"Yes, the dead man, or, perhaps, the dying man—as a Navajo might do to save the hogan from—"

"It already is a devilhouse. There'd be no object in doing that. If somebody hadn't already died in it, maybe I'd have carried the man outside—if I'd known that he was dying. Which I didn't. He was already dead when I saw him. Lying over there by that scrub cedar."

"And where was the gun?"

"Where you found it."

"Wrapped?"

"Yes."

Rogers paused; his eyes strayed to the far view through the scrub. Wicks sat uneasily before us, although attempting to cover his uneasiness by an outward show of indifference. When Rogers spoke again it was to open a new line of questioning.

"Just what has been your relationship with Norman Kimball?"

"Why, I thought you knew that he was my wife's stepfather."

"I've heard that, yes; but—"

"I'll tell you how it was," Wicks interrupted. "I was the old man's secretary. Took his dictation, wrote his letters and attended to all the small jobs a personal secretary looks after."

"How long were you in his employ?"

"Two years. It was my first job after I got out of college. It wasn't what I wanted to do, but I had to do something, you know. Take anything I could get."

"Did you hit it off with him?"

"At first, yes. He was a tough one to work for too. Stubborn. Opinionated. Dictatorial. Full of petty stratagems. At the core dishonest. Then, when I met Marian and began to see something of her, he got down on me. Just when I was about to be fired Marian and I got married. That blew the roof off. I had money enough to come out here and do something I wanted to do. I was always interested in ethnology—things like that, you know— and it seemed like the time to do it. He raised hell, of course, but what could he do? Marian had a small income —very tiny—which he couldn't touch. I had something too. And we've lived on it."

"About this property in Baltimore, the proposed sale of which, you say, is what brought Kimball out here—was there no income from it?"

"The income is all going to reduce a large mortgage," Wicks replied. "Marian gets nothing from it. Of course the equity is considerable. That's what the old man wanted to realize on."

"You've been making some studies, have you, of this region?" Rogers asked, shifting ground suddenly.

"Some, yes. I've been trying to work out a little experiment, with Marian's help. She told you about it yesterday. A white man demonstrating that he can live as primitive man lived and thrive."

"I see. Interesting, but—perhaps uncomfortable, if one remembers the more luxurious ways one leaves behind him."

"Yes."

Rogers had drawn something from his pocket as Fletcher Wicks talked. He had it balled in the palms of his hands, an edge appearing from time to time to be run through between his thumbs. I discovered that it was a dark blue headband such as was used by the Navajo men to bind up the hair. I glanced at Rogers. He seemed absorbed in the bit of cloth. At length it appeared to pop out in the open and the next instant he held it out toward Wicks.

"This is yours, isn't it?"

"Well—"

"You wore it day before yesterday when you first met Emily Millspaw and Norman Kimball over on the road."

"Well—"

"Is it or isn't it?" Rogers' manner was insistent.

"Of course it's yours, Fletcher," said Marian Wicks, speaking up for the first time. "I wondered why you put on the orange one."

"It's mine," said Wicks at last, his face paling under its tan.

"I was quite sure it was," Rogers said, pocketing the cloth.

A lengthening silence fell upon us. Rogers seemed to be waiting for Wicks to say something, but the young man sat as if he were mute. Finally Sheriff Wilson could endure the silence no longer.

"What about it, Wicks?" he demanded. Still Wicks was silent.

"You see, Wicks," began Rogers, "you're keeping something back. I've suspected all along that you're not playing fair with us. If you want to talk, all right; if you prefer not to, that's your privilege. But if you don't wish to explain how your headband came to be wrapped around the gun that was used to bludgeon Norman Kimball to death, you can't blame us for drawing certain obvious conclusions."

"Yes, I know," Wicks began slowly. "But you won't believe me."

"That depends entirely upon your story."

"Well, get this, then," the young man retorted fiercely. "Get it so you can't forget it. I didn't kill the old man! No matter how it sounds, I didn't do it."

"All right, Wicks," the sheriff put in sternly; "we're listening."

Fletcher Wicks' gaze leaped swiftly to the figure of his wife in the background, then came back to the sheriff and finally to Rogers, as if he sought the more sympathetic of the two.

"You know how it is, I guess, since you've handled things like this before. Naturally a fellow doesn't want to admit anything that might incriminate himself; he tries to put the best face on things when they are forced out of him. Well—" He paused, harrying his thoughts for the best approach to what he had to say.

"I admit that that's my headband," he went on after a moment. "I admit that it was wrapped around the old man's gun. Well—it looks bad, I know. Circumstantial evidence, though—that's all it is—"

"Now, Wicks," Rogers interrupted casually, "take it easier. We've got all day to hear what you have to say. Just give us the facts without comment."

"That's what I intend to do, Mr. Rogers," Wicks returned less nervously. "I say I admit these things. All right—I'll tell exactly what happened. Well—I believe I dozed off again after I took Andrews over to the devil-house and woke up the old man for him. As I said, I could see the shine of the flashlights through the chinks in the hogan. They talked for a long while. I was wide awake and aware of the time consumed. But I dozed off again while they were still talking."

"Did you hear anything that was said?" asked Rogers.

"I didn't even hear the sound of their voices. They were too far away. I didn't hear Andrews leave. He did leave, of course, but I don't know when. You'd think I would have heard him go, but I didn't. And then I woke

up. You know how it is when there's trouble; when someone is in extremity—your mind picks up the static, I
guess, and you come awake ready to fight or run, because
you're shot full of your own adrenalin before you know it.

"Well—that's the way it was when I woke up. I knew
something had happened. And it had. The old man came
staggering by carrying his gun——"

"How do you know that?" demanded Sheriff Wilson.
"Was it light?"

"There was some moonlight. Not very much."

"But how did you know it was Kimball?" insisted the
sheriff.

"I just knew it at the time, is all—and, of course,
from everything that happened afterward."

"Did Kimball speak to you?" asked Rogers.

"Not distinctly. He mumbled something. I recognized
his voice then. But I don't know what he was trying to
say. He ran into a tree and fell down, but got up again.
I believe he sensed that I was there with him. We were
just two shadows stumbling along together in the dark
for a few moments. Somehow I got the impression that
he was satisfied now that he had found me, that we were
pals in some great adventure in the shadow of death. You
know how swiftly things change in a nightmare. It was
like that. The next moment he tried to fight me—turned
on me with the gun and I grabbed it just in time to keep
him from killing me." The young man passed his hands
over his face and rubbed gently at his eyes. Presently he
took up again.

"You see," he said, "I didn't know what had happened to him. I didn't know that his head had been

bashed in and that he was fighting off death. I didn't have time to figure anything out. I know later I got to thinking that the old man was walking in his sleep or was having a bad dream. But, then, while all this was going on, I was confronted with a situation, an emergency, in fact, during which my actions were mostly reflex. And so I took the gun away from him. I didn't hit him; I didn't lay a hand on him, except to shove him a bit when I took the gun.

"Then he fell down. This time he didn't get up," said Wicks. "Things were sort of over by then; my conscious mind began to take over from my reflexes. I realized that it was the old man I'd been scrabbling with in the darkness, and I realized that there was something seriously wrong with him. He kept mumbling. I got down beside him and spoke to him. But he didn't hear anything I said. I shook him by the shoulder, but that didn't help him hear me. He kept mumbling something about a stope—"

"A stope?" echoed the sheriff.

"Yes. At least it sounded like the word stope to me. And I asked him what he was talking about. For an instant his mind cleared, and my question got through to him, and he said, 'We backfilled on it, Fletcher—' And that was all. He died. Gurgled, you know, and that was the last of him."

A long silence followed. I glanced at Marian Wicks. Her face was a sober mask. My impression was that she was hearing the story for the first time. Sheriff Wilson took a cigar from his shirt pocket, broke the wrapper, slowly bit off the end of the cigar and stuck it into his mouth. He pulled out a paper packet of matches but continued to hold it in his hand. Rogers' gaze was following the movements of a small flock of sheep.

"What happened next?" Rogers asked, his gaze returning to Wicks sitting uneasily on the worn packing case.

"Well—" He made a vague gesture with his hands. "What would you do in a circumstance like that? The old man was dead. Definitely. I didn't need the word of a doctor to tell me that. It was dark yet—except for a little moonlight. Trees were dimly visible; objects on the ground on close inspection could be made out. What good, though, would it do for me to run to the post and telephone a doctor who was miles away and couldn't get here for a couple of hours at least? And even a Navajo medicine man's magic—if I could have found one near by—wouldn't have brought a dead man to life.

"Besides that," he went on, "there were two women in the hogan asleep. Marian would be all right, but Emily —I didn't know. Why wake 'em up, even, when there was nothing to be done till daylight? Then I got to thinking. I still had the gun in my hand. My fingerprints were all over it. Nobody would believe that I hadn't shot the old man, if they found the gun with my prints on it. I didn't know then that he'd been beaten. Fingerprints can damn a fellow absolutely. If his prints are on the weapon, then, of course, he's guilty in the eyes of a prosecutor. But you can see how, in this case, at least, they are only circumstantial evidence.

"I did what any other intelligent person in my situation would do. I went over to where I'd been sleeping, found my blue headband where I'd left it when I went to bed, and wiped the gun clean of any possible marks. I polished it, in fact. Then another idea struck me; if I wrapped the gun the way an Indian would, it still further would divert suspicion from me. And so I did that. Then I took it over beyond the body and put it on the ground. The eastern sky had not yet begun to gray but, from the position of the big dipper in the sky, I knew that it would soon begin to get light. And so I went back to my blanket and lay down. I didn't sleep. I heard Emily when she came out of the hogan and started to run. I let her go, of course, because I saw that I had to play a part if I was to escape being connected with the old man's death."

"And that's all?" asked Rogers, when Wicks fell suddenly silent.

"That's all."

"You realize, I suppose, that you destroyed the prints of the killer along with your own," Rogers remarked.

"Yes—but how else was I going to save my own neck?"

"How—" began Sheriff Wilson, still toying with the packet of matches, "how come you haven't accused Andrews of murder?"

"Well—do I know that Andrews did it?" he replied.

"Let me put the question this way," said Rogers. "Do you know definitely that Andrews did or did not kill Kimball?"

"No. Absolutely. I can see I've set up an awfully strong circumstantial case against him. I'll swear in court to every word I've spoken as being the truth. But I'm not going to accuse Andrews of killing the old man, because I do not know that he did it."

"Have you any idea at all, Wicks, what Andrews could have wanted to see Kimball about in the middle of the night?"

The reply was slow in coming. The young man seemed to weigh his answer carefully. I thought he was on the point of telling us what might have been Andrews' purpose in visiting Kimball. He suddenly raised his head, however, and said, "No."

12

THE day that began with such promise of an early solution of the murder of Norman Kimball ended in frustration—and worse. We rode away from Fletcher Wicks' hogan feeling that much had been accomplished. Sheriff Wilson expressed his satisfaction at our progress.

"I didn't think this was going to be a tough one, did you, Professor? If you can get on the ground quick enough," he went on without waiting for Rogers' reply, "and bear down on everybody, you usually get some place. There's nothing left now to do but put the screws on Andrews and make him admit that he killed Kimball."

"I hope," Rogers said thoughtfully, "that you're right, Mr. Sheriff."

The sheriff shot him a swift glance, then dodged the branches of a juniper which reached out for him as we rode along.

"Of course I'm right. It's open and shut; there's nothing else to it. Wicks' testimony alone would convict him. I think I'll make an arrest and take Andrews down to Flagstaff and let him talk there. I had the feeling last night in the trailer that he wasn't telling us the straight of things. There must have been some

150

old grudge between him and Kimball. We've got motive —in fact, we've got everything."

It was with such thoughts as these upon the part of the sheriff that we rode up to the trading post. And I agreed with him. As for Rogers, however, he did not share our optimism; he said little or nothing that could be taken for acquiescence in the sheriff's opinion. Instead I saw him twice rubbing a forefinger along the side of his large nose, which I had learned was a sign that he was thinking deeply.

We rode by the trading post and continued on to the green trailer only to find Andrews absent. Thelma Andrews, her dark eyes boring like dentist drills behind their glasses, her sharp nose seemingly thrust deep into the motive behind our visit to the trailer, continued to stand thin and tense before us.

"It would really help a lot, ma'am," urged the sheriff, "if you could give us some idea where your husband is."

"And I said, 'What is it you want with him?' " repeated the woman.

"Well—just a little business along the line we were talking with him last night."

"Just another angle," put in Rogers pleasantly, "that needs clearing up."

The woman hesitated. "I don't know where he is," she said. "He never tells me where he's going. He'll be back for supper tonight. He took only a lunch. I suppose he went into the canyon to look at the cliff-dweller ruins. That's all I can tell you. You can chase after him if you want to or you can stay and wait for him; it's your own business which you do."

"Thank you, ma'am," said the sheriff, backing away from the trailer and mounting his horse.

It was getting on toward eleven o'clock, and a thought occurred to me as we prepared to start in search of Andrews. "Listen," I said, "why not get Peggy Easton to put us up a little lunch before we go? We don't know how long we'll have to hunt for the guy."

"Not a bad idea, Chuck," said Rogers, and so we rode over to see Peggy and waited while she made some sandwiches and cut some cake and packed it all in a saddlebag which I took on my horse.

Beyond the corral where Ernie Caldwell was camped we found the cowboy at work repairing a bridle as we rode by on our way to the canyon. Rogers reined up and spoke to him.

"Is the man you call Andrews a bald-headed fellow?" Caldwell replied to Rogers' question.

"Yes."

"He went by here a couple of hours ago, I guess." The cowboy squinted at the sun. "Didn't stop to talk; didn't even look my way. That fellow Bent caught up with him and they two went off together."

"Thanks, Ernie," the sheriff said, starting away.

" 'Most nearly everybody around Kaibito must be down in the canyon, except you fellows and me, I guess. That Patterson girl and an Indian were the first to go by, then that young Millspaw girl and Lamb followed, and now you three are headin' that way." He clipped the heavy waxed thread with a sharp knife and tossed the repaired bridle upon the ground.

Ernie Caldwell would have gone on talking indefinitely

if we had stayed to listen. He seemed disappointed when we rode away from him. As I looked back over my shoulder, he had dragged his guitar into his lap and, with his back to the piñon underneath which he sat, was beginning to pluck the strings softly. A little farther on we passed his hobbled horses, which were cropping the thin grass, and then we headed at a smart trot for the canyon five miles away.

Down in the canyon we rode for perhaps a mile without seeing any one of the several persons Caldwell had reported as having gone toward the canyon, then we came suddenly upon a horse browsing among the rocks and near by, sitting idly before an easel, was Surrey Bent. He was smoking his pipe and staring down the canyon as if he were daydreaming. He had done very little work; I noted that the prepared canvas held only the merest beginning of a painting.

"Hello," he said, looking up as we halted before him, a friendly smile baring his discolored, irregular teeth.

"Do you know where we can find Andrews?" asked Sheriff Wilson.

"Well—no," Surrey Bent answered after a moment's hesitation. "He came down this far with me, but I don't know where he is now. He went on. I've been trying to find the exact spot from which to paint a picture. From right about in here there's a most peculiar light effect about this time of day. I've been sitting here waiting for it to come on, and while I'm waiting I've been watching a bunch of eagles. Six or eight of them. They started from off on the other canyon wall there," he waved a sweeping gesture with his arm. "Probably there's a ris-

ing current of air overhead, for they went soaring up
without a single wing flap until they ceased to be birds
and became little golden dots in the sunlight, then I lost
sight of them altogether. Maybe your eyes, though—"

"Andrews, you say, went on down the canyon, did he?"
interrupted the sheriff impatiently.

"Yes."

We rode onward. A half mile or so farther on we encountered Emily Millspaw and Carter Lamb. They had
climbed high among the ruins and to our shouted inquiries about Andrews they replied that they knew nothing about him. Not a great way beyond the pair Jeff
Draper's pony was hobbled, and near it, tied to a juniper,
was the horse that Bernice Patterson had ridden into the
canyon. At first we saw neither of them, and then at a
slight turn in the trail we glimpsed Jeff Draper perched
above the canyon floor upon a boulder at the head of the
rude stairway cut in the solid sloping rock by ancient
hands. A hundred feet or so beyond him, where the ruins
clung to the canyon wall, was Bernice Patterson. Her
blue-clad figure stood out against the rough walls of the
ruins.

The sheriff reined in his horse and stared disapprovingly at the scene. "You know," he turned to Rogers, "it
looks to me like that Indian is sulking."

"Does look like it, doesn't it?" Rogers responded.

"It may be safe enough," Wilson said as if to himself,
"but an Indian is an Indian. I wouldn't want any
daughter of mine playing with fire like that."

He dismounted suddenly and dropped the reins. En-
ergetically he started to climb up into the ruins. Rogers

watched him for a moment, then dismounted and followed. I debated whether to join them, for the climb was
a stiff one up the grayish, sloping shelf, then decided
to follow.

"Oh, hello," called Bernice when she heard the sound
of our shoes on the rough way behind her. She turned
about to greet us, a smile on her lips, which faded somewhat when she observed the serious expression on the
sheriff's face.

"Is Jeff Draper mad, or something, ma'am?" he asked,
jerking his head toward the lone figure visible farther
along the ruin.

"Oh—he's just being silly." She turned to Rogers.
"You know, by all the rules there ought to be a kiva in
this particular ruin, and I can't find it. I've measured
and pried and poked around all morning. Look at my
gloves." She held out her gloved hands, the fingers of
which were almost worn through.

"Listen, ma'am," said the sheriff; "if you want me to,
I'll run Jeff out of the canyon."

"Please, don't, Mr. Wilson. He's not bothering me,
really. And I know how to handle him."

"Well, then, ma'am, can you tell me anything about
Andrews? The fellow who lives in the green trailer."

"Oh!" she hesitated. "Yes. He came by about an hour
or so after I went to work here. He climbed up to see
what I was doing. Seemed to know the ruins pretty well.
He'd evidently looked them all over."

"Did he say where he was going when he left?" persisted Wilson.

"No, he didn't—that is, not exactly. Said he was going

on down the canyon quite a way farther."

"How long ago was that?"

"Two hours, I guess," she answered, pulling up her sleeve and looking at her watch. "I'm hungry," she said. "It's past twelve. Oh, Jeff!" she called to the Indian. Jeff Draper sat for a moment as if he had not heard her, then slowly his head turned in our direction. "Let's eat. Bring the lunch," she commanded.

We did not stay to eat with them but climbed down to our horses and rode onward in search of Andrews. Half an hour later we halted and I parceled out the sandwiches and cake that Peggy Easton had put up for us. We ate sitting our horses and drank from the canteen of water we carried. When we had finished we continued our search in the canyon, although for all we accomplished we might as well have turned back, or, for that matter, never have started at all. For Lester Andrews apparently had vanished.

"I'm for turning back," Rogers said at last. "We'll not find him now. We've probably missed him along the way. Anyhow, he's bound to come back to the trailer."

"You may be right," Sheriff Wilson admitted reluctantly. "I did think, though, that this was the quickest way to get in touch with him. You don't suppose, do you, Professor, that he could have skipped?"

"Where would he go?"

"That's right. It's the next thing to suicide for a fellow with no equipment and nothing but a lunch his wife put up for him to try to ride out of here and across the Colorado. No, I guess, we might as well go back and play the cat at the mousehole when he comes out."

So we turned back. It was hot in the canyon, and not much shade. As we rode past the ruins of the ancient cliff dwellers, I caught a glimpse of the blue-clad figure of Bernice Patterson, as I suppose Rogers did also, for his eyes were upon the spot where she was working beside a wall.

There was no sign, however, of Jeff Draper, although his pony was still hobbled not far from Bernice's horse. Carter Lamb and Emily had disappeared, together with their horses, from the canyon. Farther on Surrey Bent's easel with its unfinished canvas was abandoned to the sunshine. He'd done nothing with the painting since we passed that way several hours before. His horse likewise had vanished.

A flock of sheep, tended by a shy, thin Navajo girl, was near Ernie Caldwell's camp when we passed it. Beyond them the cowboy's two horses still cropped the thin grass. There was no sign of him, however, about his camp. The guitar hung in the branches of the piñon. As we continued on toward the corral, Carter Lamb, riding the roan horse he had used on his trip into the canyon, came by, headed for the canyon trail at a gallop. He shouted something which none of us understood and rode headlong into the flock of sheep, scattering them to the accompaniment of frightened bleating, and disappeared in the direction of the canyon.

We put up our horses and relaxed in the shade of the trading post. The air was hot and still; flies buzzed irritatingly around our heads. Rogers seemed depressed by the fruitless excursion into the canyon. Sheriff Wilson was glum. He explained briefly to Harry Easton, when the trader came out to inquire after our luck, that we had missed Andrews. Presently Rogers got up and went over to the station wagon, obtained a blanket which he spread on the ground and lay down for a nap. There were more Indians about than usual. Harry went back into the bull pen to wait on the trade.

John Navajo rode up on his cream-colored pony, tied it to the rack and mounted the steps to the post. I spoke to him in Navajo and asked him why so many Indians were around, and he replied that Gray Warrior's wife was sick and that the Navajos were gathering for a healing ceremony. The sheriff asked him if he had learned anything new about the murder of Norman Kimball and he answered that he had not.

Just when the feeling of uneasiness crept over us that late afternoon, I do not know. Shortly before four o'clock a rider came up from the canyon trail, his pony whipped into a run. The rider was Jeff Draper. He went by the trading post without slackening pace, neither looking in our direction nor indicating in the least that he saw Sheriff Wilson and me sitting on the steps. His pony showed signs of weariness, as if it had been ridden at top speed all the way from the ruins in the canyon.

"What's biting him now?" muttered the sheriff disapprovingly. He said no more than that, then got up and walked toward the green trailer, although he knew as well as I that Andrews had not returned. Rogers slept peacefully on the blanket. He didn't waken until nearly sundown. When he did he put away the blanket and locked the station wagon and strolled over to where I sat smoking.

"Have a good nap?" I inquired.

"Thanks, yes. I don't know what made me so sleepy. Heat, I guess, and the trip into the canyon. Anything happen?"

"Nothing. Except that Jeff Draper rode back from the canyon hell for leather while you were asleep. Didn't stop to tell us why. Andrews hasn't returned. Carter Lamb came back before Jeff Draper did and has spent his time with Emily. Surrey Bent is still absent. I've seen nothing of Ernie Caldwell. And Bernice hasn't come in yet. The Indians are gathering for a 'sing' because Gray Warrior's squaw is sick, and—here comes Ernie Caldwell now."

Rogers made no reply. He glanced at his watch and yawned.

"What time is it?" I asked.

"Six-thirty."

The cowboy approached in his long shuffling stride, a smile wrinkling the corners of his eyes, and went inside the store. Sheriff Wilson came from the post's living quarters with word that supper would be ready soon, and Rogers and I went to our room to clean up.

Surrey Bent came in just as we sat down at the table. For once he was not talkative. To Rogers' question about the light effect he was waiting for in the canyon, he replied that he had not seen it.

"I wonder why Bernice doesn't come in," said Peggy Easton, as she brought the refilled platter of meat from the kitchen.

"Hasn't she come in yet?" Surrey Bent responded quickly. There was an odd light in the brown eyes of the artist, a worried, almost furtive expression, I thought.

"No, she hasn't," I answered.

"Did you see anything of Andrews?" asked the sheriff.

"Andrews? Not since morning."

A distinct sense of disappointment was noticeable in the sheriff's manner. It was at this point that Ernie Caldwell came knocking on the dining room door. Peggy Easton opened the screen and the cowboy stood framed before us in the dusk.

"I just wanted to say, ma'am," he began, "that a horse has come up to the corral by itself. I took off the saddle and let it in the corral. Guess it slipped its bridle—"

"What horse is it?" demanded Harry Easton, getting up from the table and going to the door.

"Black with a white left hind leg."

"That's Bernice's horse," said Harry.

"You'd better hurry and finish your supper, Harry, and go down for her," said Peggy. "She's on foot in the canyon. Maybe— No, it couldn't be that. But you boys better go," she added, turning to include the rest of us at the table.

"One's enough," said the trader. "I'll go. And thanks, Caldwell, for letting us know about it."

"Oh, that's all right. Hope nothing's happened to her." He turned away through the dusk, and Harry Easton came back to gulp what remained of his coffee and sop his plate clean with a crust of bread.

Sheriff Wilson, Rogers and I went with the trader against his protest, following the dim shadow he made in the night as he led the way toward the canyon. There was no moon yet. It would be old and dim when it did rise. Rogers had brought a flashlight but it became apparent as we rode that anything like a search for the belated girl was hopeless.

"This won't do, boys," said Harry as we paused at the head of the trail into the canyon. "We can ride down in there, but unless she's on the trail itself, or right close to it and able to holler at us, we'd not find her. Especially if she's hurt—broke a leg, say, by falling off her horse— and is lying off the trail a bit."

"Let's push on, though," urged Rogers, "and call out."

We did that, stopping our horses and shouting her name. Our voices echoed eerily from the canyon walls, dying out after faint re-echoings in the vast darkness beyond. No sound save that of our own slight movements and those of our horses was heard. Once we heard the barking of several of those half savage sheep dogs of the Navajos. And once we heard the sound of a distant voice singing a chant. We listened to its thin note coming faintly out of the vast darkness of the canyon. A moment later it had ceased.

"Some Navajo diviner," said Rogers. "He has his eyes on a star most likely while he sings, expecting the the vision which will tell him whether the patient he is singing over will live or die."

Our ears strained against the silence when the sound of Rogers' voice hushed. Then we shouted again, listening intently for some answer, but there was none. Sheriff Wilson fired his heavy revolver and the crash thundered away, growing fainter and fainter until finally silence beat it down. The only response was a renewed and excited barking of the dogs.

"I don't know what the answer is, boys, but the only thing we can do now is go back to the post and wait until daylight. What do you think, Ed?" asked the trader.

"I agree with you."

And so we turned back.

The gray light of dawn was breaking in the east when we set out once more. This time the party had grown by the addition of Surrey Bent, Ernie Caldwell and Carter Lamb. Harry led a horse for Bernice.

No attempt had been made when we returned the night before to discover whether or not Andrews had returned to the trailer. No mention was made of him this morning as we went clattering into the canyon. We shouted from time to time as we went, pausing to listen for an answer. We spread out to cover the entire floor of the canyon, but it was not until we reached the vicinity of the ruin that Carter Lamb pointed out the bridle which was tied to the juniper tree.

"I suppose that means that she wasn't thrown off," said Harry Easton. "She wasn't even on the horse. And all the time last night when we were hunting for her we were figuring that she'd got thrown off her horse as she was riding back to the post. We could have come on down here to the ruin—if that's where she is."

Surrey Bent was gazing up at the ruins on the shelf overhead. He spoke with a faint excitement coloring his words.

"She wore a blue dress of some sort, didn't she?" he asked.

"Blue slack suit," said Rogers.

"There's something blue up there in the ruins."

Harry Easton shouted Bernice's name and we waited for any response. But there was none. I saw a small spot of blue from where I was, but it didn't move in answer to Harry's shout. We dismounted hastily for the climb up the sloping shelf of rock. I was on Rogers' heels when we came out on the level of the ruins. Harry Easton and Sheriff Wilson were before us. As we approached the bit of blue on the wall, I saw that it was only the coat of the slack suit.

"She's around here, boys," said the sheriff grimly. "It won't be far and—it won't be good news."

"Oh, I say now—" began Surrey Bent.

"What are we waiting for?" I asked as we seemed to hesitate.

"Let's go," Rogers replied, pushing through the little crowd to lead the way into the maze of ruins, room upon room debris-littered and roofless save for the gray overhanging rock high above the tops of the old walls. Surrey Bent's voice rumbled behind us.

"Don't overlook any crevices or dark corners," he advised. "That's the Indian trick of hiding the body."

"Do you think she's dead, Mr. Bent?" inquired Ernie Caldwell.

Rogers halted suddenly in the doorway to a room like the many we had passed through. His attitude was one of discovery. I saw beyond on the debris-littered floor the worn, scarred box of a camera.

"Found her?" demanded Sheriff Wilson.

"Yes," Rogers answered, moving quickly into the

room, followed by the remainder of the party. A hush descended upon us; for a moment not a foot stirred among the debris. Our eyes were directed at the figure stretched full length among the shards of broken pottery, castoff sandals centuries old, feathers, broken rock fallen from the overhanging cliff. The blond hair still was bound with the dark silk scarf; the blue slacks, the blue flannel smock shirt looked as if they had been tailored to the well-formed figure which lay on its back. She appeared to be asleep; the eyes were closed. Behind me I heard Sheriff Wilson swearing softly under his breath. He suddenly poked me in the back with a finger.

"I warned her, Chuck. You heard me."

"Yes, I know you did, Ed."

Rogers had dropped of a sudden beside the girl. His hands moved swiftly as he lifted a closed eyelid, felt for pulse at the wrist, leaned down and placed an ear over the girl's heart.

"What's the verdict, Professor? Dead?" asked the sheriff.

"No. There's life! But she needs a doctor as soon as she can get one."

13

THE blue-clad figure of Bernice Patterson, covered over with our coats, lay on the wide ledge which in centuries long past had known the shuffle of the sandaled feet of the ancient cliff dwellers. Huntoon Rogers had picked up the unconscious girl in his arms and carried her out to the head of the primitive stairway, cut in solid rock, leading down to the trail below.

Already Carter Lamb had set off for the trading post carrying instructions from Harry Easton to his wife to summon a doctor, to bring the truck with mattress and blankets to the head of the canyon trail—and not to spare the horse he was riding. Below on the trail Ernie Caldwell and Harry Easton were hacking at two small piñon pines for poles with which to fashion a stretcher. When they were ready, Rogers picked up the girl once more, put her on his broad shoulders as he would a bag of meal and went down the perilous descent as skilfully as an acrobat could have done. Surrey Bent rode up the trail leading the horse that had been brought for Bernice and the horses of Harry Easton and Ernie Caldwell. We placed the injured girl gently upon the rude stretcher made of the poles and our coats, and Harry Easton and the cowboy picked it up and began a slow and steady progress on the first leg toward the trading post.

The sound of a horse behind us as they set off brought our attention around. I turned to see the square, blockish figure of Lester Andrews sitting his horse. The man seemed weary; there was a haggard, gray look about his face, despite his tan. He wore no hat, and his unsteady brown eyes seemed to shift oddly from one to another of us, and then to follow the slowly retreating stretcher-bearers and their burden. I noted that the pocket of his coat was torn so that a triangular flap of cloth hung down from the rent.

"What's happened?" he asked, nodding his bald head toward the slowly receding stretcher.

"You don't have to ask what's happened, Andrews," Sheriff Wilson replied shortly.

"Yes, I know," Andrews retorted. "But I am asking. Gad!" he said, rubbing a thick hand down over his face then looking away across the canyon. "Is it—? You mean —someone did it—killed her, I say?"

"She's not dead yet, but that's no fault of the fellow who tried it," the sheriff answered. He gazed for a long moment at the man on the horse, and the latter stared back.

"I'm glad she's not dead. I thought she was," Andrews said at length.

Rogers turned away and began to climb back up into the ruins.

"Let's look about a bit, Mr. Sheriff," he said as he climbed. "Usually there's some sort of clue remaining. Even the absense of clues can have meaning."

Sheriff Wilson followed Rogers up the rocky footholds, and I brought up the rear, leaving Andrews staring after us from the trail. We came out on top of the ledge and made our way toward the entrance into the ruins. Near the doorway to the first of the series of rooms, Rogers paused to glance at the wall of solid rock against which the ancient cliff dwellers had built their home. Here thickly scattered over a considerable area were the pecked hand prints of a vanished people, prints which first probably had been outlined on the hard surface and then with a sharp instrument chiseled, or pecked, into the rock. At the far end of this strange collection was the rude outline of a mountain sheep.

"Sort of a rogue's gallery of the former inhabitants," Rogers said.

"What was it that Bernice said about them, Hunt?" I asked.

"Only that she was interested in finding a kiva in the ruin where the pecked hand prints were. And this is it."

We turned away into the ruin and the first thing to catch our eyes was the lunch basket. It sat in a corner of the wall in the first room. There still were some sandwiches in it, wrapped in a cloth which once had been damp but now had dried out. An empty thermos bottle which smelled of coffee, two small tin cups and some unused paper napkins were all that remained.

"Only lunch was eaten," Rogers observed. "If she had been delayed and stayed late because of some work she wanted to finish, she probably would have eaten the rest of the sandwiches."

"Then she must have been slugged sometime in the afternoon, Professor," reasoned the sheriff.

"I believe so," Rogers replied. "At least, we can assume

it unless and until it can be proved otherwise."

Farther along the ruin, in the roofless room in which we had discovered the unconscious girl, we found a small notebook, which from its position might have been dropped from the startled hand of the owner. Beyond the name stamped in gold on the cover, there was nothing, not even a scribbled note or sketch or pencil mark of any kind. Beside it lay the camera.

"Well," said Rogers staring about him, "the evidence is meager, but the picture is fairly complete. Here is where she was working. Probably she was struck from behind by her would-be slayer, since there are no signs of a struggle, and she dropped in her tracks. Her notebook fell from her hand as she was about to jot down some memorandum. She didn't move, and the person who struck her concluded she was dead. We can reason, from the fact that there was no disfigurement, no unreasoning brutality, that the motive was not one of revenge or maniacal anger but merely the sudden impulse to kill arising out of the fancied or real necessity of the moment. The time, at a guess, was probably not earlier than three o'clock. Does it check Mr. Sheriff?"

"I think you've got it, Professor," responded the sheriff.

Rogers picked up the camera. He glanced overhead at the sloping cover of grayish sandstone above the roofless walls, upon which the sun was shining.

"I wonder if I can get a picture or two of the scene here. In case she doesn't survive." Rogers examined the camera. "There's some unused film."

The sheriff and I stood back and Rogers set about

using up the film in the camera, taking views of the debris-littered floor and the ancient walls.

"If we've got everything, Professor," Wilson said when Rogers concluded, "we'd better be going along. She might regain her senses and solve this thing for us."

Rogers tucked the camera under his arm, and I carried the notebook. Outside I gathered in the lunch basket. The stretcher-bearers, Surrey Bent, the horses and Andrews all had disappeared from the trail.

"We'd better have the film in the camera developed as soon as we get a chance," Rogers said as we paused preparatory to descending to our horses.

"Yes, sure, Professor," responded Wilson. "I'll probably be going in to Flagstaff this afternoon with Andrews."

"Andrews?"

"Yes," the sheriff returned as if at a loss at Rogers' reaction. "He's guilty as hell. He not only killed Kimball, but he tried to kill the girl."

"How can you be sure of that?"

"I'll make sure of it in Flagstaff. But look at the facts, Professor," he continued as if it were imperative that Rogers agree with him. "Andrews didn't come back to Kaibito yesterday evening. He was down here in the canyon all night. He looked tired when he rode up to see what we were doing. The pocket of his coat was torn. What do you think of signs like that?"

"I saw the signs. But— I'm afraid you're being hasty."

"Well, I don't know. Andrews can't talk himself out of Kimball's murder, after what Wicks said yesterday."

"You're the sheriff of Coconino County," said Rogers as if he washed his hands of the affair.

"Now, don't get me wrong, Professor," Wilson retorted. "I know your reputation, and I know that you don't agree with me. But we can talk the thing over as we go along." He started down the steep, worn series of footholds in the solid rock.

"I'd like to take Andrews on for another going over," said Rogers, following after the sheriff.

"We'll have time for that."

When we arrived at the trail Rogers walked over to the tree where the bridle still hung tied to an outthrust branch.

"Harry in the excitement forgot about this," he said as we came up. "Guess we'd better take it along."

"Let me have it," said the sheriff.

"You know," Rogers remarked as he untied it, "somebody turned that horse loose yesterday. See!" He held the bridle out to the sheriff, pointing with a long finger at the throatlatch. "Not broken at all; just unbuckled. Bernice couldn't do that after she was hurt. She wouldn't have done it before. And the horse could have broken it, perhaps, but not unbuckled it."

"That's something else to think about," said the sheriff, puzzled. He slung the bridle upon his shoulder and we mounted our horses and started along the trail in the wake of the party.

We overtook the stretcher-bearers near the head of the trail, and Rogers and Sheriff Wilson relieved Ernie Caldwell and Harry Easton of their burden. It was not long before Carter Lamb arrived in a cloud of gray dust.

The still unconscious girl was carefully placed on the mattress in the truck and covered over with blankets, and the last leg of the trip to the trading post was begun.

Sometime later we stood about in front of the post talking. Harry Easton came out to report that Peggy had put the girl to bed and was doing all that her training as a nurse suggested against the time of arrival of the doctor, who already was well on his way. Despite his obvious weariness Lester Andrews continued to stand about. I noticed that his eyes were upon Ernie Caldwell, shifting momentarily only when the cowboy happened to glance in his direction.

"You look tired, Andrews," said Rogers at length. "Why don't we all sit down on the steps?" He dropped down upon the steps himself. I sat down beside him and lighted a cigarette. Sheriff Wilson continued to stand for a few minutes. Andrews went to the end of the porch and sat down wearily, leaning his back against the stone wall of the building.

"Gosh, I'm tired," he said, rubbing his face with a thick hand. "A sandstone rock isn't comfortable for a bed even if it is flat."

The door opened behind us and Emily Millspaw stood for a moment looking out, her face sober, her manner hesitant.

"Come out, Miss Millspaw," invited Rogers with a smile. She came out upon the porch.

"It's all so awful," she said. "She's a sweet girl, but foolhardy. I'd never go anywhere alone up here."

"There's no need to, Emily," said Carter Lamb, making a place for her at his side.

"I really want to go home. I don't want to stay now."

"Please, don't," said Rogers jokingly. "Not until you've answered a few questions at any rate. Besides, this isn't such a bad country. I'll admit that you've had a most unusual and terrifying introduction to it. But this Painted Desert country gets under your skin after a while, and you feel a hankering to come back to it after you've been away from it for a time."

"I'm afraid I never should, Mr. Rogers."

All this seemed idle conversation, mere time-killing talk until the doctor should arrive, and I was left wondering why Rogers or the sheriff did not set about probing this latest of our problems.

"You and Carter Lamb went down into the canyon yesterday, Miss Millspaw," said Rogers of a sudden.

"Yes, we did."

"Tell us about it."

"Well," replied the girl hesitantly, "Carter said it wouldn't do for me to go back home without seeing the ruins of the cliff dwellers when they were so close. And, so, that's why we went."

"When did you go, how far, and when did you return?"

The girl looked at Carter Lamb and the latter answered for her.

"We left about ten o'clock. Took our lunch with us. Went down only as far as the ruins where you saw us when we waved to you, and got back to the trading post before two o'clock."

"Did you come directly back?"

"We didn't stop anywhere along the way, except to

talk a few minutes with Mr. Bent," Emily answered.

Rogers turned to the youthful artist who sat smilingly confident on the steps beside the girl.

"Anything to add, Lamb?"

"No, sir; nothing."

Sheriff Wilson leaned forward, the better to look at the young man.

"Where were you going by yourself yesterday afternoon when the Professor and Chuck Graham and I came out of the canyon?"

"Well—I thought I told you that. I shouted at you when I went by, you know."

"None of us understood what you said," Rogers informed him.

"You see," Emily interposed, "I couldn't find my gloves when I got back to the post, and Carter said he'd ride back and look for them. He wanted me to go too, but I was tired. I was so embarrassed when I found my gloves only a moment after he rode away."

"And where did you go, Lamb? Back to the ruins again?"

"Yes, of course. I didn't find the gloves, naturally. I rode on down the canyon a mile or so. I saw Miss Patterson up in the ruins where she was working. I called up to her, but I guess she didn't hear me. I rode a little way farther, then turned back, and came on in."

"Miss Patterson was all right then, was she?" asked Rogers.

"She was moving about up there quite naturally."

"What time was it?"

"I'd have to guess—two-thirty or two-forty-five."

"Did you see anything of Jeff Draper, the Indian?"

"No, sir. His pony—or, at least, an Indian pony—was near the trail below. But I didn't see anything of him. Surrey Bent was climbing up the steps to the ruin when I came back about ten minutes later, but I didn't bother to call out to him. Afraid he might slip if I startled him and he'd get a bad fall."

"Thank you, Lamb. Mr. Bent—" Rogers began.

"Now, don't get me mixed up in this thing," the middle-aged artist interrupted irritably. His voice had lifted somewhat from its ordinary low rumbling tones. "I didn't try to kill that girl. I've never killed anybody in my life, although there's an Indian or two I'd like to kill now. I'll tell you what I went up there for. I remembered that light effect I'd been looking for. I'd seen it once from the ruin where Miss Patterson was working.

"I climbed up into the ruin. I didn't say half a dozen words to her, because she was busy and the effect wasn't visible. Heavy Woman's Son—or Jeff Draper, if you want to use that name—was sitting back in one of the rooms. They'd been having an argument, but it quieted down when I showed up, and he didn't say another word while I was there. I stayed, I guess, about ten minutes, then I climbed down and went back up the canyon to where I had my stuff."

"What time was this?"

"I didn't notice the time, but if Carter is right, then it must have been around three o'clock."

"Did anybody see you either coming or going, besides Lamb?"

"Not that I know of. As you know the floor of the canyon down that far is wide enough for any number of
people to come and go, even on horseback, without seeing
anything of one another."

"Thank you, Mr. Bent." Rogers turned next to the
cowboy. "Caldwell, how about you? Were you in the canyon yesterday afternoon?"

Ernie Caldwell shifted slightly in his seat on the steps
and cast a swift glance of his smiling eyes in the direction
of his camp beyond the corral. "I hobbled my horses
yesterday morning, and I didn't take the hobbles off all
day. They've needed a little rest."

"You mean that you didn't go into the canyon at all?"

"Yes, sir."

"What we're trying to do," explained Rogers, "is to
find somebody who might possibly have seen the person
who tried to kill Miss Patterson, either on his way to the
ruins or coming from it."

"How about the Indian?" asked Lester Andrews
pointedly.

"How about you, Andrews?" retorted Sheriff Wilson.

"Me?"

"Yes, you. Seems to me you've got a lot of talking to
do."

"Well"—the man heaved a sigh—"I don't know anything about what happened to the girl any more than I
do about the murder of Kimball. I'm not mixed up in
either case. The reason I didn't get back last night, if
that's what's bothering you, was that I rode too far in the
canyon, I guess. Anyway I got lost. By mistake I went up

a side canyon, which I thought was the main one. When I saw about sundown that I wasn't going to make it back before dark, I thought it best to camp, even if it did mean trying to sleep on a rock, as I did."

"Why didn't you let your horse bring you in?" the sheriff asked suspiciously.

"I'd rather stay out all night."

"Where were you, then, from about three o'clock in the afternoon until sundown?" asked Rogers.

"I must have been several miles below the ruin where Miss Patterson was. I don't know exactly. I know I started back as soon as it was light enough to travel this morning, and I was just coming by the ruin when I saw you fellows and stopped to see what had happened."

"What did you go down into the canyon for?" asked Sheriff Wilson.

"Well—to be frank, that's a matter of private business."

"You're not telling us?"

"No."

14

A CREAM-COLORED pony emerged from the scrub beyond the trading post, carrying a tall slender rider. There seemed no hurry, no definite destination, until John Navajo espied the group we made on the steps of the stone building. Then he jerked his pony's head in our direction and continued up to the hitch rack where he dismounted leisurely and tied his pony.

"Morning, John," called the sheriff. In response to the greeting the Indian policeman fixed the sheriff with his black eyes and nodded curtly. He came over to the steps, then, and sat down. All of us, I think, except possibly Emily Millspaw, offered some greeting, which the man with a single nod of his head acknowledged.

He sat there among us a strange figure in his wrinkled blue serge suit with its tight trouser legs, the little stiff-brimmed, tan hat which sat high on top of his head because of the long hair he had gathered up underneath its round crown.

"You heard about the attempted murder of young woman, John?" Sheriff Wilson asked.

"*Ohk.*"

"Happened yesterday afternoon. Maybe after three o'clock."

"*Ohk.*"

"White folks all say not guilty. You think Indian did it?"

John Navajo studied long over the question. "Maybe. Maybe not," he said. "White man can lie. Indian can lie. Tell me more what you find out."

"It was like this, John," began the sheriff as he launched upon a description of the scene and an account of our investigation. He spoke of the lunch basket and the uneaten sandwiches, and the bridle with the un-buckled throatlatch. "That's everything, John. You want to go down to the place?"

"No."

"I haven't tackled any of the Navajos, John," said the sheriff. "You do that. You find out if any of your people guilty. Tomorrow morning you bring Jeff Draper to trading post. I want to talk to him."

"Can bring this afternoon."

"No. I go back to Flagstaff soon now. I'll come back tomorrow morning early."

"*Ohk*," answered the Indian.

We broke up at that. Ernie Caldwell started off, and so did Andrews. Surrey Bent knocked the ashes from his pipe and went inside. Emily Millspaw and Carter Lamb drifted away, and John Navajo went inside to buy some tobacco. The sheriff's gaze followed the re-treating figure of Andrews. The man seemed intent on catching up with Caldwell who walked away at a rapid pace. He succeeded in overtaking him. They could have exchanged only a few words, however, for they sepa-rated almost at once, one going toward the camp beyond the corral, the other in the direction of the trailer.

"You're not taking Andrews to Flagstaff with you, then?" said Rogers, as if he were reading the sheriff's thoughts.

"He's guilty as hell, Professor, of Kimball's murder; and I think a little more digging around might uncover some evidence that he tried to kill the girl too."

"But look at it this way, Mr. Sheriff," said Rogers. "Whether he is or is not guilty in either case, he's where you can put your hands on him at any time. If Andrews had any such notion as escaping north through the canyon and across the Colorado, he must have got it out of his head after yesterday's experience. The only way he really can go from Kaibito, by car and trailer, is south to Red Lake. He wouldn't be far on the road before your men could pick him up. So why not leave him here until we're sure you want him?"

"But I want him now."

"Will arresting Andrews clear up the attempt on Miss Patterson's life? Granted that he may have had a motive in the murder of Kimball, what is it in Miss Patterson's case? I confess I haven't the foggiest notion why he should want to kill the girl. Jeff Draper is the more logical suspect. We were just cutting out the undergrowth a while ago in our inquiry, clearing the ground, as it were, for a go at Jeff. And, anyway, Miss Patterson may come around and give us the answer we're seeking. She may have seen the killer."

"That's possible, Professor; but is there any real reason why we should hunt for one person guilty of both crimes? Can't they both occur, just as these have, and two people be guilty, instead of one?"

"It's plausible, of course. By no means does every killing, or attempted slaying, become a murder mystery; and certainly every two crimes occurring close together in time and place are not the work of a single individual. But I'm not so sure about Andrews in the Kimball affair. There's only Fletcher Wicks' story. Who lies, Wicks or Andrews? Or are they both telling the truth and there is a third person of whose identity we're ignorant? What of those pony tracks off the road for which there's no explanation yet?"

Sheriff Wilson's flinty eyes narrowed as he listened to Rogers now lying on his back on the porch. He pursed his lips, then gnawed at the under one, and finally opened his mouth.

"Maybe you're right, Professor, and I'm wrong. It's a cinch, though, Andrews can't get away from me, if I want him. I'll tell you what we'll do; I'll come back tomorrow and we'll go to the mat first with Andrews and then with Heavy Woman's Son."

The pall of this latest outrage seemed to hang over Kaibito for hours after the doctor arrived to examine the injured girl. He was a small man with a stubby gray mustache and the feel of the desert about him. His eyes seemed to lurk in the shadow of his bushy eyebrows, and their glance had the fierceness of a glare. He said almost nothing until he had finished his examination.

"Maybe she will and maybe she won't," he replied in answer to my question as to Bernice Patterson's chances of recovery. "She can't be moved. I don't see how you managed not to kill her bringing her up from the canyon."

"Skull fracture, Doctor Creelman?" Rogers asked.

"How can I tell for certain without an X-ray?" he replied gruffly. "And what chance is there to get that up here miles away from civilization? There's just one chance in her favor," the doctor turned to face Harry Easton, "and that's Peggy. She's a nurse. I can stay till morning, then I've got to go back to Flagstaff and operate a fellow."

The group at the supper table was noticeably diminished. Sheriff Wilson had left after he heard Doctor Creelman's report. Harry Easton was worried. He said, as he pushed back his plate at the conclusion of the meal, that he wondered how it would affect business with the Indians if Bernice should die at the post.

"Lord knows, of course, that's the least of the reasons for hoping she'll pull through," he explained. "But there's no more suspicious person in the world than a Navajo when it comes to the dead. All I'm hoping is that this 'sing' they're having for Gray Warrior's wife may take their minds off our troubles. I should have had a lot more trade today than I did. At no time was there more than three or four Indians in the bull pen."

Peggy Easton was silent, her mind obviously on her patient in the tiny bedroom at the post. She had attended to our wants at table, but without her usual flow of comment and banter. Surrey Bent had elected to eat in silence, and Rogers was thoughtful and had little to say. Ernie Caldwell was, therefore, a welcome figure when he came up on the porch of the post after supper carrying his guitar.

"Would it be too much like intrudin' on anyone's

feelings if I played and sung a while for you folks this evening?" he asked. The wrinkles seemed more numerous than usual about his dark blue eyes which twinkled in the leatherlike mask of his tanned face.

"If you don't sing any mournful songs about dying cowboys and the lone prairies, Ernie," said Surrey Bent. "We've had enough of that sort of thing today, if you want my opinion."

"Name your poison," was the affable reply.

We drew up our chairs in the rear of the bull pen, and Ernie thumbed the strings, twisted the pegs and finally got started on a medley of lively songs. His repertory seemed inexhaustible; he had a prodigious memory for the words, down to the final stanzas, of songs I'd not heard for years, as well as those more commonly sung in the West.

"How do you do it, Caldwell?" asked Rogers.

"Well, I'll tell you, Mr. Rogers. I always thought a white man was as good as a Navajo, even though they look down on us as an inferior race. If a Navajo can learn long chants and not miss a word, I guess I can learn cowboy songs. Besides, I have to have something to amuse me. It gets lonesome trailing through this western country. Singin' has brought me many a meal and night's lodging when I needed it, as well as more than one job."

"You've always lived in the West, have you?"

"All my life, Mr. Rogers."

"Never thought you'd like to get away from the back country into the cities?"

"Oh—no, I guess not. I did think something about it

years ago—twenty, twenty-five years, maybe—but I
got over that. I'm not cut out for a city man. Flagstaff
or Winslow is about my size, and I like 'em even
smaller."

"Never had any desire for money?"

"Guess not. Not to pile it up anyhow. You can't take
it with you. All a fellow needs is a little pocket money
for grub and tobacco, and a little gambling now and
then."

Surrey Bent knocked out his pipe against the rusty
stove. His light felt hat sat crushed and awry upon his
round, close-clipped skull. "Speaking of money," he
began, a trace of reviving humor creeping into his
rumbling voice, "I suppose you've heard the story,
Caldwell, of the lost treasure of Navajo Canyon, haven't
you?"

"I ain't sure that I know just what you mean, Mr.
Bent," said the cowboy, his fingers softly strumming the
strings of the guitar.

"It's an old story. The only reason I mention it is to
sort of get our minds off of today's happenings." He
seemed to have Emily Millspaw in view, for his soft
brown eyes were directed at her in a paternal sort of
way.

"Tell us," urged the girl.

"You know the story, Harry." The artist's attention
shifted to the trader.

"Yes, I've heard it."

"Nobody's tried to tell it to me for several years
now," Surrey Bent went on, a gleam of humor lighting
up his face, "so it's being forgotten around here. If it is,

maybe I shouldn't revive it."

"Please, Mr. Bent," said the girl.

"There's not much to it. It's all hearsay anyhow. It happened eighteen or twenty years ago. Three men came into this country on horseback from the north—from Utah, of course. They must have crossed the Colorado at the old Crossing of the Fathers, for how else could they have got into Navajo Canyon? They had seven pack horses, besides the horses they rode—which is to say that if they did come by the Crossing of the Fathers with that many horses, it was a feat in itself, for the crossing, they tell me, is just a faint trail cut in the sloping face of the canyon walls back in 1776 by Escalante and Dominguez.

"These three men with their pack train were coming along through Navajo Canyon peaceably until they got to a point three or four miles perhaps from where the trail from Kaibito enters the canyon, when a fight broke out among them. There was some shooting and two of the men came tearing out of the canyon on their horses, leading one pack animal between them.

"All this, you know," Surrey Bent continued, gesturing with his pipe held in his closed fist, "is what the Indians down in the canyon used to say. Although, I suppose, when the shooting started, the Indians all took to cover. A Navajo Indian, Miss Millspaw, is, as you perhaps know by this time, a nosy person. And while he may not know everything that goes on, he doesn't miss much that happens on the reservation. He gossips around with other Indians and if there are any missing links he supplies them.

"Well," he resumed in his rumbling voice, "what happened to the third man is the mystery. Nobody knows. Was he murdered and his body hidden? It was never found, anyhow, that I ever heard of. The Indians used to shun that part of the canyon where the fight took place, which might indicate that the third man died in there somewhere. Although again it might not. The six remaining pack horses were discovered grazing over near Inscription House two or three days later. Their packs were gone, and they had been turned loose. With the pack horses was another horse with a saddle on its back. And nobody has ever discovered what became of the treasure."

"Treasure?" echoed Emily. "How do you know that it was treasure?"

"Well," Surrey Bent's sides shook gently with suppressed amusement, "the argument used to run like this: Would those fellows have risked their necks in this rough country to bring coal, or sand, or trade goods, say, into the canyon? And would they fight over it if it were of little value? Of course, a couple of years or so afterward the argument apparently was settled when an Indian showed up with a five-pound bar of sponge gold—gold, you know, after the quicksilver has been driven off and before the remaining impurities have been taken from it."

"Where did he get it?" demanded Emily.

"He claimed that he found it in the canyon near where the fight was said to have occurred. From this fact it was argued that the three men probably had done some rather extensive high-grading—stealing valuable ore, you know—in some mine north of the Colorado River, and were making their getaway with it."

"Did anybody ever find where the gold was cached? If that's really what was done with it?" Carter Lamb inquired.

"Of course it was cached. Why would the pack horses have been turned loose without their packs, if the gold hadn't been disposed of in some such manner? But who cached it? The two men or the third man who was unaccounted for? Did the two men kill the third man and hide the gold, pretending to have been driven off by the third, or did the third man do it himself and then disappear? How are you going to fit into the picture the saddled horse grazing with the pack horses?"

"Do you suppose it's still there where it was hidden, Surrey?" Carter Lamb persisted.

"I don't know the answer to that, Carter. If those fellows were clever enough to hide it without the Indians finding it out, they'd be clever enough to come back later and take it away, wouldn't they?"

"I suppose so. What happened to the two men, though?"

"They stuck around Kaibito for a night and the better part of the following day. They wouldn't talk. They went back to the canyon that next morning, then came out and rode off."

Emily's eyes sparkled. "What if the gold is still in the canyon?" she said. "Has anybody ever really tried to find out?"

"One of the two men is believed to have come back several times in the next five or six years. Although there's no way now of checking on that, because several different traders had the trading post here in the years after Buck Weaver left, and they're scattered now. For that matter, nobody really ever had a good description of the two men. But if the gold was ever found by them or anybody else, I never heard of it. Did you, Caldwell? You're an old-timer in this country—you've heard the yarn, haven't you?" Surrey Bent turned to the cowboy who sat absorbed in the story.

"Yes, I've heard it before, Mr. Bent. I never heard, though, that anybody ever found it. It was hid too good, I guess, for it to be found."

"Do you believe the story?" Rogers asked of Caldwell.

"Yes, sir, I believe it. But—" He hesitated.

"But what, Mr. Caldwell?" asked Emily.

"I was just goin' to say that I don't see how it could have been all moved out later by the two men without the Indians in the canyon finding it out. They might be lucky in hidin' it after the fight, but they'd sure be seen bringin' in pack horses and loadin' 'em up and takin' 'em out again. And that part, if it happened, it seems to me, would be added to the story they tell. But you always hear nothin' but the part about the fight and the hidin' of it. So, my guess is that it's still where it was put in the first place, ma'am. And this fellow who came back later—if he was one of the two—just forgot where it was hid."

"Did you ever hunt for the gold, Ernie?" asked the trader.

"Me? I did a time or two, but I never had any luck. I

got to thinkin' I was wastin' my time, because if I found it I wouldn't know what to do with it. I get along all right the way I am."

Whether or not Surrey Bent's revival of the old story served to lift even in part the gloom that had descended upon us, it at least had created a diversion which lasted until we were ready to go to bed. Ernie Caldwell shuffled off to his camp under the lee of the ledge, and the rest of us soon thereafter went to bed ourselves.

"Well—you've heard the old story again, Hunt," I said as Rogers and I made ready for bed in the tiny room assigned to us in the trading post.

"Yes."

"Believe it?"

"I never thought much about it. It always struck me, though, as something belonging in the same class with the so-called lost gold mines of the West. They seem to be authentic, but people hunt and hunt for them without any luck. Why can't they be found now if they once really existed?"

"There's something in that, I suppose."

He did not reply. Instead he took an envelope from his pocket and began to figure on the back of it with a pencil stub. "Twelve ounces to the pound troy weight," he said, glancing up. "Times one hundred fifty, times seven."

"What are you figuring now, Hunt?"

"How much gold the three men could have had—if it were gold and not just high grade. In this rough country a hundred and fifty pounds is about all it's safe to put on a pack horse." He continued to figure on the envelope for some moments, then he gave a whistle. "At the old price of gold, Chuck, they might have had roughly a quarter of a million dollars in their pack train. And at the present price of gold"—he figured rapidly for several moments—"it would amount to four hundred and forty thousand, roughly."

"That's a lot of money, Hunt."

"Yes. Quite a lot."

"Sleepy?" I asked, for he yawned prodigiously.

"Yes, I am," he replied, and a few minutes later he blew out the lamp and rolled into the creaking bed beside me.

I slept well, for our day in the open air, even though it had been fraught with unusual happenings, had tired me. I was still sleeping soundly when Rogers nudged me sharply. It was dark and I did not at once waken completely. Rogers prodded me in the ribs again with his elbow, and then threw off the covers and sat up on the edge of the bed.

"What's the trouble?" I asked, getting sleepily up on my elbow.

"I thought a woman screamed— There it goes again!" He got out of bed and fumbled for the matches.

"One of the women having a nightmare," I suggested, preparing to go back to sleep. "Not surprising after what's happened."

He succeeded in striking a light and ignited the wick in the lamp. I noted that he already had on his lounging robe.

"It wasn't that kind of scream," he said. "You just sort of grunt, or yip, in a nightmare."

"Couldn't be Bernice, could it?"

"I don't know."

A moment later Rogers jerked open the door on the short hallway, just as the terrifying scream was repeated. I leaped out of bed and stepped into the hallway. It was only dimly lighted, and it seemed already filled with people. Somebody was working frantically at a lock, twisting and turning the key. Suddenly the door opened and a small, dimly pinkish figure burst out and ran headlong with a whimpering cry into what proved to be Peggy Easton's arms.

"Why, child, what is it? What's happened?" Peggy asked comfortingly, hugging the small figure of Emily Millspaw close to her ample self. For a moment the girl did not speak. Carter Lamb and Surrey Bent emerged from their room.

"What is it, Emily?" demanded the youthful painter. The girl lifted her head and cast a frightened glance at Peggy.

"Somebody—" she said hysterically. "Somebody— was in my room— And I couldn't get out— Oh! I'm so frightened!"

"Who was it? What happened?" asked Rogers severely. His voice brought the girl back to her senses.

"I don't know. I wakened, and somebody was there. I screamed and he went through the window."

15

EVENTUALLY Emily Millspaw's fears were quieted; eventually we went back to our rooms and to sleep. But not until Harry Easton, Rogers and I had examined the window of Emily's room and had gone outside to discover if possible something of the identity and whereabouts of the intruder. Which, of course, was a futile gesture, although necessary to restore a semblance of composure to the trading post. And finally, with Peggy Easton agreeing to finish out the night with Emily in her room, we got back to sleep and did not waken again until the gray light of dawn was in the windows.

The sound of shouting and shots being fired at a distance from the post roused us completely. Rogers came wide awake.

"What was that?" he demanded.

"I don't know," I answered. "Unless it's the Indians."

"Oh, yes," he said, sitting up and rubbing the sleep from his eyes. "This is the second day of their 'sing.' The party bearing the sacred wand is being met in sham battle by the forces representing Gray Warrior's sick squaw. Odd procedure, perhaps—but we're just as queer, Chuck, if we could only see ourselves." From something in his voice I realized that if it were not for our own troubles, which had absorbed all our thoughts since our arrival at Kaibito, Rogers would at this moment in all probability be an onlooker at the healing ceremony of the Navajos. But he said nothing.

It was not until Doctor Creelman had left after breakfast with word that Bernice Patterson's condition was unchanged, that we were enabled to assay completely the incident of the night just past. Emily came out to where Rogers and I were loafing on the front porch awaiting the arrival of Sheriff Wilson. Her dark eyes were filled with mystery, her face was sober.

"I've discovered something important, Mr. Rogers," she announced.

"What?" Rogers' head lifted sharply.

"Norman's traveling bag is missing from my room."

"Norman Kimball's bag?"

"Yes."

"Anything else?"

"No." She shook her small dark head vigorously. "I was keeping it, you know, until I started back home."

I reached out a hand and laid it on Rogers' knee. "We were going to look through that, Hunt—remember?"

"Yes." His eyes sought Emily's. "That was just in case there might be something that would help in untangling things." He rubbed a forefinger thoughtfully alongside his large nose. "By any chance, Emily," he said, smiling faintly, "did you know what was in it— that might be important enough to prompt someone to steal it?"

The girl shook her head again, her face still serious, her manner anxious.

"Have you any idea at all, now that the sun is shining brightly, and the terrors of the night have fled," Rogers asked, his eyes twinkling, "who the thief was?"

"No, sir. I wakened and there was a vague shape between me and the window. Everything was so dark I didn't at first realize it was anything at all but the darkness itself. Then it moved and there was a slight noise like something being dragged on the floor. Which I guess now was the bag. For a moment I was paralyzed with fright. I couldn't even scream. The thief was climbing out of the window before I could even utter a sound, and when I did he just disappeared without any noise."

"You don't know, then, whether it was an Indian or a white man?"

"No, sir."

We went around once more to the window on the rear of the living quarters. The screen had been unhooked by a sharp, slender point thrust through the wire, and the whole frame lifted off the top hooks. No skill whatever was required to do it. There were no marks on the window sill, no footprints on the hard ground beneath the window, no signs anywhere, no slightest clue to the burglar's identity.

"Well," said Rogers as the three of us returned to the porch once more. "There's only one thing that's clear, and that is that the thief wanted the bag and took that way of obtaining it. Which makes me all the more curious as to what may have been in it."

All of this was laid before Sheriff Wilson when he arrived from Flagstaff a couple of hours later. He was silent, his eyelids narrowing down upon his flinty eyes until they were mere slits in his tanned face.

"I wonder," he said when we had finished our account, "if this would have happened if I had taken Andrews with me yesterday."

Rogers gestured impatiently but said nothing. Sheriff Wilson took an envelope from his pocket. It contained the developed negatives from Bernice Patterson's camera and the prints. He gave them to Rogers without comment, and Rogers examined them briefly and passed them on to me. They were the pictures of the room in the ruins of the cliff dwellers which Rogers had taken the day before. Among them were three that Bernice had taken of walls, apparently in the room in which she was all but murdered. I gave them back to Rogers.

"Well, boys, let's go down and take on this fellow Andrews once more. This time to a finish," Sheriff Wilson said abruptly, getting up from his seat on the porch.

We walked in the direction of the green trailer, saying nothing as our feet crunched along the gravelly earth. There was no sign of life around the trailer, beyond the fact that the step was on the ground below the door. Somebody was inside, however, for as we approached the trailer began to shake slightly as if someone were moving about inside. It was Mrs. Andrews. She had seen us coming and had got up from the table where she had been playing solitaire.

"He's not here," she said defensively before a question was even asked.

"Not here?" echoed the sheriff. "Why, I came down here yesterday afternoon, Mrs. Andrews, before I left for Flagstaff, especially to tell him I wanted to see him this morning."

"He's not here," she repeated, her dark eyes boring relentlessly. "He went off into the canyon again."

The sheriff turned away swearing under his breath. Rogers appeared somewhat taken aback, but there was nothing now to do about it. I had not known that the sheriff had requested Andrews to expect him today, but I had presumed, as had Rogers, I'm sure, that Andrews was about the trailer.

"Did he say when he would be back, Mrs. Andrews?" asked Wilson, turning to her once more.

"No. But he took a lunch."

"Just what is your husband up to in the canyon, Mrs. Andrews?" the sheriff inquired testily.

"You'll have to ask him. He doesn't tell me things like that."

"Is he a scientist, or something like that, that he'd be interested in the ruins down there?"

"Not Lester Andrews," she snapped. "There's no more scientist in him than there is in my little finger."

The woman didn't soften, she didn't abate the hardness which seemed to cover her like a veneer. However, she appeared more talkative than before, but was scarcely free with information.

"I suppose you know, Mrs. Andrews, that I'm not satisfied with your husband's stories in these two crimes we've had up here at Kaibito."

"If you're still thinking he's guilty of either of them, you're mistaken. They're not on his conscience, because he's sleeping good. I know every move he makes at night, although I can't always keep track of him in the daytime."

"I don't know that I agree with you, Mrs. Andrews. I'm speaking freely, you understand. I don't mind either him or you knowing my thoughts. And when he comes back, I wish you'd tell him for me that he's practically under arrest for murder."

"Under arrest?" Mrs. Andrews snapped. "You can't arrest him for something he hasn't done."

"You just think I can't. When he comes back tell him I want to see him. I'll be around. There's no use attempting to give me the slip, either; you couldn't get this trailer out of this country without my knowing it, so don't try."

The woman did not reply, but her sharp nose seemed sharper and her dark eyes more resentful as she stared at us. We turned away and walked toward the post.

"You certainly told her, Ed," I remarked, jokingly.

"Yes, and I'm not just talking, either," he retorted in no mood for levity. Rogers had been silent all this while, a thoughtful look in his eyes.

"If you're not satisfied, Mr. Sheriff," he began casually, "with my presence in the case, please say so. I know I counseled you against taking Andrews with you yesterday—"

"Now don't get me wrong, Professor," the sheriff interrupted. "Maybe I'm talking a bit too freely this morning. But this man Andrews makes me mad, going off when I told him I wanted to see him. I thought maybe it might do some good if his old lady stewed about things today. You know how she told the guy to come clean about his visit to Kimball the other night when we had him in a corner. Of course, he told only part of the story, but it was progress. I'm hoping for the same when we get to talking to him again. I didn't mean anything critical, Professor, of you or what you are thinking about the case. Maybe I'm wrong. I'll admit that you've thought of things that don't square with my theories, and we've got to get those ironed out."

"Well, if at any time, Mr. Sheriff, you want to kick me off, don't hesitate to do it."

"I won't. I'll speak my mind. But right now I want you to stick."

We walked a few steps farther before anything more was said; then Sheriff Wilson apparently looked about him for the first time. "I haven't seen any Indians around this morning," he said. "Where are they?"

"They're all down around Gray Warrior's hogan this morning," I reminded him.

"Oh, yes; that 'sing' they're having. I understand that his squaw has been sick for some time. But—" His gaze swept on ahead to the porch of the trading post. "There's John Navajo and Jeff Draper waiting for us now. John said he'd bring him in, didn't he?"

The two Indians watched us approach without change of expression in their dark faces. The sheriff greeted them in the Navajo tongue and they unsmilingly returned his greeting. They neither moved nor made any suggestion that we sit down. I sat down at Jeff Draper's side; the sheriff and Rogers continued for a moment to stand.

"Thanks, John," Wilson said to the Indian policeman. "You said you'd bring Jeff here this morning."

"*Ohk*," grunted John Navajo.

"Jeff," the sheriff began impressively, "I want to talk to you. About Bernice Patterson. Somebody tried to kill that girl. I want to know all about it. I've talked to all the white people. Now I'm talking to you."

"Not guilty," replied the youthful Indian impassively.

"I didn't ask you whether you were guilty or not. What I want to know is what happened in the canyon yesterday. I want you to tell me what you did. Did you have a quarrel with her?"

"No."

"Did she send you away?"

"I go when I get ready to go."

"When was that?"

"Don't know. No have watch. But Bent is climbing up where we are. I am tired doing nothing. I go."

"Who left first, you or Bent?"

"I go first. He there when I leave."

We all noted the discrepancy in Jeff's statement when taken with what Surrey Bent had already told us. Rogers asked a question.

"What was your hurry, Jeff? Why were you running your pony when you went by the post yesterday?"

"No hurry. Indian like to ride fast. Plenty ponies. Too many. Kill one what's difference?"

"So you left Mr. Bent and the girl alone together, is that it?"

"*Ohk.*"

"Who else did you see down in the canyon yesterday?"

"Lamb is riding alone down the canyon."

"Did you see him come back?"

"Yes. Before I left."

"Who else?"

"Man who lives in trailer."

"When was that? When did you see him?"

"In morning, when Bernice and I went to ruin. He comes then. He climbs up. Stays and talks a lot. Asks many questions. Finally I say to him: 'Bernice can't be bothered. She has work to do.' "

"What did he say to that?" asked the sheriff.

"He got mad. Said no Indian talk to him like that. We were about to have a fight, I think. But Bernice say if we can't be quiet to get the hell out and leave her alone."

"What happened then?" Wilson asked.

"Andrews went. Shook fist at me, and I no see him again until I am ready to go."

"You saw him later?" echoed Rogers. "Where and when?"

"When I am tired of staying and decide to leave. He is down on trail, but he says nothing. He looks all time like he will start to fight with me. I pay no attention. I get my pony and ride away."

"Just a minute, Jeff," said the sheriff. "Bent is up in the ruins when you leave. And Andrews down below. Is that right?"

"*Ohk.*"

"Where was Miss Patterson's horse when you left the canyon?" asked Rogers.

"Tied to juniper tree."

"Did you unbuckle the throatlatch of the bridle?"

"Yes," was the frank answer.

"Why?" persisted Rogers. "You were mad at her, then, weren't you? You wanted to make her walk back to the post, didn't you?"

"I want her to walk. I no like the way she treat me."

"Then you were mad at her?" The sheriff took over the questioning.

"Well, maybe I am sore at her."

"Why?"

Jeff was silent.

"You're in love with the girl—is that it, Jeff?" the sheriff pressed. The Indian sat staring off through the piñon and juniper beyond the clearing about the post.

"Maybe," he admitted at length. "Three years ago she said she will come back some day. White man marry Navajo woman, why not white woman marry Navajo man? She talked like that then. But now—" he suddenly lifted his right arm and pushed away an imaginary person, "it is like that. She laugh at me. She say I am silly. I think maybe I kill her, and then I say no I do not do that, maybe tomorrow things will be different. I will make her walk to post. That will learn her not to play with Navajo man."

"Now, let's get this all straightened out, Jeff," said the sheriff. "When you left Bernice up in the ruins, Bent was there talking with her. Down on the trail below Andrews was waiting. Do you think he was going to climb up into the ruins again after you had got out of sight?"

"I think so, yes."

"And let's get this straight too. You're sweet on the girl, because she encouraged you three years ago to think maybe she cared for you. But this time she pushed you away. So you are mad at her?"

"*Ohk.*"

"You are mad at Andrews too. You quarreled with him in the morning."

"*Ohk.*"

"Also you were mad at Norman Kimball when he threatened you with a gun because you broke the girl's camera."

"*Ohk.* I despise him. He beneath Navajo. So I no kill him. I no try to kill Bernice. Andrews is alive. I no plan to kill him. So, if that is all, Mr. Wilson, I think now I am going to the 'sing' at Gray Warrior's hogan."

"Just a minute, Jeff," said the sheriff, as the Indian got up from the steps. "Did you break into Miss Mills-paw's room last night here at the post and take a traveling bag?"

"You mean steal?"

"Yes. I mean did you steal a bag that belonged to Norman Kimball?"

"I no steal. I take what I want if I can use it. But no need a traveling bag. I'm through with school on outside. I stay on reservation."

16

It proved to be a day not wholly without result, although it started badly enough. Lester Andrews continued absent and an occasional check was necessary to discover whether or not he had returned to the trailer without our knowledge.

"I don't figure that we got very far with Jeff Draper, do you?" Sheriff Wilson remarked, as John Navajo disappeared with Jeff in the direction of Gray Warrior's hogan.

"Perhaps not," replied Huntoon Rogers as if his thoughts were elsewhere than at Kaibito.

We ate noon dinner and time still was hanging heavily upon our hands, so I made a suggestion which led to an interesting afternoon, if to nothing else.

"I was just wondering, if nobody has a better idea," I said, "why we don't go to the 'sing' at Gray Warrior's hogan."

"It must be nearly over; this is the second day of it," Rogers responded, getting up from his seat on the porch.

The sheriff demurred, saying Andrews might return in our absence.

"What if he does, Ed? He'll be here when we get back," I said.

"All right."

We got horses from the corral and rode in the direction of the hogan. It wasn't more than a mile over there through the gray sage and scrub. There was a large turnout of Indians, for Gray Warrior was rich in sheep and goats and a "sing" at his hogan would draw a crowd. The canyon must have been about depopulated, as well as the area for some miles about Kaibito. Wagons, horses, sheep, dogs, men, women and children were scattered among the trees.

The "sing" had started the day before with the traditional ceremony of the making of the sacred wand. This had been done down in the canyon and the Indians had come up with it late in the afternoon and camped near the trading post so as to be ready to make the attack which we had heard at sunrise that morning. Long before we arrived, of course, the gifts had been made to the sick woman in the ceremonial hogan in the presence of those important enough to be included in the rite, and who accordingly had washed their hair in yucca suds. She later would have been blackened with charcoal in preparation for the sorcery of the medicine man.

By the time we came in sight of the place the men were singing and dancing outside the hogan, indicating that the ghost had been killed and the healing ceremony practically over, except for the entertainment which usually followed.

"What was the matter with the *bandai?*" Rogers inquired of Wilson. "It was the squaw and not Gray Warrior, I understand, who was to be cured."

"Oh—she's got a goiter. A big one."

"Think they'll cure her?" I asked.

"Yes, probably," Rogers replied. "I've seen it done. Three or four years ago over around Chinlee there was a squaw with one. They went through all the ceremonial trappings, of course. I never before saw so many gifts come flying out of the smoke hole in the hogan. There was a tremendous to-do, but I think the medicine man probably slipped her something—some sort of drug—while he was singing the seven songs at the right of the altar to scatter the ghosts of the Ancient People. Because I saw the patient about a year later and there was no sign of the goiter. They've got their remedies. The Hopis have a remedy for snake bite that really works—"

"Oh, oh!" I said, "there are the mud men. Be careful, boys."

A crowd of a dozen Navajo men accompanied by a drummer, among whom I noted Jeff Draper and John Navajo, had come tumbling out of the smoke hole of the hogan. They ran north, danced and returned to a place near a summer shade where they continued dancing about. They were naked, except for a breechcloth, and smeared from head to foot with mud. Theirs was the function of minor healing and the buffoonery that sometimes followed a Navajo "sing." They picked up a child and tossed it gently to heal it of some minor ailment. When they set it down again they pursued a youth and soon ran him to earth. They tossed him over their heads and ended by dumping him in the shallow mudhole they had made behind Gray Warrior's hogan. They dashed out of sight and next appeared with a blanket in which they rolled and tumbled a woman.

Sheriff Wilson moved off among the scattered wagons. I followed him, and for a few minutes we lost sight of Rogers. Wilson was on the watch for Andrews, thinking, as he told me, that Andrews might perhaps be an onlooker among the Indians, but there was no sign of him. We stopped to talk with some of the older men, passing the time of day with them, asking after their health, and indulging in the usual small talk that might be exchanged after a long separation.

Of a sudden the naked figure of a mud man appeared from behind a wagon, and instantly I spurred my horse and went running to safety. I looked back to discover that the sheriff had fled to safety in another direction. But beyond him Rogers was in difficulty. I rode warily back in his direction to see what had happened. An Indian had leaped upon Rogers' horse from behind and had thrown his arms tightly about his waist. The horse evidently had balked at this happening and in the instant's delay its bridle had been seized by a couple of mud men on the ground. Rogers was in for it.

My own danger being over for the moment, I rode in closer to watch the fun, yelling derisively at him, although I don't think he heard me. During the brief struggle which followed I gained the impression that Rogers had not tried very hard to escape his captors, for he probably was as strong as any two of them. A moment later he and the Indian rolled off the horse and were pounced upon by the entire muddy crew of savages.

"It was John Navajo, wasn't it, who caught him?"

said Sheriff Wilson from behind me. "It looked like John."

"I didn't notice, Ed. Funny, though, that Rogers didn't put up more of a fight."

"He could have got away from them."

By this time the naked mud men were tossing him in the air. He made a ludicrous figure, arms and legs flying at odd angles as he went high above the heads of the Indians. Again and again he was tossed over their heads to the jeers and laughter of the onlookers who enjoyed the great sprawling spectacle he made. Then struggling and kicking he was dragged to the mudhole and dumped in, where he was rolled and plastered and soused in the slimy mass of yellowish ooze until he was almost unrecognizable. At length he came grinning out of it, and the mud men ran away in search of another victim. And, now that he had been initiated into the buffoonery, Rogers joined forces with them and soon was chasing victims with the Navajos and tossing them in the air.

I should have known better, of course, than to turn my back upon Rogers for even a few moments at this time. Sheriff Wilson called to me to come over where he was. Gray Warrior's squaw had come out of the hogan and was mingling with the women and children. I was interested to see her, now that the cure had been worked over her. For when I came again next year I hoped to see whether or not it would have been effective.

"She's got a goiter all right," the sheriff was saying, but before I could single her out among the other women Wilson spoke sharply, "Look out, Chuck!" He spurred his own horse away through the scattering crowd, and I turned around in time to see the mud-bespattered Rogers, now astride his horse, riding me down.

I got away with a burst of speed, for my horse sensed my need, and we went flying off through the scrub. But fast as I was going I could hear the thudding hoofs of Rogers' horse behind me. Of a sudden he let out a blood-curdling whoop, and I glanced in alarm over my shoulder to discover his horse upon my flank. I dodged sharply to the left, but it was no use. His horse had the instinct of a polo pony.

"Get away, Hunt!" I shouted at him. "Let me alone!"

"You would laugh at me," he shouted, his teeth an unnatural white in his muddy face, and then he whooped the bloodcurdling yell again.

It's done in the movies, of course, but I'd never seen it performed elsewhere, not even on the old Lazy J ranch in New Mexico where I worked when I was younger, and where the cowboys were more than usually reckless. For to my horror when next I glanced back Rogers had got his feet out of the stirrups and in the saddle seat and he was poised in the act of springing.

"You crazy fool," I shouted, doing my best to avoid him as he launched himself at me. But the next moment he had me around the waist and the impact of his body and its dead weight were dragging me out of the saddle. Our horses sheered clear of us and went galloping away as we rolled to the ground. Over and over we went into the scraggly, twisting branches of a scrub cedar.

"You would laugh at me," he roared in my ear as we ended up with a thump. "You're not hurt, are you,

Chuck?" he inquired solicitously.

"No!" I said disgustedly. "Why don't you hire out as a stunt man to the movies, Hunt?" I said.

"I may at that," he rejoined, sitting up and hugging his muddy knees. "I didn't know that I was half as good as I must be. Now, you get a ducking like the rest of us."

"Please, Hunt."

We had rolled out of sight among the low protecting branches of the cedar. Rogers peered out of our concealment. We had not been followed by the mud men, who probably, from the faint cries that penetrated to us, had already found another victim.

"I'm ready to quit, though," Rogers said suddenly. "Let's walk on up to the post. I need a bath. The horses will have gone back to the corral."

"What a swell pal you've turned out to be!" I gibed, still somewhat nettled at his robust treatment of me.

"If you feel that way about it yet, Chuck," he grinned, "I'll take you back to the mudhole on my shoulder." He could have carried out his threat despite anything I could have done to prevent it.

"Okeh. Let's go," I said, starting toward the post.

We walked along in silence for a few minutes. The irritation the incident had caused was disappearing as rapidly as the mud on Rogers' clothing was drying in the thin air.

"You know the whys and wherefores of a Navajo 'sing,' don't you, Chuck?" Rogers asked.

"I know that it's a healing ceremony for sickness. I've seen several, but I never inquired into its origin."

"The 'sing' in reality is descended from the war dance, or *anadji*. Its purpose is to cure the individual of the diseases which he may have contracted because of war or through the evil doings of his enemies. The Navajos haven't gone to war for a great many years, of course. But the old belief was that a Navajo who killed an enemy by striking on the head would get a disease of the head; if in the chest he'd get a disease of the chest, or in the abdomen an abdominal affliction.

"But since there are no wars now, a Navajo may contract diseases by means related to the old war customs. The sight of a dead person may affect an unborn child, or seeing a slain enemy might also affect the individual concerned. Or a man may discover that his illness is due to some oversight or blunder by one or both of his parents before he was born. Neither the husband nor the wife, when the birth of a child is expected, will willingly look at the bones of a cliff dweller among the ruins for fear of what may happen in later life to the child. And so, when illness develops, arrangements are made for a singer to conduct the ceremony, a medicine man is engaged and word is sent out in advance so the crowd can come, and the necessary articles to make a show at the ceremony are accumulated."

"You think, then, that Jeff Draper didn't kill Kimball," I said.

"Well," he began slowly, and I was aware that I had hit upon one of his lines of reasoning, "it's highly improbable, I think. Did Jeff regard Kimball as an enemy after the little row down near Red Lake? And if he were to kill him might he not stand a pretty good chance of having to view the body later, and thereby lay himself open to certain bad luck—such as becoming a candidate for the lethal gas chamber down at Florence? You see, Chuck, those are factors to be weighed in Jeff's case."

"How about the attempt to murder Bernice Patterson?"

"There again, Chuck, subtle factors are involved. Don't misunderstand me—you've had more experience on the Navajo Reservation than I've had. I'm not saying that a murder can't be committed by a Navajo. Jeff's running his pony by the trading post the way he did might be an argument that he believed he had killed her and was fleeing all possibility of having to look at the body of his victim, which would indicate further that there was more than just a tiff between the two—in other words, a genuine quarrel which Jeff would regard as the beginning of a lifelong enmity. But again, it's just as likely that Jeff was displaying the usual Indian indifference for his pony and was in a great hurry to go no place.

"We've got to remember this, though, Chuck—an Indian doesn't think as a white man thinks. His psychological background is so different from ours that we can't assume that because the white man thinks and acts in a certain way the Indian will too. Where are we?" he asked of a sudden, looking about him, for he had been absorbed in what he was saying and had paid no attention to our progress in the direction of the trading post.

"We're below the corral a couple of hundred yards," I answered. "That's Ernie Caldwell's camp over there by those piñons; those are his horses hobbled to the left of it."

"Oh, yes; I see where we are. Let's drop by and call on Caldwell."

"Don't you want to clean that mud off as soon as you can?"

"It won't take but a few minutes to see Caldwell."

So we veered our course slightly and headed for the small, dingy shelter tent, the sleeping bag hanging on a line strung between the trees, the neatly piled camp equipment which the cowboy had set up for his stay at Kaibito. We were within fifty yards of the spot when Rogers' arm was flung suddenly against my chest.

"What's the trouble?"

"Over there under that cedar. Look!"

I didn't see anything unusual, and, therefore, announced the fact. Rogers went striding over to the tree. Before I had caught up with him, he was pulling something from under the branches.

"Whose is it?" I demanded, as he brought forth from its hiding place an expensive leather traveling bag. "Kimball's?"

"That's my guess, Chuck," he said, squatting beside it. He shouted, "Caldwell! Oh, Caldwell!" There was no reply. "Go see if he's over there, will you, Chuck, please."

I walked the short distance to the camp. There was no sign of him anywhere about. Twice I called his name, wondering if he could be within sound of my voice, but there was no answer. I went back and found Rogers looking through the contents of the bag.

"No sign of him?" he asked, glancing up at me.

"None at all."

"This undoubtedly is Kimball's bag," he said. "There are shirts with his monogram worked on the pockets. Sit down and help me."

We went to work. I cleared a small place on the ground of twigs and stones and we dumped the bag upside down. There was nothing in the pockets of the bag, no papers, no letters, notebooks—nothing whatever on which was written or printed a single word. There were several shirts and ties and pairs of socks, some underwear and handkerchiefs, a comb and military brushes, toothbrush, soap, talcum powder, an electric shaver as well as a safety razor and blades, slippers and a lounging robe.

Having put them all back in orderly fashion and closed the bag, we sat back on our heels and looked at each other. The mud had dried on Rogers' face and hands and had caked in yellowish masses on his clothing. He was solemn in spite of the fact that he could pass respectably for a scarecrow.

"Nothing of any value to us, now that we've found it," he said.

"Was there anything in it that made it worth stealing?"

"To the thief? Perhaps. But only the thief knows that answer. Emily, of course, wouldn't know what was in the bag."

"Then why is it hidden close to Caldwell's camp?"

"The thief could tell us that too."

"Do you think Caldwell was the burglar?"

Rogers studied over my question. "And you mean the killer too?"

"Well—why not?"

Rogers' mild blue eyes gazed at me steadily. They seemed to have changed color peculiarly against the background of his muddy face. "Well—why not?" he echoed. "Also, why not Andrews? Or Surrey Bent? Or Carter Lamb? Or Fletcher Wicks?"

"Or Jeff Draper?"

"Is the stolen bag a part of the plot? It would seem so," he answered his own question. "But if Caldwell had stolen it, would he have hidden it so close to his camp? Hidden it so bunglingly that anybody could find it? We discovered it easily enough when we happened to walk by this way." He was lost in thought for a moment. "I guess Ernie could use the things in the bag—the clothing and stuff—for his own wardrobe is meager. But our question is, was the thing stolen for the clothing and not for something else altogether? If Caldwell's the burglar, why bungle the thing as crudely as this? On the other hand, if the bag figures in the plot, wouldn't the thief attempt to plant it somewhere near enough to implicate Caldwell, say?"

"I can't figure any of it out, Hunt," I said. "I wish you'd go and clean up. You look worse than a scarecrow."

He grinned and got to his feet. He lifted the heavy bag and swung it easily along as we walked to the trading post. Harry Easton gazed for a moment at us curiously when we entered the bull pen, and then burst out laughing at the spectacle of the muddy Rogers.

"The mud men got you, did they, Hunt?" he inquired.

"Yes."

"What's that you have there?"

"It's Kimball's bag."

The trader examined it, coming from behind the counter. "Yes, I guess it is," he said. "That's the bag I carried into Miss Millspaw's room, anyhow. Oh, by the way, something happened while you were gone that may interest you, Hunt."

"What's that? A change in Miss Patterson's condition?"

"No, not that. She's just as she was—unconscious. What I had in mind was Marian Wicks—she bought some bandages and adhesive tape and antiseptics a while ago. Was anxious to get back to her hogan."

"What happened?"

"I asked her that, too, but she wouldn't say anything. She'd be buying it only for her husband, of course. So I asked her how he got hurt. She was evasive. I understand, though, that Emily Millspaw saw Wicks coming from the canyon and she said—this was after Marian Wicks had gone—that he looked like he'd been beaten up. Face skinned and eyes swelling."

17

SHERIFF WILSON was not long in returning to the trading post. Rogers had got the mud from his face and hands and had changed to clean clothes which served to restore him to respectability once more when the sheriff rode up. He inquired what had happened to us, examined with considerable interest Kimball's bag, asked many questions, and was satisfied, as were we, that for the time being the thing held little interest for us.

"I think now, Mr. Sheriff," began Rogers, "that we should pay Fletcher Wicks a call."

"Why? What's happened?"

"In our absence this afternoon, he was beaten up by somebody." He went on to tell what Harry Easton already had related to us.

"Let's go," said the sheriff, moving toward the door.

Rogers and I found our horses at the corral, standing patiently at the gate waiting to be let inside. We had forgotten them, what with the discovery of the bag, and Rogers' muddy condition when we returned from the "sing" to distract us. And although they were reluctant to start out again, we dropped in behind the sheriff, who headed for Fletcher Wicks' hogan.

There was no sign of life about the crude dwelling when we pulled up before it. Sheriff Wilson shouted for

Wicks, swung off his horse and dropped the reins.

"Oh, Wick! Wicks! I want to see you," he repeated.

Marian Wicks appeared in the doorway. She seemed more than usually attractive, the deep red color of her cheeks showing through her tan, her graceful body despite the enveloping folds of the full skirt and velvet jacket poised before us.

"He's not feeling well enough for visitors," she announced.

"That's just what we've come to see him about," the sheriff said, his flinty eyes fixed upon the young woman. "I hear that you were buying bandages and medicine for him."

A gesture of impatience escaped her. "What business is it of yours if I was?" she countered sharply.

"I'm making it my business, ma'am," the sheriff retorted politely but firmly. "I understand your husband's been in a fight. What I'm after is what for and who with?"

"I can't tell you." Marian Wicks made as if to turn away into the hogan, indicating that as far as she was concerned there would be no further information.

"Is he badly hurt, Mrs. Wicks?" Rogers inquired sympathetically.

"He was able to come home alone."

"Is he here in the hogan?"

"He's lying down."

A voice from inside called out, "Tell 'em to come on in."

Marian Wicks stood back for us to enter, and, led by Sheriff Wilson, we filed inside. Despite the outward appearance of poverty and the gossip we had heard as to the low state of fortune of this strange pair of young people, the interior of the hogan was almost luxurious, judging by what one would normally expect to find in this primitive type of dwelling.

Fletcher Wicks was lying on a bed on the hard earthen floor, but it was a bed made up of Navajo blankets of as fine a quality as I had ever seen anywhere on the reservation. There were books on a shelf and some recent magazines. There was even a bouquet of larkspur and Indian paintbrush in an old jar of redware that could have come only from the ruins of the cliff dwellers.

"What do you want now?" demanded a voice from the bed. Our eyes, when they became accustomed to the lessened light of the room, discovered a bandaged occupant who was staring at us from one dark eye, the other being hidden under a bandage that was wound turbanwise about his head. One forearm and hand likewise were bandaged. Despite this evidence of violence and the fact that he was in bed, his voice was strong and his temper not of the best.

"You seem to have got scratched up a bit," Rogers answered.

"What happened, Wicks?" demanded the sheriff.

"Nothing."

"Nothing?"

"Nothing that concerns you in any way," was the reply.

"How do I know it doesn't."

"You'll have to trust to my judgment in the matter, Sheriff."

"Now, look here, Wicks, I'm not here to beat about the bush. I understand you came back from the canyon looking as though you'd taken a beating. Who did it?"

"I'm saying nothing. It's entirely a private matter."

"Was it Andrews?"

"Andrews? I've no comment to make."

"Then why did you ask us to come into the hogan?" the sheriff exploded.

"That's the quickest way to get rid of you. You can see that something happened; you can hear me say it's a private matter—"

"Does your—accident," began Rogers slowly, "have any connection with the murder of Norman Kimball or the attempt on Miss Patterson's life?"

"I don't see how it could have the remotest connection." Wicks twisted his head about to gaze up at Rogers with his one unbandaged eye.

"Have we your word of honor on that?" Rogers pressed.

"Honor?" Wicks echoed flippantly, as if the word were strange. "To the best of my knowledge, Mr. Rogers," he added quickly, "my personal affairs have no connection with either the killing of my stepfather-in-law or the attempt on Miss Patterson."

There seemed to be nothing further that Wicks was willing to tell us, but Rogers was not done with him yet.

"I suppose you've heard of the burglar at the post last night."

"So?"

"Kimball's bag was stolen from Emily's room. It was recovered, however, this afternoon, and so far as we know its contents are intact. Perhaps you know whether or not he had any personal papers, letters, documents, or anything of the kind in the bag."

"How would I know that?" Wicks said irritably.

"I thought perhaps you might have seen inside the bag, or observed him putting something of the kind in it, or heard him say that he had such things with him. It would be of help if we knew why the bag was important to a thief."

"No."

"How about you, Mrs. Wicks?" Rogers asked, turning to the young woman who stood near the doorway.

"I'm sure I can tell you nothing," she answered firmly, then added: "If you've asked all your questions, I think you'd better go. I want my husband to rest now."

"There's just one more." Rogers smiled. "Your step-father brought some papers from the coupé that first afternoon. I saw him take them from the glove compartment when he left the car to come here to the hogan. Where are they now? And what were they?"

"Oh, those," she said, and went to a box in the hogan and took from it a thin packet of papers held together with a rubber band. "Here they are. He left them with me that night. He said he was leaving them just in case I changed my mind and was willing to sign them. Of course, I didn't. It's an agreement to sell the property back home." She gave them to Rogers who glanced through the packet and passed them to Sheriff Wilson.

"So far as you know, this is all he had with him?" Rogers asked.

"Yes."

The sun was dropping rapidly as we rode back toward the trading post, and the wind was beginning to strengthen. Rogers and the sheriff were both silent for the greater part of the distance. Once the latter swore roundly and slapped his horse with his hand, which startled the animal so that it went tearing off through the scrub. We caught up with him and Wilson looked back at us in disgust.

"I hate to be made a sucker by Fletcher Wicks," he said.

"So do I," Rogers agreed, but there was no such feeling in his tone as there was in the sheriff's voice; rather, I thought, he said it as if his tongue were in his cheek. "Supposing it was our friend Andrews who beat him up, Mr. Sheriff," he asked, "what's the answer?"

"Search me. You don't think that Wicks possibly was on the point of discovering Andrews' secret, say, and that started hostilities?"

"By Andrews' secret you mean his connection with the killing—his guilt—that—?"

"Hell, I don't know what I mean," said Wilson. "I'm all mixed up in this thing, Professor. Do you see any head or tail to it yet—except that Andrews is our man?"

"Nothing's clear yet. There are certain facts beyond dispute; they point to other suspected, but as yet unknown, facts. And until all of these are discovered, there's little to be gained by trying to interpret what we have."

"Well—I'm hungrier than a wolf," responded the

sheriff, as if he preferred to shut the whole thing out of his mind. "But as soon as I've had something to eat, I'm going down and sit on Andrews' doorstep, and I'm not going to move until that fellow shows up. He'll be home tonight; that's certain," he concluded with a vast confidence in his prediction.

We rode up to the corral and unsaddled. Carter Lamb arrived before we had finished, riding a horse and leading another. He shot a hasty glance at us and began talking.

"I say," he said, "you didn't hear what happened to Surrey Bent, did you?"

"No, what?" responded Sheriff Wilson, not greatly interested, despite the young man's obvious but suppressed excitement.

"He got hurt this afternoon."

"Hurt?" echoed Rogers.

"I found him on the trail below the steps—you know, the steps that lead up to the ruin where Miss Patterson—"

"What happened?"

"He—well, I don't know exactly. I wasn't there at the time. He said he was going to climb up and look for that light effect he's anxious to see. So I rode on down the canyon. When I came back I found him at the bottom of the steps. He was groaning a little. I think he'd been unconscious. I wasn't gone, though, more than half to three quarters of an hour. He was vague about what happened. I don't think he knew. I figured he'd slipped and fallen when he was part way up the steps, and that probably knocked him out. He was scratched a little. I couldn't get much out of him, though. Haven't yet, for that matter. I got him on his horse. He was able to sit in the saddle, although he wobbled a bit as we came, and I had to stop now and then to let him rest. He was sort of dizzy—"

"Where is he now?" demanded the sheriff.

"I took him to our room and put him to bed."

"Come on, Professor, we'll find out about it." Wilson set off at a smart pace toward the living quarters of the post.

I followed in the wake of the pair, believing that we were on the threshold of an important discovery. Before we had reached the stone building, however, Lamb had caught up with us.

"I don't think he needs a doctor," he continued. "It just knocked his wind, and the fall sort of shocked him. He's not a young man, you know. He's fifty-one and can't stand a great deal."

The room at the post where Surrey Bent lay in bed was already filling with the dusk. The man's soft brown eyes seemed luminous, almost feverish in the half light. Doctor Creelman, who had returned to Kaibito, was in the room. He was taking the artist's pulse.

"I'm telling you, Doctor," the rumbling voice of the artist was saying, "you're fired before you begin."

"Pulse normal. No fever," said Doctor Creelman tersely, glaring at the man in bed. "I don't think there's anything the matter with you."

"I know there isn't."

"How are you feeling, Bent?" Rogers asked.

"Hungry."

"We'll see that you're fed, Surrey," Carter Lamb said, crowding into the room. "You're lots better already, though, aren't you?"

"I started all of a sudden to get better after you rolled me into bed. Can't be anything serious. I'm eating supper at the table."

He thrust his bare legs out from under the covers and sat up on the edge of the bed. "Hand me my pants, Carter," he directed, and when his trousers were passed to him, he thrust his legs into them.

"How's Miss Patterson, Doctor?" Rogers turned to Creelman.

"No change," was the gruff answer. "Holding her own, though."

"Still unconscious, of course?"

"Oh, yes," Creelman answered. He glared at Rogers and left the room.

"What happened, Bent, down in the canyon?" asked Rogers.

"That's what I'm asking myself."

"You know what hit you surely," said Wilson. "Was it Wicks?"

"Wicks?" echoed the artist in astonishment. "No; I saw that fight, though. He and Andrews put on a real go, to judge from the results. I was there only in time to see the finish. Andrews is quite a boy. Wicks is a lot younger and more active. Should have got the best of the argument, but Andrews packs an awful wallop. They were slugging away at each other down there when I came along. I'd have stopped the fight, of course, but Wicks had had just about enough and was quitting when I rode up."

"What were they fighting about?" demanded Wilson.

"They didn't tell me, and I didn't ask. Wicks was in a hurry to get out of the canyon."

"What did Andrews do?"

"Disappeared. I don't like that fellow. There's something oily—slick, I guess—about him. I said to him, 'What are you, a white hope in disguise?' and he told me to go to hell. So I guess he was all worked up about something. A fellow'd have to be to put up the fight he was putting up with Wicks. It was brutal."

By this time Surrey Bent was dressed. Peggy Easton already had appeared anxiously in the doorway, not only to inquire after Bent but to announce that supper was waiting. The artist smoothed his hair on his round head at the little mirror over the washstand and pushed us ahead of him out into the hallway and in the direction of the dining room. Our appetites were enormous by this time and we fell hungrily upon the food before us.

"Well, then, what happened to you?" asked Rogers after the plates all around the table had been filled.

"As I said a while ago, I don't know," responded Bent.

"What could have happened?"

"I've tried to figure that out." The artist finished buttering a biscuit and glanced across at Rogers. "The only certain thing about it is that I rolled almost all the way down those steps."

"Goodness, gracious!" exclaimed Peggy, concern manifest in her dark eyes. "Why, you might have been killed!"

"Yes, I might," Bent agreed with her. "But I wasn't. As I was saying, I was almost at the top of the steps. I remember catching at handholds and slipping and catching again. Then after that there's a blank in my mind. For the next thing I knew positively was that Carter was trying to get me on my horse. I don't know how long the interval was, or what happened. I know that there's a sore spot on my scalp," and he reached up to touch tenderly the top of his head; "and I've got a few bruises here and there on my body, from the way I feel, but that's all the damage."

"Could a small piece of the overhanging rock have broken loose and come down on your head, Mr. Bent?" suggested Rogers.

"It could have. I've thought of that. And again somebody could have been lying in wait behind that boulder at the head of the steps and reached out and tapped me."

"Who could that have been?" asked Wilson. "Andrews?"

"I'm not accusing anybody. I didn't see anybody on the ledge above, although somebody could have been concealed there behind the boulder."

The matter was left about at that point, although we continued to discuss it for some time after we had finished our supper, sitting about the table. Emily Millspaw, who had been a silent listener throughout the meal, left the table as soon as she had eaten, and Carter Lamb, with first a proprietary glance at the older artist as if to verify the genuineness of his recovery, got up and followed her.

It was quite dark, therefore, when we finally shoved back from the table and went out into the bull pen for an after-dinner smoke, with no inkling of the terrifying night that lay just before us. Part of the mystery surrounding the injuries Fletcher Wicks had sustained earlier in the day had, of course, been cleared up by what Surrey Bent had seen in the canyon. But it left obscure the reasons why Wicks and Andrews should have fought each other, just as it left us with what amounted to a new mystery—namely, what had happened to Surrey Bent? Bent could throw no further light upon the incident. As a matter of fact, he did not join us in the bull pen but went to his room instead. Later we heard him as he went outside.

We were totally unprepared for what was to follow shortly, however, when the door opened and Lamb and Emily entered. They now sought the light and comfort of the bull pen in preference to the darkness outside.

"It's chilly out and the wind's getting awfully strong," said the girl. There was a little fire in the stove at the rear of the room, and the two came back to where we were.

"Come up and get warm," Rogers invited, moving his chair.

"I say," said Lamb, holding his hands out to the rusty warmth of the stove, "I think that fellow Andrews is cockeyed."

"Why? What's happened?" Sheriff Wilson's jaw dropped a trifle and he shoved back sharply from the stove. I realized that he had forgotten having said earlier in the evening that he was going to camp on Andrews' doorstep until he should return. There was a twinkle in Rogers' eyes, and I knew that he shared my own thoughts with amusement.

"I wouldn't want to drive a trailer out of here after dark. A car's different, of course——"

"Trailer?" demanded the sheriff open mouthed. "Is he——?"

"I said trailer. He pulled out, trailer and all, about half an hour ago."

"Toward Red Lake?" I asked.

"Where else would he go?" Harry Easton asked.

"Come on," said Rogers, already on his feet, and starting in the direction of the door.

18

I swung down near the corral and around past the spot where the trailer had been parked as we started away in the station wagon. It was Rogers' idea, just to make sure that the trailer was gone, although Carter Lamb resented the implication that we doubted his statement that Andrews had pulled out. The lights shone for a moment on Ernie Caldwell's horses hobbled near his camp; then the darkness swallowed them up.

Sheriff Wilson was silent in the seat beside me. Behind us on the extra seat were Rogers and Lamb. We had rushed outside at the word that Andrews had pulled out of Kaibito, hesitated a moment beside the sheriff's coupé, and decided that three of us were too many for the single seat.

"Let's take the station wagon," I suggested. "It's all ready to go." And so we had crowded quickly into it, Carter Lamb included. Since the sheriff had not objected to Lamb's presence, and, also, since there was plenty of room, I said nothing. It was just as well, perhaps, that Lamb did come along, for he had an interesting bit of information yet to tell us.

"You know," he began, as the station wagon started rolling along the road which skirted the two-hundred-foot ledge at the edge of the mesa, "I don't know what all was going on down there at the trailer—"

"What happened?" asked the sheriff from the darkness beside me. Lamb lighted a cigarette. His match flared and then was extinguished before we went on.

"Well—I didn't see it, understand. But Emily did. She was telling me about it after supper."

"That was when the two of you went outside?" Rogers asked.

"That's right. She'd seen it before supper, you understand. She'd been strolling about. Been down to the corral, and around among the trees. Trying to find wild flowers for her room, she said. Well, anyway—" He paused to order his thoughts. "I'm trying to tell it just as she said she saw it. First she met Ernie Caldwell and he stopped and looked at the flowers she had found. He told her about the flowers you can see and smell over on the trail to Rainbow Bridge. Sort of a little paradise in there, you know. Well—they talked a few minutes, and then Caldwell went off in the direction of the trailer. She didn't see him go to the trailer, but just in that direction, she said."

"When did Andrews come back?" interposed Wilson.

"Well—I— Better let me tell the story, Sheriff, the way I got it."

"Go ahead."

"Emily said that she walked farther through the scrub, but didn't find any more flowers and so she turned back. The sun was down and she thought she ought to be getting back to the post. When she was about a hundred yards from the trailer, she saw Mrs.

Andrews. The woman was running like hell. Toward the trailer—"

"Mrs. Andrews?" echoed Rogers. "I haven't seen her outside the trailer all the time I've been here."

"It was Mrs. Andrews. I said the same thing to Emily about her that you did. Mrs. Andrews didn't see Emily, or, if she did, she paid no attention to her. She was hell bent to get back to the trailer, like a rabbit running for its hole. And just as she got pretty nearly to it, Ernie Caldwell popped out of the trailer, saw Mrs. Andrews running for it, stepped aside in order not to get knocked over, and Mrs. Andrews jumped inside and slammed the door."

"She didn't speak to Caldwell?" asked Rogers.

"Apparently not. Caldwell stood outside for a few seconds, Emily said, as if he didn't know what to do exactly, then started walking toward his camp, which brought him close to Emily again. He saw her when their paths were about to intersect, and stopped and waited for her. When Emily came up, he said to her, 'That's a most peculiar woman, Miss Millspaw.'

" 'What happened?' Emily asked him.

" 'I guess she don't like me. I went over to ask if they'd like to have me come and sing some cowboy songs for them tonight, seein' as they hadn't been up to the bull pen any evening. I like to be friendly with folks. Trailer was open, and I just naturally went inside to wait. When I saw her comin' I stepped out to meet her, and I guess you saw how she acted. I figure I'm not welcome.'

" 'It is a bit doubtful, Mr. Caldwell,' Emily said, and

they separated, and Caldwell went on over toward his camp."

"Where was Andrews all this time?" the sheriff asked again.

"Well, now, that's the funny part of it," Lamb replied. "Emily told me the incident I've just told you when we started out for a little stroll. And I suggested that we walk down to the trailer and sort of snoop around and see what the excitement might be all about. I even had it in mind that we could make a call on them. Somehow I missed the fight Surrey Bent said Andrews and Wicks had this afternoon, and I was interested in what Andrews might have to say about it. At least I could sort of size up how he fared."

"And did you call on them?"

"We didn't have a chance to. They were all set to go. The trailer was hitched to the car. The trailer was dark. Before we could get up to the car the motor started, and as the outfit pulled past us I saw Andrews at the wheel and her beside him. I called out, 'Are you on your way?' "

"What did they say?"

"Nothing. No answer. Emily shouted good-by as they pulled out. They couldn't have helped seeing us and knowing who we were, because the lights of the car were on us for a few moments. To show how big a hurry they were in, they hadn't even fastened the trailer door securely. Of course, it was at dusk when it's hard to see, but I'm sure I saw the door swing shut as they started off."

"Well, when did Andrews come back? That's what I

want to know." The sheriff's voice was caustic. "You haven't told me."

"I don't know, Sheriff. But here's the funny part I mentioned a while ago. A woman ordinarily isn't as observant of things like horses, say—just horses in a corral—as a man is. Andrews today, you know, had that horse with the white left hind leg; the one Bernice Patterson rode the day she was hurt. Well, that horse was in the corral when Emily went down that way just before supper. Funny thing, none of us noticed that. We were all there at the corral about that same time. Of course, I was excited, telling you about Surrey, you know, and I didn't notice."

"If that's so," said Rogers, "then where was Andrews when Caldwell was at the trailer? Was he inside with Caldwell?"

"I can't answer that question, Mr. Rogers. Caldwell, you know, didn't mention it to Emily if Andrews was inside."

We speculated upon the possible whereabouts of Andrews, and also dwelt upon the reasons for Mrs. Andrews' strange actions. The other three in the station wagon, however, did the talking, for I was busy driving. By this time we had left the tiny trading post well behind us. It was very dark and a strong wind was blowing, although we were in the lee of the mesa and somewhat protected from it. There was no moon yet. The lights of the station wagon bored through the blackness. The road was none too good. It was better at other times of the year than now, for a recent rain had washed the surface in places. I hoped, as we drove along, that I

remembered where the worst spots were, but even so anything like speed was impossible.

"Can you speed it up a little, Chuck?" suggested the
sheriff.

"A little, perhaps," I answered. "Not too much. If
we're going to overtake the trailer we don't want to bust
anything." I pressed down slightly on the accelerator
and our speed increased, but soon I hit a hole in the road
before I could brake down for it, and those on the extra
seat were thrown upward to the roof.

"Not so fast," shouted Rogers. "I don't want a
broken neck."

I slowed somewhat, and we went on for a mile or two
in silence. Sheriff Wilson muttered something under his
breath and Rogers asked him what he had said. "Nothing," the sheriff responded. "Except that I don't see
how in hell Andrews thinks he's going to make it at night
with that trailer. He'll never get through the sand down
around Red Lake if it's blowing hard there." He turned
back in the darkness to Lamb. "You think it's a half
hour's start he's got, Lamb?"

"About that, I guess."

"Why the devil didn't you tell me he was pulling out
at the time, instead of waiting half an hour?"

"How was I to know you were that interested in Andrews, Sheriff? Neither you nor anybody else said a
word to me about him. Is he the—the killer?"

"Whether he is or not, I'd like to have known it at
the time."

"You were lucky to hear it as early as you did. If
Emily hadn't got chilly and the wind been so strong,

I'd not have suggested coming in when we did. You might not have heard it until tomorrow morning."

"Oh, yes, I would," said Wilson, dropping the matter. "I was planning to go down there in just a few minutes when you and the girl came in."

We settled back once more in our seats. There's a hypnotic something about driving at night in the desert. There was no white line to mark the center of our road, no well-defined edges; there were only the hum of the motor, the whisper of the tires on the unpaved surface, the steady sweep underneath of roadway, punctuated occasionally by rough spots which jolted us back to reality.

We were silent for a long while together. Carter Lamb continued to smoke cigarettes. Sheriff Wilson lighted one but soon threw it away. An occasional rabbit appeared on the road ahead, wavering uncertainly in the rays of the headlights but managing always to escape to safety as we passed. Wilson began to fret as he sat beside me, his eyes straining ahead beyond the lights to discover the first glimpse of the trailer. Still in the lee of White Mesa, we were dropping slowly down the enormous benches toward Red Lake, benches which required the perspective of miles to reveal them in this vast country.

"Why'n hell hasn't he busted down before now, or got off the road, or turned over in a rut or something?" asked the sheriff of us generally, and then, not waiting for an answer, continued, "We're not making any time ourselves, but even so he can't go as fast as we're going, and we ought to have overtaken him before now."

"There's another road, you know, direct from Kaibito to Tuba City," suggested Rogers.

"That road!" exclaimed the sheriff. "Why it's impossible with a trailer on that road. 'Tisn't even a road; it's just a trail. You couldn't possibly drive a car down through that sandy desert. You'd be lucky to get through horseback. I was over it several times years ago, and I know what I'm talking about."

"Yes, I know," returned Rogers. "That's what I was thinking. If Andrews knows about that road, and is trying to give us the slip, perhaps he's already riding along it on horseback."

"What would he do with the trailer and car?"

"Drive them off the road somewhere near where he had his horses waiting, and then he and the sour Mrs. Andrews would be off."

"I can't believe it," said the sheriff. "You haven't noticed any tracks where they've pulled off the road, have you, Chuck?"

"No, Ed. I've been noticing fresh tire tracks, though, besides those I think Andrews' outfit is making. They overlie his."

"Andrews would have to be an old-timer in this country, even to attempt that road, Professor," said the sheriff still intent upon his subject. "He'd have to know landmarks—and at night—"

"He told me several days ago," Lamb spoke up, "that he knows this country like a book."

"He did!" Wilson exclaimed. "What else did he tell you?"

"I don't remember that he told me anything in particular along that line, Sheriff; but he did give me the impression that he was familiar with this region."

"Maybe he is," the sheriff answered. "Well—anyhow, if he's riding the old road, we'll meet him when he comes out at Tuba City."

Once more we settled back into silence. I looked at the speedometer. We had covered twenty-two miles since we left Kaibito; therefore, we couldn't be far from Wild Cat Peak. I shared this information with the others but it brought no response. About five miles farther on the lights of the car picked up the figure of a lone horseman on the road. He was coming toward us, but almost at once he pulled his pony off the road, kicking it vigorously in the flanks. Indians not infrequently ride at night, especially in the summer months. The sheriff touched my arm.

"Stop, Chuck. I want to talk to that fellow."

I made a quick stop, and the sheriff, leaning out on his side of the car, shouted at the horseman.

"Hey, you! Navajo! Come here!" There was no response. The horseman already was beyond the rays of the headlights, but we could hear the sound of his pony's hoofs. "Hey, Navajo! Have you seen a car and trailer tonight?"

For answer there was the quickened tempo of the pony's feet as the alarmed horseman kicked his mount into a run. The sound faded rapidly as the rider fled in the darkness.

"Go on, Chuck," said the sheriff.

I started the car once more, and the road, grown more sandy now, recommenced its monotonous flow underneath us. We had left the protection of White Mesa, and fine sand was blowing along the surface of the road now like snow before the wind, obliterating tire tracks but recently made.

"The fellow couldn't have been going far," remarked Rogers. "Did he have a bridle on the pony, or a halter? I didn't notice."

"I didn't either, Hunt." I said.

"I don't see what difference it makes," said Wilson fretfully.

"He was using a rope halter," said Lamb.

"Sure?" asked Rogers.

"Yes; I saw it."

We passed two hogans close to the road a couple of miles farther on. The headlights playing off the curving road for a moment shone briefly upon a rude corral in which some six or eight Indian ponies slept, heads drooping, in a huddled bunch. And then of a sudden, and without warning of any kind, at about a mile beyond the corral, we came upon the car and trailer stopped in the road, around a curve, taillights and headlights still shining.

"Hold her!" shouted the sheriff.

I stepped hard on the brake, and the tires skidded gratingly on the sandy surface. The sheriff and the other two were climbing out almost before we stopped rolling, the former with his heavy revolver drawn and ready.

"Be careful, fellows," he said warningly; "he may put up a fight."

We advanced cautiously upon the trailer, which, because of the curve, was only partly in the rays of our headlights. Its green bulk was like a huge shadow in the night, with a baleful red taillight at the rear and green markers on either side. The sound of our footsteps on the unpaved road was deadened by the growing cushion of sand. Sand already was drifting about the tires of the trailer.

"I don't understand this. Do you, Mr. Sheriff?" said Rogers who followed in the wake of Wilson, "unless the sand is too much for them." There was no response. We went forward along the left side of the trailer toward the driver's seat in the car.

"Hey, Andrews!" the sheriff called out, as we reached our destination. "Put 'em up! I've got you covered."

In the dim light from the instrument board, I saw him thrust his revolver in at the open window. A moment later he hastily withdrew it and moved away from the car precipitately.

"What's the trouble, Ed?" I asked.

"Get back in the dark, boys! There's nobody in the seat!"

We retreated hastily into the darkness beyond the rays of the station wagon lights, which partly illumined the trailer and the car, and for a moment strained our eyes to discover the whereabouts of the man we sought. "I don't want to get plugged in the back," Sheriff Wilson muttered. "Where's his wife? I don't see anything of either of them," continued the sheriff softly. "Lamb," he turned to the young man, "you weren't kidding me about Mrs. Andrews being in the car when they pulled out, were you?"

"No, sir. She was sitting beside him."

For a few minutes we remained concealed, buffeted by the wind and the blowing sand, awaiting developments. Rogers grew restless. I could feel the sheriff's tense body beside me; he still held his revolver.

"Haven't you boys got anything to shoot with?" he asked.

"No," I answered. "We didn't bring any guns on the reservation."

"I haven't anything with me," said Lamb.

"Fine lot of help you'll be," growled the sheriff. "If any shooting begins, you boys get back out of the way."

Rogers of a sudden started away in the direction of the station wagon and the sheriff called after him softly to know what he was up to.

"We're not getting anywhere like this. I want to have a look around," he answered.

We heard him walking and saw him dimly at the station wagon. A moment later he snapped on a flashlight. Somewhat discomfited at this move of his, we reluctantly left the comparative security of the shadows and walked in his direction. Rogers crossed between the trailer and the station wagon, bathed in the latter's lights, and walked along the trailer on the dark side. We caught up with him.

"What could have happened to both to them?" I asked.

"Maybe this is where they picked up horses," suggested Lamb. "I noticed an Indian corral full of ponies back on the road a mile or so."

"Nonsense," said Rogers. "They might have done it

farther back, but not here. If they were making a get-away and had any sense, they wouldn't leave the outfit on the road and go away leaving the lights burning."

He threw the beams of the flashlight not only under the trailer, but to the side and off the road. I pounded on the door of the trailer and found that it was fastened. Abruptly Rogers quitted the side of the trailer, his flashlight beams on the ground. He walked rapidly in full stride into the sage brush, following alongside footprints which were rapidly being filled in by drifting sand. A moment later he froze in his tracks, waiting for the rest of us to overtake him.

"Look here!" he said, and his voice carried a tremendous something in its grim tones. "Look! Here he is!"

The grisly sight was picked out in the white rays of the flashlight. Sheriff Wilson grunted, gazing at the figure lying face down in the sand, which already was drifting about it, arms thrown out, bald head with a great bruise oozing blood.

"He staggered out this far, and died," said Rogers.

19

FEW investigations of murder ever got under way in stranger surroundings than did our inquiry that night into the death of Lester Andrews. Overhead was the star-filled sky; around about us the incredible pinkness of the Painted Desert was now blotted out in windy darkness and mystery. The lights of the two cars on the road, the feeble rays of the flashlight which Rogers held upon the dead man were all we had with which to combat the enveloping blackness. If anything, they seemed to make for a greater loneliness and a more heart-chilling mystery. Rogers shut off the flashlight.

"Don't do that," protested Carter Lamb. His voice held a startled note. "I'd rather see him in the light like he is than be shut up in the dark with him."

Rogers snapped on the light once more, directing its rays slightly away from the body. "The poor chap was running away from death, wasn't he?" he remarked soberly. "Have you seen enough, Mr. Sheriff? I mean, you're satisfied as to the cause?"

"I guess so."

"Like Kimball," I commented. "Head bashed in."

"The killer doesn't vary his technique, does he?" said Wilson.

We drew back a little from the gruesome spot and

241

continued to stand not more than twenty feet from the trailer. We were on the inside of the sharp curve which the road made and almost on a level with its sandy surface.

"Where is the woman, though?" asked Sheriff Wilson, mystified. "Why are we standing here? Is there another body?"

Rogers on the instant turned on his heel and directed the shaft of the flashlight upon the trailer windows, bringing it to rest upon the middle one.

"Look!" he said.

I wheeled automatically, but even so I almost missed the vision in the small window. The face was strained and fear-ridden—ghostlike in fact. But I made out dimly the sharp nose, the gold-rimmed glasses behind which I knew lurked the dark, sharp eyes.

"Oh! Inside!" exclaimed Wilson. "Why didn't she answer us a while ago?"

"I heard her in there as I came by to get the flashlight," said Rogers.

As if of one mind we moved slowly toward the trailer, abandoning for the moment the murdered man to the darkness and drifting sand.

"We'll get her out and settle right now what all happened here," said the sheriff grimly. "Mrs. Andrews!" he called. There was no answer. The trailer was as silent as the dead man lying in the sand behind us. "Mrs. Andrews! Open up! I'm the sheriff!" he banged his fist upon the side, shaking the whole trailer.

"The door's on the other side," Rogers pointed out.

"Mrs. Andrews!" roared the sheriff. "We'll have to

break in, if you don't open up."

We started around the rear of the trailer. But from the other side I heard the door opened softly. A light footfall sounded on the road, and then terrified feet fled into the darkness.

"Chase her down, boys," shouted the amazed sheriff. "Run after her." We bolted behind the trailer and into the sand on the opposite side of the road. "Be careful! She may have a gun," warned the sheriff.

We ran blindly in the darkness. Rogers had the only source of light and we soon were following the dancing rays of the flashlight, instead of separating fanwise in our groping search.

"Spread out more, boys," commanded the sheriff. "Lamb! Spread out."

It was an astonishing thing that a woman like Mrs. Andrews could have eluded us so easily. However, it was very dark. We had only the single light, which, after all, probably was a handicap, because she had only to observe its whereabouts and run away from it. This thought must have occurred to Rogers, for he snapped it out, and we continued in the darkness.

The minutes slipped by—ten of them, at least. We all had raced away in pursuit at right angles to the road. It occurred to me that in that fact was a possible source of error. I turned now and ran at a dog trot to the rear, paralleling the road. I'd gone perhaps a hundred yards when I stopped to listen. There was a gasping breath near by in the darkness, the sound of cautious movement. I lunged at it and stumbled over the crouching figure of Mrs. Andrews. My fingers clutched, closing upon a shoulder and an upper arm. There was little strength left in her.

"Here she is!" I shouted. The flashlight was snapped on.

"Please let me go," begged the woman.

"Let you go?" I echoed. "You're with friends," I added melodramatically. "Didn't you hear the sheriff say who we were?"

She did not reply; she made one weak effort to free her arm, then subsided, trembling violently. I called out several times to direct the others to us, and in a few moments they all came panting up. Rogers flashed the light upon Mrs. Andrews. Her gold-rimmed glasses still sat defiantly upon the sharp nose, but her eyes were closed.

"Now, Mrs. Andrews," began Sheriff Wilson, dropping on the ground beside her, "I'm Ed Wilson; I'm the sheriff of this county. You're entirely safe from danger. Of course—" he added hesitantly, "of course—you know what's happened to your husband. But—we're here to help you—"

"I don't want your help," said Mrs. Andrews defiantly, although in a frightened, subdued voice.

"Don't want it? Well, you're going to get it whether you want it or not. I can't neglect my duty. When there's been murder I have a duty to do, and I'm going to do it. Can you walk? If you can't, I'll carry you."

"I'll walk," she said. I helped her to her feet, but she was weak from the terror she had suffered and reeled against me. Rogers handed the flashlight to Lamb and picked the woman up in his arms. He went striding toward the cars with her, while the rest of us followed.

"What do you want to do now, Mr. Sheriff?" Rogers asked when we had reached the cars.

"We'd better go on into Red Lake. Can't be more than two or three miles now, can it?"

"About three, I think, Ed," I replied.

"We'll take Mrs. Andrews in the station wagon, Chuck," he directed. "Professor, will you and Lamb stay here with the trailer—and the body? The trader at Red Lake's got a truck and we'll come back for it."

"Why not load it in the trailer and all go in together?" suggested Lamb, a vague uneasiness in his voice.

"No," objected Rogers, firmly.

It was arranged that way. Rogers put Mrs. Andrews upon the second seat of the station wagon, and the sheriff climbed in beside her. I started the motor and pulled around the trailer and the black sedan. The going was heavy now, because of the drifting sand, but soon the few lights which marked Red Lake showed up before us. Not a word was spoken between the sheriff and Mrs. Andrews. So quiet was she that it was difficult for me to realize she was a passenger.

"Drive up to the trader's," Sheriff Wilson directed as we rolled into Red Lake. "He can take care of Mrs. Andrews tonight. I want to put in a call to Flagstaff. We'll bring the body in, and then we'll do a little talking, Mrs. Andrews. You can explain everything then. I want Professor Rogers to hear it too."

The woman did not reply.

There was a light in the trading post when I stopped

before it. Sheriff Wilson climbed out on to the ground. I slipped from my seat and pounded on the door, calling out to the trader.

"Stacy! Oh, Stacy!" I shouted. "Open up!"

I heard slippered footsteps shuffling inside the stone building, and a few moments later the door was unbarred and Stacy James appeared in the doorway.

"What's the trouble?" he demanded. "Oh, hello, Chuck. Hello, Ed. What's going on?"

"Plenty," said the sheriff. "Here's a woman for your wife to look after. She's Mrs. Andrews. I've got to call Flagstaff. Chuck will tell you what it's all about. Then get out your truck, Stacy."

The round, freckled face of Stacy James was filled with growing interest as I related briefly what had happened. Before I had finished he excused himself to go put on his boots and get out his truck. Mrs. James appeared from the living quarters and took charge of Mrs. Andrews, and I went outside.

I stood alone by the station wagon. The motor was shut off, but the headlights were burning. I fished out my cigarettes and waited in the shelter of the car for the sheriff to finish his telephone call and for the trader and his truck. As I stood on the deserted road I realized that there was no need to drive the station wagon back to the trailer. I could go in the truck. So I reached in to turn off the lights. As I was on the point of pushing the button in, my eyes fell upon a car coming toward me. It was moving without lights, approaching on the highway from Cameron. I did not know whether it had just come in off the desert like this, or whether it had been standing with lights out and I had not noticed it until it began to move.

I kept the lights on. The car passed within a few feet. An odd, prickling sensation tingled along my backbone, for I was looking at Norman Kimball's gray coupé. In the seat, suddenly revealed through the windshield by my lights, I saw the bandaged head of Fletcher Wicks, and at the wheel sat his wife Marian. Their lights suddenly flashed on and I ducked my head so as not to be recognized if their lights should strike me. The next moment they had rolled past, the motor was opened and the car went roaring by the turnoff to Kaibito and on up the highway in the direction of Marsh Pass.

Here was something interesting. When had the pair left Kaibito? How did it happen that Wicks, who a few hours earlier had been in bed in his hogan, kept there apparently by his wife who had insisted that he was too ill to get up, was now at Red Lake, riding in the gray coupé and heading up the road which led deeper into the reservation?

I puzzled over these things as I rode back to the trailer in the truck. I kept what I had seen to myself, not that I had any intention of concealing anything of importance from the sheriff, but rather because I thought it best not to confuse an already puzzling situation by introducing into it a new mystery.

Rogers and Carter Lamb were sitting in the front seat of the sedan when we arrived. They climbed out to greet us. Nothing had happened in our absence. I asked Rogers if any cars had passed while they sat there, thinking of the Wickses, but he replied that none had gone by.

Stacy James had brought along some old blankets and we took them and, with the extra flashlights he had provided, walked out through the sand to the body of Lester Andrews. We placed the blankets on the ground and lifted the body, which was half buried in the sand, upon them, then rolled them about it, tied them securely, and carried the gruesome burden back and loaded it into the truck.

"All I'm hoping," said Stacy James, "is that we get back with this thing and get it out of the truck before the Indians see us. I'll have to get me a new truck otherwise, for they'd never buy anything that's hauled in it again."

"Do you have a shovel with you, Stacy?" I asked, looking at the sand that had drifted about the wheels of the trailer outfit.

"A couple of them. I thought we'd need them."

For almost half an hour we shoveled sand. The wind seemed to have increased in violence. For a few minutes we thought we might have to give up the idea of taking the trailer into Red Lake, but Rogers insisted that it could be done. He took the wheel and we were off. It was hard going, fighting through the drifting, sandy stretches with the cumbersome trailer a drag behind the none too powerful engine of the sedan. The truck followed, in case we got into difficulty, but was not needed, and we finally pulled up in front of the trading post.

"If there's a key to this thing," Rogers said to Wilson, as he climbed out, indicating the trailer, "it should be locked up."

"Locked up? What for?"

"Just a hunch," was the brief reply.

"All right, Professor; I'll see to it. And, Stacy," the sheriff turned to the trader, "if you want to put your truck in the garage with the body in it just as it is, the boys will be up here from Flagstaff long before daylight and can take it off your hands before the Indians know you've got it."

"Okeh, Ed; I'll take a chance."

We went inside and found that Mrs. James in our absence had persuaded Mrs. Andrews to lie down on a couch in the living room. She was awake, of course, and sat up when we entered the room, her dark eyes smoldering with the emotions engendered by the terrifying events of the night.

"Now, ma'am," began Sheriff Wilson with the air of a diplomat, sitting down in a chair and resting his hat upon the floor beside him, "I'd like to know what happened."

For a few moments I thought the woman was not going to make any response. Her eyes were cast down. She put her handkerchief to her lips but there were no tears in her eyes, and none in her voice when she finally replied.

"You already know all I know. Maybe more."

"Well, now," parried Wilson, "maybe we do and maybe we don't. I'll be the judge of that after we've heard your story."

"Well—" She lifted her hands suddenly in a hopeless sort of gesture. "Lester's dead—and that's all I know."

"Mrs. Andrews," began Rogers quietly, "you don't

seem to understand. We know your husband's dead, but if we are to discover who is responsible for his death, we must have your help. Who killed your husband?"

"I don't know."

"How did it happen? Your outfit wouldn't have stalled in the sand if you hadn't stopped. Did somebody stop you, and then kill your husband, say, from the running board of your car?"

"No."

"Tell us just exactly what occurred out there on the road."

The woman hesitated, her fingers picking at the edges of the handkerchief in her lap, her dark eyes downcast.

"Lester stopped the car to see what was wrong with the trailer—and it happened."

"What was the matter with the trailer?"

"I don't know; he never found out. At least if he did he didn't have a chance to tell me."

"I—" Rogers began thoughtfully, "I drove the trailer into Red Lake myself, and I didn't notice anything wrong with it."

"Didn't it sort of bounce around behind you like there might be something wrong with the hitch? Or a flat tire?"

"No; the sand was the only concern."

"Lester must have fixed it, then—before they got him."

"Who do you mean by 'they'?"

"Somebody was following behind us all the way from Kaibito."

"That was our car."

"They pulled around us two or three miles before we

stopped."

"Oh," said Rogers. "That's different."

"Yes."

"Do you think, then, that somebody in the other car waylaid you when you stopped?"

"I don't know what else could have happened."

"Did you see the other car again after it pulled around you?"

"No. But—it must have been those people."

It suddenly occurred to me that I had something of importance to communicate to Rogers and the sheriff. But I didn't know whether they would want me to tell it before Mrs. Andrews; so I interrupted the questioning, and Wilson and Rogers followed me out into the bull pen, where I told them about seeing the Wickses in the coupé when I was about to turn off the station wagon lights.

They listened in silence; then the sheriff rubbed the stubble of beard on his tanned face and his eyes narrowed.

"Now, we're getting somewhere," he said.

"They'll stall in the sand on that road before they get to Marsh Pass," said Rogers, "with the wind blowing like it is now."

"But you were so doggoned sure, Ed," I said, "that Andrews was the man who killed Kimball and tried to kill the girl."

"I'll admit now that I was wrong, Chuck. Andrews is dead. The fellow we've been wanting all along is Wicks. Followed Andrews down here to finish the fight they started in the canyon, and killed him—"

"Now, wait a minute, Mr. Sheriff," interrupted Rogers. "Let's not jump to any conclusions about this thing yet. I'd like to hear what else Mrs. Andrews may have to tell us."

"Well—all right, Professor," agreed the sheriff, "but it looks pretty plain to me right now."

We returned to the living quarters and Rogers took up once more.

"We were wondering, Mrs. Andrews," he began, "if we have the story straight so far. You and Mr. Andrews left Kaibito shortly after dark. And after you'd gone some distance you noticed another car following you. You began to have trouble with the hitch on the trailer and finally you stopped to investigate the trouble. But before this happened, the car that had been following pulled around you and went on and you didn't see it again. And when your husband got out to investigate the hitch he was set upon and slain. Is that right?"

"Yes, sir."

"But you say that 'they' must have waylaid you— been lying in wait for you, in other words. Now, then, did you see that other car or anybody on foot beside the road when you stopped, or have any warning of what was about to happen?"

"No, sir."

"Was there a hitchhiker there? Or anybody on horseback when you stopped?"

"No, sir. We thought for a while it was the wind making the trailer act up."

"How long was your husband back at the hitch before he was killed?"

"It happened almost at once. He didn't have more than a minute to make the examination. I heard the blow struck—"

"Did he call out any names, as if he recognized the person?"

"There wasn't any sound except the blows—there were two or three, maybe more. Then I heard feet running on the road—running away. I called out to Lester. He didn't answer, so I got out to see what had happened. He'd taken the flashlight when he went back. It was on the ground turned on, and—and I picked it up—and found him out in the sand. He was dead, of course. And that scared me so that I ran and climbed in the trailer. Then you came along. I thought it was the murderers come back to kill me. That's why I ran from you."

"Yes, I know," murmured Rogers. Then he said: "When you pulled out of Kaibito this evening, did you notice the gray coupé that's been parked there the last few days? I mean whether or not it was there?"

"It was there, yes. This man here and the girl rode around in it several times," Mrs. Andrews pointed accusingly at Carter Lamb. The young man stirred uneasily in his seat at that.

"You're not accusing him," the sheriff spoke up, "because if you are, ma'am, it's no use. He sat right beside me in Chuck Graham's car all the way down from Kaibito."

"I'm not accusing him."

"Do you accuse anybody, Mrs. Andrews?" Rogers asked.

"No," she replied quickly. "But they might have done it."

"You mean the 'they' in the gray coupé?"

"Yes. I don't see who else it could have been. That young fellow—Wicks, is his name—killed Kimball—"

"How do you know?"

"Lester was sure of it."

"Mrs. Andrews," Rogers began slowly, "about sundown—a short time before you left Kaibito—you were seen running very fast toward the trailer. What was the reason for that?"

"That?" echoed Mrs. Andrews blankly, although I thought her tone a trifle forced. "That's not important. I'd left some things cooking and I was afraid they might burn."

"Wasn't your husband sitting in the trailer at the time?"

"Ye-es—but he was the kind who would sit right beside them and let them burn. Then blame me for it," she said, an odd resentment rising to the surface once more.

"Thank you. I don't think of anything else to ask you now."

"Maybe you'd better get some rest now," advised Sheriff Wilson. "You've told us enough for the present, I guess."

20

A NEW day dawned in the desert, and with it came a sense of reality which made the happenings of the night just past seem like a story that had been dreamed. Stacy James had put us all up for the night, which proved to be one of broken rest, for the undertaker's car came in the small hours, and Rogers, the sheriff and I had gone with Stacy James out to his garage. The coroner was out there, standing thin and tall in the uncertain light, and we talked for some time after the body had been removed from the trader's truck and the undertaker's car had been driven a short distance down the road.

"Ed, how much longer is this killing going to go on up here on the reservation?" the coroner inquired seriously of the sheriff, shoving back on his forehead the huge hat which seemed always threatening to fall about his ears.

"I wish I knew the answer, Tom," Wilson answered. "Maybe the professor does, although he hasn't said yet."

Rogers was silent. He rubbed his nose thoughtfully and looked away through the windy darkness. "I wish I could say truthfully that I knew," he remarked, "but I don't. If there's to be still another, and perhaps another, I'm sure I can't name the victims. I hope this is the last, but I'm still in the dark. By the way, what are you going to do with Mrs. Andrews?" The question was directed at Wilson.

"I hadn't thought. I suppose she'll want to go home to Tucson and bury her husband. What do you think ought to be done about her?"

"Let her go."

"How's she going to get her trailer and car down? She won't want to drive it herself."

Stacy James spoke up, his round, freckled face ghost-like in the faint light of the lantern. "I was planning to go to Flagstaff this morning with the truck for some things. I've got a Hopi boy who helps me. He can drive the truck and I'll drive Mrs. Andrews' outfit as far as Flagstaff—if this wind will drop."

"That'll be fine, Stacy," said the sheriff.

Rogers cleared his throat lightly. "The interior of the trailer should be examined for fingerprints," he said. "Can it be done at Flagstaff, Mr. Sheriff?"

"Sure. Do you think it's important?"

"As a precaution, yes. I don't know what we'll find, though. I don't know just how we'll interpret anything we may discover. Has that outfit of yours at Kaibito got an ink pad and blank cards?"

"Yes."

"I want to make some fingerprints of the folks there. It will be necessary to print Mrs. Andrews, of course— and to take the prints of Andrews' fingers too."

"I guess maybe I'd better go down to Flagstaff instead of back to Kaibito, fellows," the sheriff said. "Thanks, Stacy, for offering to drive Mrs. Andrews'

outfit down. I guess I'll do it. My car's still at Kaibito.
I'll get back up as soon as I can, of course. And—Professor, these two Wickses driving around in the coupé
—I'm picking them up and holding them for investigation—"

"I wonder if that's the best thing to do," said Rogers
slowly. "If they're not stalled between here and Marsh
Pass, and should be on their way back to Kaibito when
you find them, wouldn't it be just as well to let them
return to their hogan?"

"You mean not let them know we suspect them?"

"We haven't got the weapon that killed Andrews, you
know. We haven't looked over the ground thoroughly
where the killing occurred. If you're going into Flagstaff with Mrs. Andrews, Chuck and I will do that on the
way back to Kaibito."

"All right, Professor, I'll leave that to you. What
else now?"

"What time is it?" Rogers asked, holding his wrist
watch to the lantern. "It's about an hour until daylight
yet," he answered his own question. "As soon as we can
get a call through to Harry Easton at Kaibito, will you
ask him to check up on everybody at Kaibito and see if
they are there— Humph!—there's only Surrey Bent,
Ernie Caldwell, and Miss Millspaw left there. And Jeff
Draper. The two Andrews are accounted for. We're
here, plus Carter Lamb, and the two Wickses are stalled
somewhere probably in the coupé. Anyhow, I'd like
Harry to check on everybody up there as soon as he
hangs up."

"Okeh."

"Well, Ed," the coroner dropped his cigarette and stepped on it, "I guess I'll be going. You and Stacy here can drop around when you get down to Flagstaff, and I'll hold an inquest. You saw the body. Two of you will be enough. You other fellows, I see, have important stuff to look after."

"Better stay and eat breakfast, Tom," urged Stacy James.

"No, I won't do that. I can be an hour or two on my way. I'll stop and get something at Cameron. Sand doesn't bother on this stretch, you know. I think that wind is going to drop soon."

He walked briskly to the waiting undertaker's car, and we lingered until we saw its lights flash on and heard the motor and saw the taillight receding into the windy desert. Whereupon we went inside the post and tried to sleep again.

Breakfast over and the telephone call put through to Harry Easton, Rogers and I prepared to leave. Mrs. Andrews, despite a touch of make-up, obviously had not slept at all. Mechanically she drank several cups of coffee, ate sparingly of the bacon and eggs, all the while seemingly lost in thought, for her dark eyes behind the glasses no longer were sharp, but instead were fixed as if on scenes beyond the Painted Desert.

Rogers shook hands with her when we separated, expressing not in words but in his manner a genuine sympathy for her.

"How long were you and Mr. Andrews married?" he inquired gently, still holding the tense, thin fingers in his large hand.

"Twenty-two years next month," the woman replied promptly.

"Twenty-two." He seemed to dwell upon the words. "Well—good-by, Mrs. Andrews. Mr. Graham and I must be on our way."

"Good-by," she said.

I climbed into the station wagon. Carter Lamb got into the extra seat and Rogers slipped in beside me. I touched the starter. The sun was dazzling; the bizarre colors of the Painted Desert were emerging from the shrouding haze of early morning; the soft blue-black shadows of the night were giving way before the mounting sun. The strong wind had suddenly died away to a light breeze. Rogers gazed about at the early morning scene and said lightly:

"Well—Johano-ai, the sun carrier, has mounted his turquoise steed, as a Navajo might say. In other words, the blue sky is free of storm clouds. The Navajo legends are as many and as fanciful as those of the ancient Greeks. Some day, I suppose, they'll be collected and written down for us. The first stop, Chuck, is at the spot where Andrews died," he ended, his voice taking on a businesslike tone.

In daylight the distance was nothing. I halted at the edge of the road and we sat for a moment surveying the scene before we got out. Our tracks in the sand on the right where we had gone pell-mell into the desert in pursuit of the panic-stricken Mrs. Andrews were entirely wiped out. On the other side the confused tracks, made the night before in the discovery and removal of the murdered man's body, no longer existed.

"Well," Rogers opened the door and thrust out his long legs, "it looks like a clean slate, but let's see what we can find, Chuck. From all signs no one even stopped here last night, no one was murdered."

"Why didn't you want Ed Wilson to arrest Wicks?" I inquired.

"What's the hurry? You know, Chuck," and he included Lamb with a glance, "more trouble and confusion result in a murder investigation from hasty action than from almost anything else. Of course, a quick solution is greatly to be desired, but the pressure for immediate action, the demand for the quick solution, the ambitions of rival detectives to score a beat, police politics and what not sometimes need more unraveling than the mystery itself. Obtain the facts and study them carefully is the only sure recipe I know in solving a murder mystery."

"Haven't we got all the facts in the Kimball killing?"

"Not all; and almost nothing in the attempt on Bernice's life; while with last night's bloody occurrence we're just beginning."

Rogers walked off the road and halted at approximately the spot where the body of Andrews had lain. He stirred the sand hopefully with his heavy boot as if to uncover some sign in the loose sand, but there was no sign.

"What did he kill him with?" Carter Lamb asked.

"The usual blunt instrument which figures in so many autopsy reports," Rogers replied. "In Kimball's case it was the butt of a pistol, indicating that the killer's weapon was the choice of the moment. In Bernice's case she probably was struck with a stone, or even battered against a wall in the cliff dwellers' ruin. The chance weapon is the favored one of the killer. I'm interested in what we find here, Chuck."

A careful search, however, of the area revealed nothing. We gave it up for a time and walked for some distance down the road. It was Rogers' idea that, if the gray coupé had stopped and the occupants waited to waylay Andrews, there might still be some sign, despite the drifting sand. But there was none. There was no evidence now that the coupé had pulled off the road, no track, of course, in the sandy surface, of anyone walking either forward or back to the murder scene.

"Well," Rogers remarked as we turned back, "we have exactly nothing, no picture whatever of what happened. But what became of the weapon that killed him?"

We were swinging along toward the station wagon when Rogers halted suddenly, his eyes fastened upon a stone that lay a couple of yards from the edge of the road on a hard surface swept bare by the wind.

"Found something?" Lamb asked. Rogers pointed with the toe of his boot at the stone. We stood for a moment looking at it. Rogers dropped to a squatting position, his eyes surveying the stone and the area about it. The stone was a yellowish gray in color and somewhat rounded as if it at one time had lain in the pathway of running water. It weighed about four or five pounds.

"The most interesting thing about it," observed Rogers thoughtfully, "is that it doesn't belong in this particular part of the Painted Desert. The rocks around here are all red, but there's no red in this one." He picked up the stone and turned it about in the sunlight. The stone was dusty. If there had been any fingerprints upon it they had been obliterated by the sand and dust.

"There may be blood on this—if it's the weapon the slayer used. But the dust has blotted it, and it would take a chemist to settle the point."

"You're not thinking that this is the weapon, Hunt?" I asked.

"If it isn't," he answered, turning back toward the station wagon, "I don't know what else to look for, or where to look for it. We're within a short distance of the scene of the crime—about a hundred yards, perhaps, I'd say. It's a plausible assumption that the killer, under the excitement of his crime, would carry the weapon from the scene and, when he discovered the fact, would throw the thing down. Who, anyway, would look for one particular rock among so many rocks in a sandy, rocky desert?"

He put the stone in the back of the station wagon and climbed on the seat beside me, while Carter Lamb got in behind us.

"Kaibito the next stop?" I asked.

"Yes. To see what Harry Easton has to report on the few remaining inhabitants of the community."

I started the motor and soon we were rolling along the road. Another few miles and we would be out of the sandy valley in which Red Lake lay. We all were silent. I was thinking, of course, as I suppose were the other two, upon the murder of the night before, and of the scene as we had just left it. It was incredible that anything would ever come of the meager evidence we had

been able to uncover. It might be better if we went back
to the murder of Norman Kimball and started all over
again, or made a more intensive study of the attempted
murder of Bernice Patterson than we yet had had time
to make. Either way might prove an easier solution than
by wasting time on the murder of Andrews.

"Do you think, Professor Rogers," asked Lamb suddenly, as if the question had just occurred to him, "that
the same person is guilty of all three crimes?"

"There's no doubt of it, Lamb. As Wilson observed
last night, the fellow doesn't change his technique. He
uses the bludgeon, or what amounts to it, in each in-
stance."

"But why does he kill these particular people? Why
not some of us others? What has Kimball in common
with Andrews, or either of them with Miss Patterson?"

"There you touch upon the real problem, Lamb. If
I knew the answer to that one, I could soon put my hands
upon the man we want. How far is it to Kaibito, Chuck,
from where Andrews was killed?" Rogers asked, suddenly shifting the conversation.

"About thirty-three or four miles."

This interlude of conversation was over almost before it had begun. Ahead of us at a curve of the road
appeared the rude corral where, on the night before as
we passed, we had seen some half dozen or so Indian
ponies sleeping.

"There's an extra one in there now," said Rogers as
we swept by the corral. "It wasn't there last night."

"Listen, Hunt," I began jokingly, "you don't mean
for us to believe that you count the ponies in every In-

dian corral we pass."

"I happened to count these last night," he replied.
"There were seven then. And now there are eight," he
added as we were passing the two hogans. "Wait a
minute, Chuck! Stop!" he called out. We were well past
the hogans by the time I had brought the car to a stop.
"Back up. I want to show you why there's an extra
horse in the corral now."

I backed the car wonderingly and halted opposite the
door of the first hogan. There seemed to be no one inside, but several children were playing behind the other
hogan, not far from a small spring which explained this
little Indian establishment.

"What do we do now?" I asked, as we stood on the
road before it.

"Oh, Jeff!" Rogers shouted. "Jeff Draper!"

"Are you crazy, Hunt?" I demanded.

"Of course not. Jeff's inside. I saw him. Jeff!" he
shouted.

"Hello," answered a voice from inside the hogan, and
a moment later Jeff Draper came outside. He walked
slowly to the car and rested one foot on the running
board.

"I just wanted to show you, Jeff," began Rogers,
"that I got the mud all off yesterday. You certainly
helped souse me in the mud when you had a chance to."

"*Ohk*," smiled the Indian. "No hard feelings, Mr.
Rogers?"

"None at all. I had it coming to me. Did you stay
until the 'sing' was over?"

"Yes. I stay. 'Sing' over before sundown. I go home

and clean up."

Rogers was silent for a moment, gazing at the Indian who stood beside the car. "Is this where your relatives live?" he asked, nodding toward the hogans.

"Yes. My sister live here. I finish visit I make when Bernice come to reservation."

"When did you come down?"

"Last night."

"Is that your pony in the corral over there?"

"*Ohk.*"

"What time did you leave Kaibito?"

"It is just dark."

"When did you get here?"

"I come fast."

"Did you hear about Andrews—the man with no hair? Murdered last night. Two miles south of here."

"I hear this morning."

"Do you know who did it?"

"No."

21

WHEN we drove up to the trading post at Kaibito that Sunday morning, I was still turning over in my mind the fact that Jeff Draper easily could have been at the scene of Lester Andrews' murder at the time the man was slain. I remembered Jeff's statement when he was being questioned about the attempted murder of Bernice Patterson, which was to the effect that Andrews had climbed up into the ruin where he and the girl were and that he and the man now dead had quarreled. They were "about to have a fight," to quote what Jeff had said. I ticked off these significant facts in my mind—Jeff had quarreled with Norman Kimball, with Bernice Patterson, and with Lester Andrews, and two of them were dead, and the third seriously injured.

We climbed out of the station wagon and walked over to the trading post. Harry Easton was in the bull pen. Carter Lamb went on back to his room, while Rogers and I stopped behind with the trader.

"What did you find out this morning, Harry?" inquired Rogers. "As to the whereabouts of the various residents of Kaibito?"

"Oh," replied Harry casually, "they were all here. Emily Millspaw and Surrey Bent were both at breakfast. Bernice Patterson, of course, is still unconscious."

"How is she, Harry?" I asked. "Any change?"

"Well, Peggy thinks there's a little change for the better. I hope she's right."

"So do I," Rogers said quickly. "But how about Ernie Caldwell? Was he at Kaibito?"

"He was at his camp. I went down there first, right after I got Ed Wilson's call. Ernie was just getting up. I knew the others were here. I didn't bother to wake 'em up. Just waited till they came out to breakfast, which they did. Why?"

"I wanted to know where everybody was last night, or, at least, that everybody was here where he was supposed to be and not down at Red Lake where Andrews was killed."

"Killed him just like Kimball?"

"Beat him to death. With a stone, I think. Mrs. Andrews was unable to give any description of the killer. The Wickses were down that way. Jeff Draper was within a couple of miles of the spot. Mrs. Andrews, of course, was on the ground—"

"You don't suspect any of them?"

"Everybody, more or less, Harry, is under suspicion."

"Including those up here—Caldwell, Mr. Bent and Emily?"

"Until it's proved that they couldn't have done it."

"Well—I can speak for the folks who were in Kaibito last night. Ernie, as I say, was just crawling out of bed when I went down there. And Emily and Mr. Bent came in to breakfast as usual."

"That settles several things, but by no means all. Let me see that fingerprint outfit the sheriff left with you."

The trader produced it and Rogers lifted the box lid and took out an ink pad and some blank fingerprint cards. He opened the pad and reached across the counter and took one of the trader's hands.

"What's the idea?" he asked, resisting Rogers for a moment.

"We fingerprint everybody now at this stage of the investigation," the latter replied unsmilingly, pressing in turn upon the pad and then upon a card the thumb and finger tips of the trader. "A little gasoline will take the ink off," he said when he had finished. Outside we found Emily Millspaw and Carter Lamb. Rogers did not pass up Lamb as I had expected him to, but made his prints as well as those of the girl.

"Where's Surrey Bent?" he inquired of Lamb.

"He's down in the canyon, they tell me."

"We'll go down into the canyon, Chuck," said Rogers, as we started toward the corral for horses.

"Is it as important as all that?" I asked, for I was feeling the lack of sleep.

"It must be done," he said firmly. "The sooner the better. I want to stop and print Caldwell on the way."

But there was no need to visit the cowboy's camp, for we found him sitting on the top rail of the corral smoking a cigarette, his shoulders hunched, his eyes mere slits as he squinted dreamily out across the corral and the six or eight head of saddle horses dozing in the sun.

"Hello," he responded in answer to our greeting. Rogers climbed up on the rail beside him while I stood on the ground leaning on the gate.

"Your horses are getting a good rest," Rogers said,

opening the conversation.

"The mare sure needs it. Her leg ain't gettin' over that sprain as quick as I thought it would."

"You're staying on a Kaibito a while longer?"

"I guess so." The cowboy filled his lungs with smoke, then slowly expelled it. "Understand there was another killin' last night."

"Who was telling you?"

"Harry Easton. He dropped down to see me when I was just gettin' up this morning. He thought I'd be interested in hearin' the news. I went over to the trailer last night with my gittar to spend the evenin' with 'em, seein' as they hadn't ever been up to the bull pen when I was there singin'. Found they'd pulled out. Do they know who done it yet?"

"No." Rogers took the ink pad and a card from his pocket. "The idea now is that everybody up here is to be fingerprinted. Ready?"

"Sure. You can have mine right now."

They climbed down off the rail and Rogers found a smooth place on top of a corral gatepost where the card could be placed in order to make a perfect print, and the cowboy's fingerprints were taken. Rogers stowed the pad and card in his pocket.

"Gasoline will take that ink off," Rogers reminded him."

"It'll wear off," grinned Caldwell, climbing onto the fence again. "Goin' some place?" he asked as we selected a couple of horses.

"Little ride into the canyon," I replied.

"So long," he said, lifting inky fingers in salute as we

rode away.

We went directly away from the corral, crossing the parklike grounds in the general direction of the trail to the canyon. Our way led us near the spot where the trailer had stood. I was wishing that Rogers had put off this trip to the canyon, for I could have slept if only I had had the opportunity. But I was not willing to let him go alone. Suddenly he halted his horse and turned its head back along the path.

"What's the trouble now?" I asked, riding back. He was gazing at the ground at a spot about ten feet from where the trailer had stood. There around the base of a piñon pine was a small grouping of stones done for decorative effect. The grass had grown up around them. They were stones of a yellowish gray, as were most of the stones around and about Kaibito.

"There's one missing," he said. "See where the grass didn't grow, and the little depression in the center of the spot."

"Yes, I do. Hunt. But—"

"I'm wondering if we have the stone that will fit that spot?"

"Do you want me to get it?"

"Please."

Rogers was waiting when I returned from the station wagon with the stone. He dismounted and carefully fitted the stone in place.

"That—" he said, standing back to survey it, "that's excellent. The rustic effect that Harry Easton had achieved has been restored. I'm wondering, though, how that particular stone got down to the spot where we found it this morning—"

"Listen, Hunt," I interrupted, "do you believe Mrs. Andrews' story? She can't prove it. What's more natural —if she were thinking of killing her husband—than for her, just before she climbed into the car last night, to pick up this rock and take it with her? The Wickses were following, and so she didn't dare kill him until after they pulled around the trailer. Then she let him have it."

"Mrs. Andrews," Rogers said, "must be presumed to be innocent until we have more evidence than this to prove she's not."

"But isn't this stone evidence of it?"

"We'll waive the answer to that, Chuck, for the time being," he answered. "And," he picked up the stone and remounted his horse, "I guess this should be given to Harry to keep."

Once more we got under way for the canyon, this time without interruption. The air was still cool and the horses moved along at a brisk trot. "I'm still hoping," Rogers said, "that there'll be time to spend exploring among the ruins in the canyon."

"Going to hunt for the lost treasure?" I inquired jokingly.

"Don't be foolish," he said, taking me seriously. "I'd sooner start hunting the Lost Dutchman Mine down in the Superstition Mountains. There'd be a better chance of finding something worth while."

"You don't believe the story Surrey Bent was telling, then?"

"I neither believe it nor disbelieve it. I know this, I'm not going to waste any time looking for something as vague and indefinite as this lost treasure of Surrey Bent's."

We reached the edge of the canyon and began the descent. Rogers led the way. Ahead of us a couple of Indians were on the trail, which reminded me that the many Indians who had participated in the "sing" at Gray Warrior's had disappeared; dwellers in the canyon and on the mesa had scattered to their hogans.

"It's just a bit of hard luck," Rogers said, "that the canyon was so nearly deserted the day Bernice Patterson's life was attempted. If it hadn't been for the 'sing' some interesting, if not vital, information might be forthcoming by now from among the Indians. However, I think I've got John Navajo gossiping among them, in addition to what detective work he may be attempting."

"Gossiping?"

"Yes. I was talking with John at the 'sing' as one mud man to another. I asked him particularly to find out for me what us white folks have been doing the last few days. Odd bits of Indian gossip here and there, you know, of our comings and goings. May be of value."

"You may have something there, Hunt."

"I hope so."

We had reached the floor of the canyon before we had exhausted the various angles of this interesting device. We rode down the canyon now, keeping an eye out for Surrey Bent. The spot where he had set up his easel on a previous occasion held no trace of him now, and not until we reached the shelving, sloping bench, with its ancient footholds carved in solid rock, did we discover his horse.

"Our man seemingly is up in the ruin," Rogers remarked. "Still trying for the mysterious light effect." I glanced at him quickly, wondering whether or not there was a question in his own mind concerning the assertions of the middle-aged artist. But his face was sober, his mild blue eyes thoughtful.

We dismounted, tied our horses to the juniper, looked up at the long sloping climb, and then started. I said again that I would have preferred to wait in the shade at Kaibito for the artist's return, rather than undertake the excursion we had embarked upon. But Rogers continued to climb upward without appearing to have heard me.

There was no sign of Bent when we reached the top. Somehow this ancient shelf with its superb view out across the canyon and up and down its length now seemed unusually lonely. The sound of our feet echoed faintly against the sounding board of overhanging rock as we picked our way along among the debris of centuries.

We reached the room in which we had found the unconscious Bernice Patterson, and still no sign of the artist had been discovered. The floor was covered by a foot or more of debris made up of shards of pottery, pieces of adobe, small stones that had fallen from the overhanging rock, turkey feathers and bones, worn, discarded sandals of yucca, whose onetime wearers long since had crumbled to dust—mute evidence of a vanished race.

"You know, Chuck," said Rogers gazing about him at the wreckage, "they were a remarkable people who once lived here. This whole region, while still a wilderness, now has its connections with the outside world, and can be fed by it and cared for if need be. But these people lived here centuries ago, when there was no outside world. While life no doubt was primitive beyond belief, as we look at life now, yet it must have been a really remarkable civilization. These towering, fantastic cliffs, the great isolation, the very nearness to Nature must have wrought mightily with the psychology of these people.

"They had their little farms where they grew corn and beans; they had domesticated the turkey; they had cotton and cotton loom cloth as well as turkey feather cloth; the yuccas yielded fiber for sandals and basketry. Wild life was plentiful and they didn't kill it out as we killed out the buffalo, say. And so they survived here for many more years than the white man has been on this continent. They inhabited this whole region of what in reality is a Painted Desert all the way from the Mesa Verde in southwestern Colorado clear on down into Mexico, and then west to the opposite bank of the Colorado River. Apparently they worked down the San Juan River into this country. Study of the kiva points to that fact, I believe. Architecturally the kiva reached its highest development in the Mesa Verde region. There it is a circular subterranean room with ventilators and deflectors, pilasters and banquettes, fireplaces and ceremonial openings. But as you come down the San Juan River you find a gradual simplification until there is little left except the large banquette.

"That kiva there," and he pointed to the opening in the wall near the floor where the debris had been dragged back, "however, is a most unusual one. I imagine that it originally was a pothole worn by water in centuries long past, and the cliff dwellers adapted it to their needs. Curious that instinct in people, which can be seen in the modern boy who enjoys a secret hide-out where he can crawl away with his companions and indulge in what to him are esoteric and mystic rites. Is this the room where we found Miss Patterson?" he asked of a sudden, an odd note in his voice.

"Don't you recognize it?"

"I do and I don't. There are so many rooms in this ruin and all are so nearly alike." Rogers thrust his hand into the pocket of his coat for a handkerchief. A small packet of kodak prints dropped on the debris at his feet. I stooped to pick them up.

"These are the pictures, aren't they, that you and Bernice took of the room here?" I asked, handing them to him.

"Yes, thanks, Chuck." He put away the handkerchief, and for a few moments shuffled the prints through his large fingers. He straightened their edges and would have returned them to his pocket but stopped midway and brought the pictures back before his eyes once more. He shuffled through them slowly, studying them, glancing up once at the opening of the kiva.

"Do you see what I see, Chuck?" he said, the same odd note in his voice. "Look at them." He gave me the prints.

I took the pictures and ran them through. There were the three which Bernice had taken before she was set upon in the very room in which we stood; the others were the ones that Rogers had taken to show the scene of the crime. The first time I missed the discovery he had made, and then I saw what he meant.

"I guess so, Hunt," I said. "The pictures of that wall were taken before the kiva was opened, both yours and Bernice's."

"Right," he said quickly.

"What does it mean, though, Hunt? Didn't she say something the other night at the post about a ruin without a kiva. And that there ought to be a kiva in it and that she intended to find it?"

"You're right, Chuck," he said. "But Bernice didn't open that kiva. She may have suspected its existence, but she not only didn't have any tools to do the job the day she was here, but her photographs and mine show that she didn't."

"Well—the thing has been opened since we were here and found her unconscious. Andrews spent the night in the canyon, the night Bernice lay here in the ruin," I reminded him.

"Yes, but the kiva wasn't opened that night, and anyway, Andrews is dead. We might assume," he said, rubbing thoughfully along the side of his large nose with a forefinger, "that the person who opened that kiva was the person who tried to kill Bernice Patterson. It can be only an assumption, though, a sort of working hypothesis. Let's go down into the thing." He pulled the inevitable flashlight from his pocket and approached the small opening. He got down on his hands and knees among the debris, snapped on the flashlight and thrust it into the dark opening. His large person quite filled the entrance, so that I could not see into the thing. For a moment he stuck there, gazing down into the pit, then he backed abruptly out. His face held a curious expression.

"Somebody's down there," he said, his voice strangely subdued.

"Who could be down there?" I replied, infected with the excitement that had assailed him.

For reply he leaned into the hole again, and the flashlight went searching the eerie depths of the kiva.

"Is it Surrey Bent?" I asked, the recollection of the artist's horse tied to the juniper tree below flashing into my mind. "Is he dead? Has the killer got another?"

"No—he's alive," was the answer, muffled and rumbling from the kiva. "Hey!" he shouted. "Hey, Bent! Are you all right?" He waited for a reply which was slow in coming. "Bent! I'm coming down there and pull you out if you don't come."

"Well," was the reply, rumbling hollowly from the hole, "why do you have to come snooping around here?"

"Give me your hand," commanded Rogers. "Give it to me."

Rogers suddenly backed out of the opening clasping a wrist which soon became an arm, and then with steady pulling the stoutish figure of Surrey Bent. The man stood there before us, his soft brown eyes now blazing with anger. In one hand he was holding a couple of small pigs, like pigs of iron, only they were yellow. My eyes, as well as Rogers' were upon them instantly. Bent noted the fact.

"The sucker's moved it out on me," he flared.

"Interesting," said Rogers. "Very interesting indeed."

"I tell you it's the truth!" Bent shouted. "The gold's gone."

22

Huntoon Rogers stood gazing steadily at Surrey Bent. The latter stared back as if he suspected Rogers of some trickery. That he resented our presence in the ruins was all too apparent, but that he did not know what to do, now that he had been discovered, was equally plain.

"I'm not lying," he said more quietly. "The gold's gone."

"I accept your word for it, Bent," Rogers returned.

"I don't know why I should have to account to you, though——"

"Neither do I. I didn't ask you for any explanation."

"What do you want, then?"

"Your fingerprints." Rogers took the ink pad and cards from his pocket.

"Fingerprints? What for? And why do I have to give them to you?"

For reply Rogers held out the deputy sheriff's badge he was given by Sheriff Wilson that first day of the investigation, and Bent offered no further objection. They sat down on the debris-covered floor, and with one of the two pigs of gold for a makeshift base for the card Rogers took Surrey Bent's fingerprints.

"What else?" demanded Bent when the job was done. "Are you arresting me for anything I have or haven't

278

done?"

"I'm through with you for the present."

The artist by this time had recovered his usual poise. The fire of resentment had gone out of his brown eyes, and there was now something of the familiar glint of humor in their soft depths.

"Let me tell you this much, Rogers," he began, pulling his pipe from his pocket, "I wasn't exactly trying to hide out on you. As a matter of fact, I didn't know you were looking for me. I didn't know it was you even. I heard somebody coming and I merely dropped down into the kiva until you'd gone. I've thought for a long time that somewhere in this ruin there could be a hiding place for that gold I was telling you about. If you'll look outside along the rock shelf which makes a floor for this ruin, you'll discover that you can ride a horse up in here; it's narrow in spots and dangerous, but it can be done if you'll start a quarter of a mile or so up the canyon and ride along the outcrop of the ledge. Of course, it's quicker to climb up, if you're not bringing in pack horses loaded, say, with gold."

"So you really believe it was done that way, and that this is the place?" Rogers asked.

"Of course. I was just too late, though. The gold's gone without a trace. Only these two bars were down below; they'd fallen into the sipapau—the hole, you know, in the floor of the kiva, symbolic of the entrance to the underworld."

"You're not through searching, of course?" Rogers smiled.

"The new hiding place must be somewhere around.

But where it may be and how much gold is left is plain guess work."

"Well—good luck, Bent. I'll see you this evening, I suppose."

"Yes. So long." He struck a match on the wall and touched the tobacco in his pipe and we turned away and climbed down to the trail.

"I can't understand, Hunt, why you didn't arrest him for murder," I remarked as we untied our horses from the juniper tree.

"Whose murder?"

"Attempted murder—Bernice Patterson's."

"Think he's guilty?"

"Don't you?"

He did not reply at once. We mounted and I fell in behind him on the narrow trail. When I came abreast of him once more his mind was elsewhere than upon Surrey Bent.

"I still don't know who stole Kimball's bag from Emily's room, Chuck; there is as yet no explanation of those hoofprints on the east side of the road which were made the night Kimball was murdered. Wicks has not yet told us all he knows, and by running away in the coupé within the last few hours he has made still further explanations necessary. Why did Mrs. Andrews race back to the trailer and slam inside? Why was a stone from Kaibito used to kill Andrews thirty-three miles away at Red Lake, when there are actually thousands of stones available there for the picking up? Why wasn't Ernie Caldwell's pack horse limping when he rode into Kaibito that day? And is Jeff Draper telling the truth when he says he went back to Red Lake to finish an interrupted visit with his sister?"

"If you had the answers, Hunt, would the thing be solved?"

"Yes, of course. The answer to any one might prove to be the key I'm looking for, Chuck." We climbed out of the canyon, and as it was now past the noon hour we urged our horses into a smart trot. "By the way," Rogers said, "did I tell you that Mrs. James down at Red Lake last night gave me Barbara W.'s address in London?"

"The little girl who lost the diary?"

"I got to talking to the trader's wife and discovered that the girl had given it to her."

"What are you going to do?"

"Send the diary back to her, of course. I'll wrap it up this afternoon and mail it the first chance I get."

We found when we got back to the post that Peggy Easton, in spite of all her pronouncements to the contrary, was keeping dinner warm for us. And we ate it while Peggy sat by to attend to our wants.

"I saw Doctor Creelman's car outside, Peggy, as we came in," Rogers said. "How's Miss Patterson?"

"The doctor just got here, Hunt. He hasn't said yet how she is," Peggy answered. "Did you see Mr. Bent down below?"

"Yes, we did."

"I guess his fall down the steps in the ruins didn't hurt him any," she observed, "but I was worried this morning when I found his bed wasn't slept in last night. He was here for breakfast, though, but he'd gone back to the canyon before I found it out this morning, and I didn't get to ask him where he was. I worried about him all morning. You're sure he was all right?" she asked anxiously.

"Oh, yes; seemed perfectly normal," Rogers assured her. But there was an odd look in his mild blue eyes when he said it, and I wondered if his thoughts were not running with mine. I couldn't reasonably picture the stoutish, middle-aged artist at the spot where Lester Andrews had died. That is, I could not understand how he might have contrived it.

Peggy Easton's eyes lifted suddenly and she half started to her feet at the sound of a footfall behind us.

"What is it, Doctor?" she inquired anxiously.

Both Rogers and I twisted about in our chairs to glimpse the small figure with the stubby mustache and the bushy eyebrows.

"Our patient," Doctor Creelman said, his fierce gaze directed at Peggy Easton, "has regained consciousness. She's much improved."

Rogers got to his feet quickly. "Is her mind clear, Doctor?" he asked anxiously.

"Yes," was the gruff answer. He glared up at Rogers who towered above him, reading his thoughts. "Two questions are all you can ask."

"One will be enough," was the reply.

I stood in the doorway as Rogers and Doctor Creelman approached the bed where the injured girl lay. Her eyes were alert in her pale face as she smiled up at Rogers.

"Can you tell me what happened, Mr. Rogers?" she asked in a low voice.

"Oh," Rogers replied casually, "you got a knock on the head."

"Yes—I guess so. I don't understand how it could have happened."

"Was anybody with you in the ruins when it happened?"

"I was alone. Did I fall? I don't remember."

"Well—I'm happy to see you so much better, Miss Patterson. I'll talk with you when you're stronger. Good-by."

Rogers withdrew from the room and we went outside. Obviously there was nothing of value to be gained from the injured girl.

"She knows nothing that will help," Rogers said and I detected a note of disappointment in his words.

Later on in the afternoon I spread a blanket on the ground under a piñon near the station wagon, and was about to take a nap when Rogers came out to the car.

"I'm still wondering about Surrey Bent," I said. "I mean, where he was last night. Have you any ideas?"

"We'll add that one to the problems I was telling you about earlier," he replied. I saw that he had the diary in his hand. I rested my head on my elbow, looking off through the trees, while he stood with one foot on the running board thoughtfully fingering the leaves of the diary.

"Here comes John Navajo," I said, looking beyond him to the familiar figure of the Indian policeman mounted on his cream-colored pony riding in our general direction. He wavered between us and the trading post as if uncertain of his destination, until Rogers hailed him, whereupon he rode over to us and dismounted and tied his pony.

He nodded curtly in answer to our greeting when he came up. I indicated the blanket, and drew my feet up under me. Rogers sat down and the tall slim figure, in its tight blue serge suit and little stiff-brimmed hat which perched on top of his head, dropped down beside me. I remarked upon the fineness of the day, in Navajo, which observation he responded to solemnly and continued to sit silently beside us.

"You heard about the killing last night near Red Lake?" Rogers asked.

"That on Moqui Reservation. I no investigate what things happen there."

"That's right," returned Rogers, glancing at me as if to remark on the Navajo habit which still persists of referring disparagingly to all things Hopi as Moqui. "I'd overlooked that fact. And yet," he went on, "a man is killed who was here at Kaibito. His death belongs with the other one here—and the attempt on Miss Patterson's life."

John Navajo's black eyes in their narrow slits were fastened upon Rogers' face. He seemed to be searching out the innermost thoughts behind the mild blue eyes.

"You know that?" he inquired at length.

"I'm sure of it."

"Who killum?"

"We don't know yet. We're counting on you, on what you find out from your people about white men at Kaibito. You talk?"

"Some."

A long, lean arm unwrapped itself from about the thin knees and brown fingers reached beyond the blanket's edge to gather several twigs. He slowly put one on the blanket between us; all the while his lips were as tightly sealed as if they had been molded of copper. His hand swept back to a spot an inch or two beyond the blanket where he stuck another twig upright in the earth.

"Wicks," he said, indicating the twig on the blanket. "Canyon," he said, pointing to the upright twig in the earth. "Wicks go many times to canyon," and his arm swept between the two. "He go old trail only Navajo and Wicks know about."

"Was he in the canyon the day Miss Patterson was hurt?"

"He go every day." He dropped another twig beside the one which represented Wicks. "The man who paints," he named it. "He go many times." He dropped a third twig. "Caldwell," he said. "He go in canyon. Talk long time with man with no hair."

"Does he go to the canyon every day?"

The Indian looked at Rogers. "Warband-comes-home not know. He go to *anadji* at Gray Warrior hogan. No in canyon for two days."

We sat silent for some minutes. John Navajo still held several twigs in his brown fingers. Presently he dropped a twig apart from the others. "Bear-leaps-out find dead pony near his hogan. Today. No belong Kaibito."

This strangely assorted information meant little to me. Whether or not it had any meaning for Rogers, I had no way of knowing at the time. His eyes were intent upon the figure of John Navajo; he followed his every movement, the slightest expression upon the almost masklike face. The Indian dropped another twig.

"White woman Wicks," he announced, and then was silent for a moment. "She tell Tall Woman soon she leave reservation. Never come back. Before sunup she hide bag near Caldwell tent. Run away."

"Humph!" Rogers said, and looked off through the trees. John Navajo's eyes were upon him appraisingly. He held one more twig in his brown fingers, and he was long in dropping it on the blanket among the others. At last he did so.

"Young man who paints," he said, "takes stone out of shoe pack horse belong Caldwell."

John Navajo continued to sit on the blanket, his black eyes all but concealed by the narrowed lids, the little stiff-brimmed tan hat perched on top of his head at a ridiculous angle which, however, seemed to accentuate his immense air of gravity. Ten minutes went by while we waited to learn what else he might have to offer. Finally, however, he got up on his knees, then stood up straight and slim.

"I go," he said simply, and walked away to the trading post without waiting for Rogers' thanks which were called after him.

"Well," I said when the door had shut behind him, "it seems to me, Hunt, that he merely enlarged your collection of things you wanted explained."

A faint smile appeared on Rogers' lips. "There are some puzzlers in what he told us, Chuck, and no mistake."

"What has Lamb's taking a stone out of the pack horse's hoof got to do with Bernice Patterson's attempted murder, say?"

"Perhaps nothing. But we'll fit what we can into the picture. Some, of course, will be left out, and probably have no meaning. John was only doing what I asked him to do in finding out what the Indians had seen us white people doing—"

"But what's the dead pony down near Bear-leaps-out's hogan got to do with it? That isn't any activity of the white people."

"Maybe not," he answered. He took the diary from his pocket, crawled across the blanket to the piñon, where he sat with his back to it and began to leaf through the pages, stopping here and there to read the observations of the youthful diarist. I lay on my back observing him out of the corner of my eye.

"Hunt," I said after a while, "have you no shame?"

"What?" he answered vaguely, only partly aware that I had spoken. "Oh! I intend wrapping it up soon. I got interested in it. I'll have to part with it, you know. It's almost good enough to publish. Listen to the grown-up philosophy in this paragraph: 'I think the Navajos are a strange people,' " he read. " 'They live in a country too barren for white men to live in. I guess that's why it is not so crowded as England is. I have my pockets so full of funny colored rocks that I rattle when I walk—' " He looked away, dropping the diary in his lap before he had finished the paragraph. "Oh, Lamb!" he called. "Lamb! Will you come here, please?" I followed his gaze to where Carter Lamb and Emily Millspaw were just emerging from the post.

"At your service," said the young man drawing up before us.

"You've been spied upon by the Indians," Rogers

began.

"Spied upon? I don't follow——"

"You were seen taking a stone from the shoe of the pack horse that belongs to Ernie Caldwell. How about it?"

"I did, yes. But there wasn't a soul around anywhere when I did it. I made sure, because I thought Caldwell might be around and I was going to call his attention to it and let him take it out. But when I didn't see him, I removed it. That's why the horse was limping about so."

"Funny that Caldwell didn't know what was wrong," I said. "He's been calling it a sprain."

"Isn't it?" Lamb returned. "Of course, I don't know. A horse will pick up stones like that, but I had a feeling that the horse didn't pick it up—that it might have been put there."

"So?" echoed Rogers. "What makes you think that?"

"The horse was limping again a couple of hours later when I passed, and Caldwell was in his camp sitting looking at the horse."

"What day was that?"

"Yesterday."

The conversation drifted to other things. The two young people finally moved off and I began to doze again. Rogers picked up the diary to read. When I wakened an hour or so later, John Navajo had come for his pony in my absence and ridden away, and Rogers was over at the station wagon, wrapping up a small package and tying it securely with a piece of string.

"Well, Hunt," I said, sitting up, "did you finish your shameless prying into the secret thoughts of a young girl?"

"Yes," he answered brusquely. "I'm wrapping the thing up now." He cut the string with his knife, took out a fountain pen and a small slip of paper from his billfold and copied an address on the package. "Take a look, Chuck, and see what you see," and he nodded off to his left. I rolled over on my side.

"The gray coupé!" I exclaimed.

"Mrs. Wicks drove it up a while ago, climbed out and walked away."

"Where was he?"

"She was alone. Gone almost before I was aware of the fact. Listen——" he said, and I looked at him in some astonishment, for there was in his manner a tenseness he seldom displayed. "As casually as you can, go over and take the distributor head off that car. And keep it. I'm going inside and telephone Sheriff Wilson."

"What's going on?" I demanded, getting promptly to my feet.

"I want him up here."

"Something happened?"

"Plenty has happened here in the last few days. I don't want the Wickses running out on us again, so get that distributor head."

He climbed down from the seat of the station wagon and set off in a long stride toward the trading post, while I walked over to the gray coupé. I looked inside. The rubber floor mat was deep with sand. There were no keys in the ignition switch. I raised the hood, unsnapped the distributor housing and removed the head. It was of a special make and couldn't be replaced from any other car then at Kaibito. I pocketed the thing and, for a few minutes, in case I was observed, continued to look under the hood, as if I were merely satisfying my curiosity, then shut it down and walked to the post.

Rogers was at the telephone in the living room when I entered. He had just got through to Flagstaff and was waiting for the sheriff at the other end. I stood by to hear the conversation.

"Hello! . . . Hello, Mr. Sheriff. . . . This is Rogers at Kaibito. . . . Bernice Patterson has regained consciousness, but can tell us nothing. . . . How did you make out with the fingerprints on the inside of the trailer? . . . That's good. I've got everybody printed here. . . . Now, listen, I need you back up here. . . . When? . . . Make it the first thing in the morning. As early, anyhow, as you can get up here. And bring your fingerprint man along. We may need him. And, listen, Mr. Sheriff, where's Mrs. Andrews? . . . Still in Flagstaff? That's fine. Bring her along. . . . What? . . . Of course, I want her. It's important. . . . Everything clear? . . . You, the fingerprint man, in case we need him, and Mrs. Andrews here early tomorrow. . . . And one more thing. Do you remember those two hogans about a couple of miles north of where Andrews was killed? Jeff Draper is there visiting his sister. Stop and get him. Bring him along too. I'll blow this open for you. . . . Yes. . . . What's that? . . . Yes, I know who did it, but I'm not telling anybody over the telephone. . . . That's all. . . . Good-by."

Rogers hung up the telephone receiver and turned around. I extended the distributor head. "You keep it," he said.

"So it's come to the showdown, Hunt?" I inquired.
"Yes."

23

THAT final day at Kaibito is one I'll never forget. I wakened with a start, long before daylight, at the click of the door latch, and lay awake listening to the sound of heavy breathing like that of a man who has had a hard run. My hand went out to touch Rogers in the bed beside me, but the place was empty.

"Hunt!" I said, "is that you?"

"Yes," he said, breathing heavily. "Sorry; didn't mean to wake you."

I started to get up, but he seemed to read my thoughts.

"Don't do it," he cautioned. "Don't light any lights." He came over to the bed and sat down on the edge.

"What's happened?" I demanded

"Nothing much," he answered, beginning to breathe easier. "I've been having a little fun. Kaibito is cut off from the outside world, except for the telephone and shank's mare."

"Are you crazy?"

"I've put a chain and padlock on the corral gate. I took the hobbles off Ernie Caldwell's two horses and put them in the corral, too, before I locked the gate. Can't get a horse out now. And I've got the distributor heads of the other cars—Harry Easton's car and truck, Bernice Patterson's, Bent's and the station wagon too.

Nobody's going to run out on us now, Chuck, before we've had our say."

"Why are you all out of breath?"

"Somebody was snooping around outside while I was getting the distributor heads. I thought it was Bent. So I went loping off for a run and doubled back on him, and got inside——" He suddenly put his hand on me in the darkness. "Listen," he whispered. There was a soft footfall in the passageway outside, and then the careful closing of a door. "He's come back," Rogers said.

"Why didn't you say something to me before you went out alone, Hunt?" I asked peevishly. "Supposing it was the killer trying to knock you off, and he had succeeded in doing it?"

"Sh-h-h!" he whispered. "Get a little sleep. It must be three o'clock."

Sleep was long in returning and was not sound when it did. I could not help thinking of the chance Rogers had taken. I was awake at dawn, however, and dressed, leaving Rogers to sleep as late as he would. I went out and made a round of inspection of Rogers' activities in the night, and as I was coming back from the corral I met Surrey Bent strolling among the trees. He stopped me.

"What's going on around here, Graham?" he asked, pulling out his pipe and beginning to fill it from his tobacco pouch.

"How do you mean?"

"Somebody was monkeying around the cars out here about two or three o'clock this morning. I heard a noise and came out to see what was going on. I thought the fellow was about the size of Rogers; couldn't see much in the dark, though. He started running, and I followed as best I could, but he got away from me."

"Surely it couldn't have been Rogers," I said, striving for an effect. "I'm sleeping with him, you know."

"Probably an Indian. I came out just now to look things over." He walked to his car, and gave it a cursory examination, kicked the tires, looked at the gasoline gauge, and stood back from it critically. "Don't see anything wrong, do you?"

"No."

"I guess everything's all right. Can't figure what the fellow was up to, though."

The effect of Rogers' action was not felt until after breakfast when Surrey Bent prepared to go to the canyon and found the corral gate padlocked. He came back to Harry Easton in the bull pen and inquired why it was.

"Ask the professor here," the trader replied. The artist turned to Rogers for an explanation.

"No one is to leave the trading post until the sheriff gives permission," Rogers replied. "That means everybody—"

"Why not?"

"Personally, I believe you'll be more interested in what is about to happen at Kaibito than anything down in the canyon."

"You're spoiling a day of my stay up here," grumbled the artist.

"Every day of mine has been ruined so far." Rogers smiled.

There was some chafing at the restriction Rogers had placed on us all at the post as the hours lengthened toward noon and still the sheriff had not arrived. Our im-

patience grew as we sat idly on the front porch. Ernie
Caldwell came up to buy some cigarettes. He remarked
that he had seen nothing of his horses that morning and
that if they didn't graze back toward his camp he would
look for them later on in the day. Neither Rogers nor I
mentioned the fact that he could find them in the corral if
he'd only look. And then we saw the sheriff's car round
the turn in a cloud of gray dust.

"Well," said Sheriff Wilson, climbing out and coming
up to the porch, "we'd been here sooner, but Jeff Draper
delayed us. Had to hunt for him down at his sister's."

"Did you bring Mrs. Andrews and your fingerprint
man?"

"Yes. Brought along Deputy Humbolt too. Get out,
everybody," he called to the others still in the car, and
they began to climb out.

Harry Easton, who had come out on the porch, pulled
his thick watch from his pocket and studied it for a moment. "I'd suggest, Ed," he said to the sheriff, "that we
better all eat something. Peggy's got it about ready, and
it's close to noon now."

"All right, Harry."

"The Wickses are not here," said Rogers. "We want
them."

"I'll send Humbolt down and get them. He can take
somebody along to show him the way."

It was then that Rogers yielded the key to the corral
gate, drawing the sheriff aside and talking to him in
tones too low to be heard by the others.

Deputy Humbolt and Jeff Draper set off for the
Wicks' hogan, and the fingerprint man, whose name was
Johnson, Sheriff Wilson, Rogers and I went inside where

soon there were spread out upon the counter the fingerprint cards that Rogers had made at Kaibito and those
of Thelma Andrews and her dead husband, together with
numerous photographs of prints taken from the interior
of the trailer.

Rogers began a careful inspection of the prints, su-
pervised by the fingerprint man, an inspection which was
not concluded until some minutes after Peggy Easton
had announced that dinner was ready.

"Well," said Rogers soberly, "I don't know, Mr.
Sheriff, that this really tells us anything after all." He
pushed two groups of cards to one side. "Both Mrs. Andrews' and her husband's prints naturally would be
found in the trailer, since it was their home. But here
are the others." He picked up the groups of assorted
cards and photographs. "Ernie Caldwell's," he said.
"Surrey Bent's, Sheriff Wilson's, one that's probably
mine, although it's smeared badly. Chuck, what's the
matter, don't you touch anything with your hands?
Yours are not here, yet you visited the trailer just as I
did. And Carter Lamb's," he said, dropping the last of
the prints on the counter. "I hadn't taken prints of the
two Wickses, but," he shrugged his shoulders, "there's
nothing to match them up with from the interior of the
trailer. Those are all accounted for."

"Aren't you men through?" called Peggy. "Dinner's
getting cold."

The fingerprint man scooped up the prints, evened
their edges and carefully put them in an inside pocket,
and we went in to eat.

It was an oddly assorted company that assembled
later among the trees. There were blankets on the

ground, and chairs for some, including Mrs. Andrews and Emily Millspaw and Marian Wicks. Rogers sat on the running board of the station wagon. The finger-print man was up in the seat. John Navajo sat silently in our midst, wearing with great dignity the small, stiff-brimmed hat.

Harry Easton had locked the trading post and brought a couple of chairs with him. One was for Peggy and Surrey Bent claimed the other. Deputy Humbolt lingered in the rear behind Ernie Caldwell and Fletcher Wicks. A nervous sort of hush fell upon us as Sheriff Wilson from the running board beside Rogers spoke up.

"I guess there's no use telling you folks why we're all here. You all have sense enough to know that it's got to do with the killing that's been done here at Kai-bito and the one down at Red Lake. There's been some mighty puzzling things about them. We've got a lot of facts that don't seem to lead nowhere in particular. You're all under suspicion. The professor thinks maybe if we talk things over we might know more about what's happened after we're through than we do now. That right, Professor?"

"I quite agree with you, Mr. Sheriff," said Rogers soberly. He glanced about the circle of faces before him as if uncertain for the moment how to begin. The silence grew prolonged. His eyes seemed to be on no one in particular.

"There's been some gold hunting going on around here," he said tentatively, as if testing out an approach to what he wanted to get at. "I think by this time we're all aware of the old story that has floated around Kai-bito for many years. Mr. Bent revived it the other night, but whereas he was the first to speak of it openly, I think that several, besides Mr. Bent, have been secretly engaged in searching for it. Bernice Patterson, for one, but only in an incidental way. Lester Andrews for another, and—Fletcher Wicks—"

"Me?" interrupted Wicks, his dark eyes glowing with resentment, for he had arrived at the post openly hostile and vigorously protesting what he considered his arrest.

"You've been going and coming from the canyon by a trail supposedly known only to the Indians; you evidently have spent much time in the canyon."

"What of it? It's my privilege, isn't it?"

"Certainly." Then came a question fired at the young man like a bullet: "Just what was your connection with Lester Andrews?"

"Why—well—"

"Go on. I want the story you've been holding out on me all this time." Rogers' voice was hard.

"Andrews and I were planning to hunt for it together," Wicks began, resentment in his voice, if not in his words. "That's why he was here in the trailer. He wrote me he was coming."

"How did you get in touch with him? How did you two know anything about the gold? How did you happen to decide to look for it?"

"I can't answer that all at once," he flared. "Andrews was blackmailing Kimball. That's the way he had lived for years."

Mrs. Andrews sat opposite me. I noted the sharp nose, the boring, dark eyes behind their gold-rimmed glasses, which were turned belligerently upon the young man.

"What's the whole story," pressed Rogers. "That's what I want."

"I told you I was Kimball's secretary until Marian and I were married. I used to send the checks to Andrews. Kimball would write them out and I'd send them with a note 'Herewith check enclosed.' That was all. And then one day when the old man was angry he called Andrews a leech and a blackmailer, and he swore he was through with him. Later I saw him looking over a hand-drawn map which he kept under lock. About that time the old man and I fell out, and I married Marian. A few months later I wrote Andrews—sort of experimentally. A correspondence developed. He said the old man had a map he wanted. Described it sufficiently for me to identify it as the map I'd seen in the old man's possession. We'd go shares if I could get hold of the map—there was a fortune in it. But I'd severed relations with Kimball by then and I couldn't get hold of it. I came out to Tucson and saw Andrews, and he convinced me he knew what he was talking about. I mean about the gold. That's why I came up here to Kaibito and brought Marian. I was to be the active man in the field. Andrews said he couldn't be seen here for too long a time. Of course, we gave out a different reason for our being here—"

"I'm right in assuming, am I, that you then tried to lure Kimball out here with his map?"

"Yes, of course. He wrote about this other proposal—selling the business property in Baltimore—and I replied that if he came he must bring the map. We wouldn't talk on any other basis. When he got here, though, he swore he didn't bring it—"

"And, then, after his death, you, not having had opportunity to search his luggage, burglarized Miss Millspaw's room? Still hoping to find the map."

Fletcher Wicks' face drained slightly of its color. "You've got me there," he said. "Either the old man was telling the truth about not bringing the map with him, or else Andrews got it the night he killed him."

"Andrews killed Kimball, you mean?"

"He certainly did."

"You're sure of it?"

"I accused him of it—"

"Was that the reason for your fight in the canyon?"

"He was trying to double-cross me. I accused him of having rifled the old man's luggage that night, and he socked me."

"I see. And you managed somehow to discover that he was pulling out bag and baggage night before last, and you followed him—in the coupé?"

"We discovered they were pulling out. Marian and I were coming up to have a talk with Andrews—peaceable, you know. We wanted to reach an understanding. I was feeling better. I wasn't as badly beaten up as Marian thought. But just as we got to the post, Andrews, trailer and all, pulled past us. We had Kimball's keys to the coupé, and we decided on the spur of the moment to follow and have a showdown with Andrews. But I decided we couldn't do it out on the road, the wind was blowing so hard and the sand was drifting so badly. So we pulled around the outfit and kept on into Red Lake. Something happened; the trailer didn't come. And we got scared—well, maybe not scared, but suspicious—and started up the road toward Marsh

Pass where we got stuck in the sand."

"Did you, before you reached Red Lake, waylay him and kill him?"

"Certainly not!"

"How about the attempted murder of Bernice Patterson?"

"I don't know anything about it."

"Mrs. Wicks," Rogers turned to the young woman, "is this all something new to you, or can you confirm your husband's statement?"

"So far as I know," she answered quickly, "every word is true. You can't accuse us of Lester Andrews' murder. Fletcher didn't do it, and I didn't. The same goes for my stepfather's death."

"How about the attack upon Miss Patterson?"

"I know nothing about it. Neither does Fletcher, I'm sure."

"Do you, too, believe that Andrews killed your stepfather?"

"Yes."

"Mr. Bent," Rogers turned suddenly upon the artist, "you didn't sleep in your bed here at the trading post the night that Andrews was killed down at Red Lake. Where were you?"

"I spent the night in the ruin. Hunting gold."

"I see," Rogers replied, his eyes engaged with Jeff Draper. "Jeff, your sister lives about two miles from where Andrews was killed. You were down there at about that time. But tell me how many ponies did your sister have in the corral?"

The Indian seemed to brood for a moment over the question. I thought he was wary of possible trickery in it. Finally he said,

"She have eight pony. But she have only seven when I put mine in corral."

"Is it a tight corral?"

"Good corral. Too high for pony to jump out."

"What did the missing pony look like?"

"Bay with two white feet and star on forehead."

Rogers' eyes roved over the circle of faces and stopped at the bronze mask of John Navajo.

"John," he said, "is that the horse that Bear-leaps-out found dead yesterday morning near his hogan?"

"*Ohk*. Same horse," replied the Indian policeman.

"Thank you." Rogers turned back to Jeff Draper. "Jeff," he began slowly, "you have told me that before you left the cliff dweller ruins the afternoon you quarreled with Miss Patterson, that Surrey Bent climbed up into the ruins, and that you left them together."

"Yes, sir. That's right."

"Thank you," and Rogers turned next to Bent. "Mr. Bent, your statement the other day was that you came away, leaving Jeff with Miss Patterson. Now, which of you is right?"

The middle-aged painter removed the old pipe from his mouth, holding it in his hand. His voice was heavy, rumbling slightly even in the open air.

"Well," he said, "you can believe one of two things, Mr. Rogers. Either I lied, or Jeff lied. And again I could have been mistaken in what I said. I didn't think it was important. I don't think it is so very important now that you've brought it up again. If the Indian left before I did that doesn't necessarily make me out a murderer."

"You didn't go up to the ruins looking for a light effect that you had been seeking, did you?" Rogers quizzed.

"To be truthful I didn't. Miss Patterson was up there and I was curious as to what she might be doing. I was pretty well convinced that I knew about where the cache was, and I didn't want her stumbling on it after all the work I had put in searching for it."

"And she hadn't uncovered it?"

"No. She was working in the room, though, making some photographs. I didn't think she would get anywhere, but I stuck around and talked with her half an hour or so. Maybe the Indian was gone when I left. I didn't really notice, and of course I didn't give a damn. Because who am I to know in advance that the girl is in danger of being murdered? Maybe the murderer was concealed in the ruins at the time. Over in some one of the other rooms, perhaps, and waiting for me to go. If I'd stuck around a little longer he might have decided that I should be numbered with the girl. And the more I think about it, the more I incline to the belief that the murderer bounced a rock on my head that day I rolled down the ledge to the trail."

"Yes, I see. Thank you. Mrs. Andrews," Rogers turned abruptly to the woman who had not yet opened her mouth, "You were seen running very fast back to the trailer the evening you and your husband pulled out. You told me that you'd left something on the stove and that it might burn. That wasn't the real reason, was it?"

"Yes. But also I had decided we must leave. I was afraid for my husband's life."

24

"How do you mean afraid?" Rogers inquired.

"It just came over me all of a sudden that we should get away. I'd gone for a short walk, it looked so pretty at that time of day. I didn't intend to be gone long, and I wasn't. But before I was ready to return something came over me all of a sudden, a presentiment that something was wrong. That we had to leave just as soon as we could get rolling. I never felt so strange before in all my life."

"Did your hunch—if I may call it that, Mrs. Andrews—indicate the source of danger? Did some particular person seem to be a threat?"

"No, not that. Just something inside that said: 'Get going! Get going, or it will be too late!'"

"Yes, I know; but just what was the real reason?" Rogers persisted. The woman cast an odd look at him, opened her lips, then closed them. "Go on, please."

"Well—Lester told me that morning that Edmondson was here—"

"Edmondson?"

"Yes—Lester had everything wrong. He believed that Fletcher Wicks killed Kimball, but he couldn't prove it. He thought he had something to do with the attempt to kill the Patterson girl. You see—Lester thought the girl was dead. He went up there in the ruins after Mr. Bent left and she was all laid out like she was dead. Lester lost his nerve—that's why he stayed in the canyon all night. He knew the sheriff was trying to pin Kimball's death on him, and he was afraid some Indian might have seen him coming away from where the girl was murdered, and they'd pin that on him too. But it was while I was taking that little walk that I saw through the whole thing—saw that Lester was wrong about everything. I ran back to tell him and I made him see it my way. Then he couldn't get away fast enough. I told him to go to the sheriff, but he wouldn't listen to me. He argued that it would bring up all the past and he'd be involved. The girl probably would get all right again. And Kimball had needed killing for years. So why not let the whole thing sleep? He argued the best thing for us to do was to pull out. If Edmondson was going to kill him, we'd get away before he had a chance. He didn't trust the sheriff. And so—"

"I see," Rogers interrupted the torrent of words. "And now tell me: Down near Red Lake, after you discovered your husband was dead, you fastened yourself inside the trailer. Was the trailer door standing open at the time, or was it closed?"

"I hadn't thought of that! I remember now; it was open."

"Another thing, was the trailer door locked when you pulled out of Kaibito?"

"We never locked the door unless we were both going to be away from the trailer for a time."

Rogers was silent for several moments, his eyes seemed to see into the distance beyond the figure of the thin, tense woman in the chair. He rubbed the side of his large nose thoughtfully with his forefinger and of a sudden snapped back into the semblance of a dynamic, insistent prosecutor.

"Mrs. Andrews," he began incisively, "I want the story that you've been keeping secret all these years—the part your husband was afraid to have come out."

"The story?" The woman returned uneasily.

Rogers smiled faintly. "I can guess what it is, but I want you to tell me. I want to know why your husband could successfully blackmail a man like Norman Kimball for a long period of years; why your husband should be hunting a long-hidden cache of gold, and what there was in his background that should build up eventually into his murder. Come! You were married to him for twenty-two years. This is not the time to hold back any secrets, if we're going to get to the bottom of this thing."

"Well—" the woman hesitated, "I—I don't know how you know I have any such story. But—it took me years to pump it out of him. I nagged him until I had it all—then wished I didn't know anything about it. You see, Lester was one of the men who brought the gold in a pack train across the Colorado. There were three of them; Lester and Norman Kimball and this man Edmondson I spoke of. Bob, I think, was his first name."

"Where did they get the gold?"

"From a little mine in the mountains not far from Cedar City in Utah. It wasn't their mine, you understand. It belonged to a fellow named—" The woman's dark eyes shifted suddenly to the girl sitting beside Carter Lamb. "Well—his name was Millspaw. He was the owner of the mine—"

"Why, that's father," said the girl strangely. "It must be."

"I don't know about that," said Mrs. Andrews. "He was away at the time, Lester said—that is, when they struck the rich pocket. In a single afternoon they took out several hundred thousand dollars worth of very rich ore. Lester was the millman—there was a little ball mill at the mine, which he ran. Norman Kimball was the engineer and was in charge when Millspaw was away, and this man Edmondson was the underground foreman.

"When the three of them realized what they had and that the boss was away, the temptation was too great. First they fired all the other miners and the three of them ran the rich ore through the mill and got what Lester said at the old price of gold was worth around a quarter of a million dollars. They wanted the gold for themselves. They planned for several days how to get away with it. Of course, they couldn't send it to the mint in San Francisco, for then it would have to be credited to Millspaw, the owner. They had hidden the gold which they had melted into small bars, and while they were still arguing how to cash in on what they had, Millspaw came in on them unexpectedly.

"It didn't take him long to smell a rat, the mine being shut down. He assayed some of the stuff on the tailing pile and, since the mill would only recover about eighty-five per cent, he knew that some very high-grade ore must have been run through it, but he didn't know how much. He went over to the bunkhouse where the boys were and accused them of high-grading while he was gone. The boys had been drinking some, and Edmondson was drunk and abusive. Something happened;

there was a fight; they all three more or less jumped onto Millspaw, but it was Kimball who killed him when he hit him and knocked him so that his head struck against the stove."

The gathering among the trees had hushed as the woman talked. Three or four Indians who had come to the trading post were sitting patiently on the porch waiting for the time when it would be unlocked and they could make their purchases, but few if any of those listening to Thelma Andrews had any knowledge of the fact. I glanced at Emily Millspaw. She was sitting forward in her chair, her small face white and strained as she listened to this strange story.

"What happened next?" inquired Rogers quietly.

"Well, Bob Edmondson was too drunk to know what was going on. Lester said that Bob had been swinging his arms like a cyclone but not hitting anything. He passed out just before Kimball hit Millspaw the lick that killed him. Lester, I'm sure, always regretted what happened to Millspaw, and what they did about it. The mine was out in the sticks away from everybody. Nobody but the three of them had seen Millspaw and knew that he was at the mine, and Edmondson was drunk. Kimball was the leader; it was his idea what to do about the murder they had committed. He persuaded Lester, who was always a weak character, to help him put the blame on Edmondson. So they doctored up some evidence—I don't know just how they did it—and then sobered up Edmondson and told him that he had killed Millspaw, and he believed it.

"Edmondson had grown up in this country; he knew it like a book almost, and it was his idea how to get away with the gold. But first they had to dispose of the body of Millspaw. They took it into the mine, which was three hundred feet down, then, and took it out in one of the drifts and put it up in one of the stopes. They were stoping up to the two-fifty level. Then they back-filled tons and tons of rock on top of it. They took Millspaw's car and got it down into the mine somehow and then dynamited the timbering and collapsed the mine on it.

"Never in this world—or, at least, not without spending thousands of dollars—could the law get the body out, even if they knew where to look for it. And, as Lester said once, if they can't produce a body it's hard to convict for murder.

"The three of them then, with Kimball and Lester holding the murder over Edmondson, but all promising to keep still about the whole thing, loaded the gold into an old truck and drove as far as the roads would let them. Then they bought enough horses for themselves and for a pack train—ten altogether, I think—and with Edmondson guiding them, came across the Colorado at the Crossing of the Fathers. The plan was to pack down to some place in southern Arizona, pick up a small mine, and work it for a while and pretend to make a rich strike and in that way cash in on the stolen gold.

"It was Kimball's greed, though, that spoiled everything. He wanted to freeze out Edmondson. Edmondson got wind of it somehow, and that's what started the fight down in Navajo Canyon just a few miles from here. Edmondson got the drop on them, took their guns away from them and ran them out of the canyon. Edmondson and the gold disappeared. The other two went back next day, expecting to be killed at almost every turn, but there was no sign of Edmondson. Kimball drew a map and then they pulled out and went down in the southern part of the state, and got a little mine and worked it, and pretended to strike a rich pocket of ore, and in that way got rid of the gold on the one pack horse they'd managed to get away with.

"But Kimball beat Lester out of that and went East and married a woman with a lot of money, I understand. Lester, after four or five years, traced him, and I guess that's when he began to get money out of him. It was his; it was Lester's just as much as it was Kimball's, since they'd both stolen it. Kimball would never come back to this country, and the reason was that he was afraid of Edmondson. Lester wrote him once that he had seen Edmondson and told him the truth, and that Edmondson, who was supposed to be around this part of the country, had sworn to kill him if he ever stuck his nose north of the Little Colorado River. But Lester made that up. He never saw Edmondson again until we came up here this time. Lester, of course, wanted the field clear to hunt for the gold himself, which he did after a few years. But he didn't have time or money to hunt every year. He had to earn a living; we couldn't live off what he was able to get out of Kimball. He couldn't let an outsider in on it, because that would most likely bring up the old murder story. He didn't remember very well where they were at the time of the fight, but he did the best he could. He always wanted to get the map that Kimball made, but didn't know how. He thought it might help him, but until he got in touch with Mr. Wicks, there didn't seem to be any way.

"What he went down to see Kimball about that night

was about the map. He'd decided to let Kimball in on it, if he'd help."

"And what about Edmondson?"

"I never knew, except what Lester said, and that was that he'd completely disappeared. This time, though— I mean almost as soon as we got here—Lester acted funny. Like he'd seen a ghost. I tried to get him to tell me what it was, but he was as mum as an oyster. And I knew that he was scared. It wasn't till last Saturday morning that he told me Edmondson was here. He was turning over in his mind, I think, whether he and Edmondson could make a deal and find the gold. Of course, he didn't realize that Edmondson was his enemy and was planning to kill him too."

Mrs. Andrews came suddenly to the end of her story, her eyes fixed upon the heavy, solid figure of Surrey Bent.

A sort of sigh went round the circle. John Navajo wrapped his long arms tighter about his knees. Bent knocked the ashes from his pipe and Harry Easton cast a glance toward the post, seemingly indifferent that customers were waiting outside. Rogers rubbed the side of his nose thoughtfully and then began to speak.

"The unfortunate part of it all, Mrs. Andrews, was that Edmondson knew what you were up to. He was watching, determined to kill your husband. If you'd only asked protection of the sheriff, if you'd only locked your door that night, your husband might still be alive."

"Locked it?"

"Edmondson is a clever person; he can turn an opportunity to his own uses automatically. As you pulled away, Edmondson picked up a stone from the ground, stepped into the trailer, and closed the door, which Carter

Lamb saw swing shut and which he thought was caused by the movement of the car. So the murderer rode with you all the way. His plan was simple. By jumping about inside the trailer, shifting his weight suddenly, teetering the trailer up and down and creating the rhythm that would rock the trailer, he attracted your attention in the car, so that your husband was impelled to get out and examine the hitch. Edmondson was waiting to kill him when he came back.

"After he had struck him the fatal blows, he ran back along the road, tossed away the stone, and continued on up to the corral near the hogan of Jeff Draper's sister, selected a pony, managed somehow to obtain a rope for halter, mounted and came riding back to Kaibito. Incidentally, Jeff Draper, that let's you out of it. You couldn't be Edmondson. You're Navajo. And, besides, you didn't reach your sister's hogan until after Edmondson had stolen one of her ponies from the corral.

"Edmondson rode bareback those thirty odd miles to Kaibito, or almost to Kaibito, for the pony died under him near the hogan of Bear-leaps-out. He walked the rest of the way to Kaibito. I know now why the lone rider we saw Saturday night, before we discovered the murder of Andrews, wouldn't answer the sheriff's call to stop. The rider was Edmondson. And because of the darkness we didn't recognize him." Rogers' eyes seemed to rove about the circle of faces. They stopped at Harry Easton. "You're counted out, Harry," he said. "You were never even a suspect. Carter Lamb out; you don't fit anywhere. All the women are out; it was a man's job. Fletcher Wicks —" He paused significantly. "I could wish that you had been more helpful. There is no saying whether or not

Andrews might now be alive if you had told me frankly in the beginning everything I know now. You're out of consideration, of course—too young to be Edmondson."

"Thanks, Rogers," said Wicks.

"Mr. Bent," Rogers' eyes were upon the artist for a long moment, "you're movements have been a bit mysterious. I can't say truthfully that I suspected you at the time of killing anybody. Your bed wasn't slept in the night Andrews was murdered. You said you were in the canyon, but there's no way to prove that. But if you had been the rider who rode a horse to death in your haste to get back to Kaibito you'd have gone promptly to bed. Out, Mr. Bent—and, while I'm not a court of law to impose judgments, my guess is that the gold bars you found in the kiva belong to Miss Millspaw. As does the cache when and if it is ever found.

"Edmondson," Rogers' voice snapped in the warm air, "you've kept quiet throughout hoping that somewhere there would be a slip, that I couldn't name you, hoping that you could fade away when the talk was over."

My eyes had traveled to Rogers and thence to Ernie Caldwell; the others were almost as quickly staring at the lean, hunched figure of the cowboy as he sat rocking gently back and forth on the blanket, hugging his knees to his hollow chest, his eyes mere slits set amid a thousand wrinkles in his weather-beaten face. Rogers went on:

"You sat beside the road down near White Mesa the day that Kimball and Emily drove to Kaibito in the gray coupé. You recognized your old enemy—just as he realized who you were and refused to stop. You knew where Fletcher Wicks lived. You said so that first time we met you down the road near Red Lake, and Chuck

Graham told you who Kimball was. You made camp that night about twenty miles below here, borrowed a pony from an Indian herd, rode until you found the coupé parked at the roadside, tied your pony, found your way over to Wicks' hogan, were waiting uncertain, perhaps, in just which hogan Kimball was sleeping, when Andrews showed up. You waited until Andrews had gone, perhaps not recognizing him in the darkness, then entered the hogan where Kimball was and left it a few minutes later after you had fatally beaten your old enemy. You walked back to the pony, mounted and rode back to White Mesa.

"Indian gossip puts you in the canyon the afternoon that Bernice Patterson was almost killed. From what she said that first night when you asked her what her business was, you realized that she might easily discover your gold cache. You came upon her that afternoon, struck the blow that all but killed her and left her to die in the ruins. For a couple of days you lay low; then, on the afternoon you moved the gold cache, you discovered Mr. Bent climbing up to the ruins. You lay in wait for him at the top of the steps, hit him a blow which might have resulted in his death, and he rolled down to the trail. I've already described how you contrived the death of Lester Andrews. Now—"

Suddenly the cowboy was a bundle of fighting, straining energy, as he rolled up on his knees and sought to regain his feet. The gun in the sheriff's holster leaped out, but there dropped from behind upon the escaping man the two-hundred-pound bulk of Deputy Humbolt and the two rolled together against the trunk of the piñon pine near which we sat. When the brief, fierce struggle was ended Caldwell was handcuffed with arms about the six-inch trunk, his snarls growing less as he realized it was all over.

"You'll never find what's left of the gold now," boasted the captive. "I've spent all but a few bars—gambled it away."

"There's only a point or two more I want to mention," Rogers said when Caldwell had subsided. "You might have escaped suspicion altogether, Caldwell, for I was predisposed in your favor from the beginning because of what a little girl wrote in her diary. She said of you 'he smiles all the time, which I think is a good sign in strangers.' But—there were several things that didn't square. Your pack horse didn't limp when you rode into Kaibito that first day. That was your excuse for staying —until the horse was able to travel again. Carter Lamb removed a stone from the horse's shoe later, and said that it looked to him as if it deliberately had been put there. More interesting than that, the horse was limping again two hours later.

"Incidentally, before I wrapped up the diary yesterday to return it to England, I reread a paragraph the little girl had written. I'll quote from memory: 'I stayed and played checkers with a cowboy and almost beat him twice. He had crinkled eyes and smiled all the time, which I believed is a good sign in strangers, although when I asked him his name he said he'd tell me his Indian name which the Indians gave him. He said he didn't tell it to everybody. I couldn't pronounce it, though. But he said it means; "Man-borrows-horse." '

"Perhaps, Caldwell, in getting about to cover up your crimes, you borrowed one horse too many from the Navajos."

www.ingramcontent.com/pod-product-compliance
Lightning Source LLC
Chambersburg PA
CBHW020644030726
47498CB00002B/365